in women's fiction today, than that of Kathleen Gilles Seidel."

—*Romantic Times*

PRAISE FOR
KATHLEEN GILLES SEIDEL:

FOR *AGAIN*

"A delicious ready—witty, romantic, and wise, and original as only Kathleen Gilles Seidel can be. Don't miss it!"
—Mary Jo Putney

FOR *TILL THE STARS FALL*

"Extraordinary! One of the most moving novels I've read in years . . . I couldn't bear for it to end."
—Susan Elizabeth Phillips,
author of *Fancy Pants* and *Honey Moon*

"Kathleen Gilles Seidel is a truly gifted writer and this is a truly wonderful book. I literally did not put it down, and the characters are with me still . . . complex, compelling and memorable."
—Katherine Stone, author of *Promises*

"Seidel is one of the most insightful romance writers around. . . . She writes with precision, a keen sense of the value of reality and develops relationships and interrelationships with infinite care."
—*Fort Wayne News Sentinel*

"A consummate craftsman, Kathleen Gilles Seidel illuminates the human heart with exquisite precions."
—Melinda Helfer, *Romantic Times*

by

Kathleen Gilles Seidel

ONYX
Published by the Penguin Group
Penguin Books USA Inc., 375 Hudson Street,
New York, New York 10014, U.S.A.
Penguin Books Ltd, 27 Wrights Lane,
London W8 5TZ, England
Penguin Books Australia Ltd, Ringwood,
Victoria, Australia
Penguin Books Canada Ltd, 10 Alcorn Avenue,
Toronto, Ontario, Canada M4V 3B2
Penguin Books (N.Z.) Ltd, 182–190 Wairau Road,
Auckland 10, New Zealand

Penguin Books Ltd, Registered Offices:
Harmondsworth, Middlesex, England

First published by Onyx,
an imprint of Dutton Signet,
a division of Penguin Books USA Inc.

First Printing, September, 1994
10 9 8 7 6 5 4 3 2 1

Printed in the United States of America

Not many people anymore call my sister and me "the Gilles girls." Our brother's two oldest daughters are that now. In hope that they will always be as dear to one another as their aunt and I are, this book is dedicated to—

Erica and Alison Gilles

Acknowledgments

"You don't know me, but you went to college with my neighbor's sister. Would you please talk to me?" "I'd love to," said Caroline Franz, and writing this book suddenly become possible. Currently a scriptwriter on *As the World Turns,* Caroline has also written for *All My Children*, *Search for Tomorrow*, and *Another World*; she was a source of incalculable value.

Then a whole crowd of very short people—and their mothers—helped me beyond imagining. Laura Brookhiser and Claire Matlack, Emily Boone, Sophie Burtoff, Nicole Fallone, Brian and Michael Grey, Caroline Hightower, Hope Hurley, Katie Mullen, Sarah Myers, Courtney and Zachary Roberts, Elizabeth Smith, and Austin Thomas—these are my children's friends, and the hours the girls spent at their houses was much appreciated work time.

Two people deserve no thanks at all. My older daughter's first and second grade teachers, Carmen Wilkinson and Darnell Wise-Lightbourn, turned their classrooms into such magical places that I could not keep away.

Virginia Story was the most cheerful, insightful typist you could imagine . . . even after she fractured her elbow. Jennifer Enderlin did everything that the best editors do. She had a strong vision for this book, she knew of wonderful restaurants, she believed in me more than I did, and she changed jobs. I am grateful to her for most of these.

One

"You know what they say about him, don't you?" This was from George, the executive producer. He was more or less Jenny's boss.

"I know, but he's terrific."

"He's supposed to be impossible, very demanding." This was from Thomas, the show's casting director. He and Jenny had been friends since their days as lowly production assistants.

"Maybe the people calling him impossible are impossible themselves."

"But you've never met him. We could be letting ourselves in for all kinds of trouble. It can't be worth it." This was from Brian. He was Jenny's boyfriend.

These were reliable people, George, Thomas, and Brian. Jenny trusted their judgment and their taste. But she had instincts. *This is it*—the knowledge would flash along her arms. She would feel bubbly and confident. This was what she loved about her job, about her life.

"I don't get it," Brian went on. "Why are you so sure?"

"I like his eyes."

* * *

Two years ago two daytime soap operas debuted on network television at the same time—the big, splashy, generously budgeted *Aspen Starring Alec Cameron* and the quiet, quirky *My Lady's Chamber*. No one except the people on *My Lady's Chamber* thought of the two shows as being in competition. *My Lady's Chamber* had too much against it. It was only a half hour, it was scheduled against daytime's number-one show, it had an historical setting. "Quixotic" was the word most often used to describe it, followed right by "doomed."

But in spite of the predictions, the offbeat, little underdog held on. Slowly it built an audience. Its attention to historical detail and the elegant BBC-*Masterpiece Theatre* tone of its production brought in new viewers, people who had never watched soaps before. Lawyers with expense accounts, college professors, graphic artists, and symphony volunteers programmed their VCRs and watched *My Lady's Chamber*.

And the megabudget *Aspen Starring Alec Cameron*? It was a bomb. No one watched it.

Alec Cameron hadn't asked anyone to produce a show starring him. The network had approached him with the idea, and he hadn't thought it a very good one. He said so frankly and clearly. Soaps shouldn't have one particular star; the cast should be an ensemble. Daytime should never feature one actor so prominently.

Of course if daytime was going to feature one actor so prominently, Alec would just as soon that it be him rather than someone else. The network executives kept talking about his proven audience appeal, his unquestioned talent. The idea started sounding better and better. Pretty soon Alec was persuaded that it was downright excellent.

It wasn't.

The network hired a new writer, a playwright who had never written for television, much less for daytime. The man watched three weeks worth of soaps and then, based upon that vast experience, announced that he was going to revolutionize the structure of the soap opera. There would be no core families, no super couples, no amnesia.

"What do you mean, my character has no family?" Alec asked during his first meeting with the man.

"Oh, we're not going to be doing families. We're not interested in families."

A soap that wasn't interested in families? That's what soaps were about: families, connections, blood. The family stories held everything else together. A soap had to have families.

Jenny Cotton knew that. She was a creator and head writer of *My Lady's Chamber,* and she was very interested in families. Her show was set in the past, her characters wore intricately tied cravats and flowing high-waisted gowns, but they still belonged to families. Jenny wasn't interested in revolutionizing the structure of anything. The structure of the soap opera was fine. She worked on what needed to be worked on. *My Lady's Chamber* had better writing and more consistent, believable characters than anything on daytime.

Day after day Alec would get his scripts for

Aspen, and he would stare at them, disbelieving. Everything was wrong. There wasn't enough recapping of prior episodes; viewers who had missed a few shows got lost. Two, sometimes even three, stories peaked at the same time, diluting the intensity of all of them. The characters were glamorous, but not engaging. Whoever was writing these scripts didn't know anything about soaps.

If he had been just another actor in the cast, Alec might have kept his mouth shut, but his name was part of the title, his face was featured in the credits, so his reputation was on the line. With the morale of the cast dropping like stone, he had to do something.

He tried to play fair with Paul Tomlin, the writer. He kept his criticisms out of the greenroom and the dressing room corridors where the actors hung out. His business was with the writing staff and the production staff. He met with them, reasoned with them, pleaded with them. This was his fourth soap role, he had won back-to-back Emmys. He knew a lot about what made soaps work. *Get back to basics*, he urged. *Characters that the viewers care about, stories that touch the heart. And families, please give us some families. Mothers, grandfathers, unknown half-sisters, adopted third cousins, anything.*

"Families are *passé,*" Paul said with a sniff. "No one cares about families anymore."

No one cares about families? Alec could only stare at him. Where was this guy from? Didn't he know anything about the daytime viewer?

Alec kept on. He wasn't doing this only for

himself. *Aspen Starring Alec Cameron* employed a lot of people. Actors, craftsmen, tradespeople, gofers, and hairdressers would be out of work if the show got canceled. Just as surely as if he had to meet the payroll himself, Alec felt responsible for these people's livelihoods.

At the end of the first year the network became desperate too. Alec found himself working five days a week, with forty pages of dialogue to learn a night. The show started going on location, expensive jaunts to Peru and Finland. It didn't help. A story that was boring at home was going to be boring in Italy.

My Lady's Chamber, on the other hand, actually had a foreign setting, Regency England. But it never went on location. It couldn't afford to. It didn't need to.

At last after a wearying, mind-numbing eighteen months Alec's ordeal came to an end. *Aspen Starring Alec Cameron* changed its title to *Aspen!!* and Alec's character skied into an avalanche. He was fired.

It was a relief. He could stop feeling responsible. Someone else was taking the sword out of his bloodied hand. "You have fought long enough, my friend." The doctor was closing the chart. "You may die in peace."

Alec slept for a month and then went home to Canada to visit his own family. He returned to New York, renewed, refreshed, ready to work again, and discovered that he might just as well have stayed home. His name was as muddy as his father's potato fields. No one would hire him. He was finished at the age of thirty-two.

He was being blamed for everything that had been wrong with *Aspen*. He was difficult—the reports went—temperamental, obstinate, a perfectionist.

He couldn't believe it. He had always been one of the good guys, punctual, professional, dedicated. How could anyone call him difficult? He was Canadian. The world's longest unprotected border and all that. Canadians didn't know how to be difficult.

"But these people know me," he protested to his agent. "They know I'm not like that."

"They also know that you were part of a bomb."

There was no quarreling with that. In fact, he hadn't just been "part of" a bomb. He had starred in it. *A Bomb Starring Alec Cameron.* Not a perfect career move.

Putting bread on the table was not a problem. He did voiceovers for commercials, work that wasn't very satisfying but was quite lucrative. He got a decent-sized part in a good movie, but he had never liked film work, standing around and waiting while people fussed to get the lights exactly so. Nor did he like the space ship/desert island atmosphere of a movie production. He belonged on a soap. It suited his acting style; it fit in with his desire to be a regular guy, someone with a job, a person who went to work every morning, saw the same people, was a part of a team. Acting in the soaps was clearly what he was meant to do with his professional life, and all of a sudden no one was letting him do it.

Then that strange, little, historical show, *My*

Lady's Chamber, needed to recast the part of His Grace Frederick Charles Edmund Stairs, the fifth Duke of Lydgate, and an instinct flashed along Jenny Cotton's arms.

My Lady's Chamber was housed in an old, three-story brick warehouse in Brooklyn. The network's other daytime shows were taped in a modern, midtown Manhattan facility, but *My Lady's Chamber* had expensive costumes, expensive sets, and a very limited budget. Everything from lumber to midmorning danish was cheaper in Brooklyn than in Manhattan.

The network did provide limousines to bring the actors out to this wilderness of a location, but Alec decided that he would get to Brooklyn on his own. He didn't want to begin his stint here sharing a car with other cast members. He didn't want to get too chummy.

Things were going to be different this time. He was going to come in, do his job, and go home. He wasn't going to be responsible. He wasn't going to carry the weight of the world on his shoulders. If two of the actresses loathed each other, well, that was a shame, but he was going to keep out of their way. If one of the directors was too hard on the gay men—or on the straight men—again Alec would be sorry, but he wasn't going to fix it. It was someone else's turn to play savior. It was someone else's turn to be crucified.

The security guard sitting inside the warehouse's street door recognized him. "Mr. O'Neill wanted to know when you got in." The guard picked up the phone that sat on his desk. "He'd like to show you around."

"That's not necessary." Alec did not want to be led around like some kind of returning prince who had failed to distinguish himself on the Crusades. This was his fifth soap. He could probably tell the makeup room from the wardrobe department. "Just point me toward the dressing rooms."

"But Mr. O'Neill, he said that you were to wait." The guard was looking worried. He had his instructions.

And Alec was making it hard. His agent had warned him to be careful. "Everyone will be watching you," she had said. "Stop at the water fountain, and someone will say that you're being difficult."

This really stank, that he should have to be so careful at this point in his career. But that was the way things were. No use in pretending that they were otherwise.

He beamed at the security guard and spoke in good hearty tones. "If Mr. O'Neill said I should wait, then wait I shall do." He folded his arms and moved to the wall to wait.

He assumed that "Mr. O'Neill" was Brian O'Neill, an actor he had met several times over the years. Alec didn't really know the man, but he had a good reputation in the daytime world. He was known to be pleasant and hardworking, particularly able to do something with a character who wasn't getting much of a story.

Indeed it was Brian O'Neill who approached the security desk a few minutes later. He was a slender man with a willowy torso and the sort of slim, long fingers seen in Renaissance paintings. He had the fair skin and very dark hair of the black Irish.

Alec's own ancestry was Scotch, and he had a firm, broad-shouldered build, warm skin tones, and auburn hair. He had wideset, sea-green eyes and clean, strong cheekbones.

He shook hands with Brian and let the other actor show him around. There were no surprises. Wardrobe, the greenroom, and the studio floor were on one. Makeup and the dressing rooms were on two. The rehearsal hall and the production offices were on three. The walls were painted cinderblock, the floors sheet linoleum and vinyl tile, the stairs concrete. Clearly the money was being spent on the sets and costumes, what the viewer could see.

Brian directed Alec to Dressing Room Six. "You're sharing with Ray Bianchetti," he said as he opened the door. "He's a nice guy."

"I'm sure he is," Alec replied.

"In fact we all get along pretty well."

"I'm sure you do."

Brian paused. "This isn't *Aspen,*" he said quietly. "Jenny is nothing like Paul Tomlin."

"How could she be?" Alec's answer was brisk. He didn't want to talk about *Aspen*. "She writes a show that people want to watch."

"It's also one people want to work on."

Brian's voice was still quiet, but there was warning in it. *Don't be difficult. Don't cause problems. We don't want your kind around here.*

Alec fought down his resentment. Brian had

a right to say this. He wasn't simply another cast member. He was Jenny Cotton's boyfriend, her longtime "significant other," her live-in companion. That must give him a special place on the show. He would be the one in the middle, defending the writer to the actors, the actors to the writer. He would be the one who negotiated, advised, and warned. It was a thankless job. Alec had done it on *Aspen,* and he was very glad that someone else was doing it on *My Lady's Chamber.*

"We all hope you like it here," Brian continued. "Jenny certainly did go out on a limb for you."

"Oh?" Someone went out on a limb for him? Alec did not like the sound of that.

"She was the one who pushed to have you cast, and now she's really looking forward to meeting you. People assumed that she already knew you because she was so willing to discount . . . well, you know. . . ."

Yes, Alec knew. She had been willing to discount everything Paul Tomlin was saying about him.

Alec was a middle child in a family of six. The first three children had been born one right after the other. Then there had been a gap of six years, after which had come three more closely spaced children. Alec had been the first of the second wave; he was the oldest of the "Littles."

He had always felt responsible for his younger brother and sister; he was the one who spoke on behalf of all three of the "Littles." He supposed that was why he had felt so responsible for what happened to the people on *Aspen*. He had always felt responsible for Ross and Meg.

While he had had an oldest child's sense of responsibility, he hadn't had an oldest's self-assurance. Watching out for Ross and Meg didn't keep him from comparing himself to Bruce, Gordon, and Jean. He couldn't measure up to them because they were years older than he was, and he hadn't liked that. As a kid, he had sworn that people would never patronize him, and they would never have to make allowances for him.

But now, thanks to *Aspen,* that was exactly what was happening.

"I'm looking forward to meeting her too," he answered smoothly, if not quite truthfully. "What day does she come in?" Writers worked at home and usually came into the studio only one day a week.

"She's here all the time. She likes being in the thick of things." Brian had his hand on the dressing room door, motioning for Alec to pass through. "She had some early phone calls to make, but she should be done now."

Alec could hardly object. He followed Brian up to the third floor and down a short hall. Brian stopped at a door that was ajar and pushed it open without knocking.

Alec had a quick impression of clutter—bookcases wedged tight with books, maps and drawings taped to the walls, piles of dog-eared legal pads, and stacks of colored index cards. But his eye skated over the clutter. He was interested in the person behind the desk.

She hadn't noticed them come in. She was

staring at the computer screen, intent, concentrating. It was probably very grown-up work she was doing, but she was sitting like a kid, one leg drawn up, her arm wrapped around her knee, her chin resting on the back of her hand.

"Jenny, here's our new duke."

She looked up. The leg dropped, the chin lifted, and a smile flashed across her face. Alec had to admit that it was a cute smile, bright and gamine. "Hello, hello." An instant later she was out of the chair, in front of the desk.

She was small. Her light brown hair was full and short, rumpling around her ears. She had freckles across the bridge of her nose, and everything about her sparkled with energy. Alec knew her to be twenty-eight; she looked at least ten years younger.

She was dressed casually, her trousers were wheat-colored, light and loose. The collar of her white shirt was open, and her cuffs turned back. They were good garments, well-cut, nicely fitting, but she wore no accessories—no earrings or bracelets, not even a belt although her pants had belt loops on them. Clearly she was not one of life's better dressers.

She banged her elbow against Brian's ribcage. It was a nice gesture, lighthearted, affectionate. *I like you*, it said. *I'm glad you're here.* Then she put her hand out to Alec. "Welcome to the nineteenth century." She was lightly tanned and her voice was a little husky as if she had been outside all afternoon playing ball in the wind and the sun. "I'm so glad to finally meet you. I think you'll love it here. I mean I *hope* you will. You should. Everyone's so great, we're—"

"Jenny," Brian interrupted, "you're bragging."

"No, I'm not," she protested. Then she made a face, wrinkling her nose, laughing at herself. "So what if I am? A half-hour show is really great. You've only been on the hours, haven't you?"

Alec realized that she was speaking to him. "That's right."

These were the first words he had spoken.

"I think you'll be surprised at how much more fluid and flexible we can be here, how much more—"

Brian interrupted again. "It's just that *she* loves the show," he explained to Alec.

"I gathered that."

He had to smile. No one on *Aspen* had had fun. Jenny Cotton was still having fun.

Why didn't a person meet more women like this? She seemed fresh and uncomplicated. Alec was enchanted. He could imagine her on that limb she had supposedly crawled out on for him, a compact little nugget of a person sitting up in a tree, her feet swinging, her bright eyes and freckled nose peering down among the leaves.

He had worked with many gifted, successful actresses; he had been married to one of daytime's most gifted, most successful. As astonishingly lovely as some of these women were—his ex-wife was almost supernaturally exquisite—he couldn't recall any of them making such a marvelous first impression as Jenny Cotton.

As long as your career was perched out on a limb, you might as well be in the tree with someone who is having fun.

The daily routine on a soap had been developed in the days when shows were aired live. What was taped in a single day aired on a single day. If a Friday show ended with a character rushing in a room shrieking that the building was on fire, then Monday picked up two seconds later with everyone scrambling to get out. The two parts of the scene, even though all the actors were in the same costumes, standing on the same places on the same set, were taped on two different days.

The day began in the rehearsal hall with the cast sitting at a long table reading through the script. Rehearsal halls were usually bare, vinyl-floored rooms furnished with folding chairs, a couple of tables, and a trolley for coffee. The one at the *My Lady's Chamber* studio was no different.

The show had two core families, the Varleys and the Courtlands. The Varleys had raised two nieces, a wealthy one and a poor one. The rich one, Amelia, had married the Duke of Lydgate, Alec's part. Amelia was a sympathetic character, played by Karen Madrigal, a lovely swan-necked actress with clouds of dark hair. The viewers were crazy about her. Ray, Alec's dressing room-mate, played another popular character, the duke's younger brother, Lord Robin Stairs, a dashing and gallant calvary officer. An actress named Trina Nelson, a pretty strawberry blonde, was the duchess's maid, Molly, and Brian played Hastings, the family's butler. There were about ten actors getting themselves coffee and finding places at the table in the rehearsal hall.

Alec didn't know any of them. Except for Brian—and now Alec himself—everyone in the cast was new to daytime. But they were all welcoming. "Oh, you *are* going to love it here." "Yes, yes, that's right. We're one big happy family."

One big happy family. Alec listened to the cast talk. Most actors had little experience with happy families. They usually confused such superficial pleasantries as the absence of spurting blood with family happiness. Since four of the six children in Alec's family had been boys, there had been a great deal of spurting blood as well as prolonged dearths of superficial pleasantries, but as family they had gotten along, a condition far too complicated to compare to anything else, especially a professional situation.

Moreover, how did any of this cast know that a half-hour show was so much better? None of them had ever been on an hour show.

But Alec let these suspicions drift away. It was so good to be back at work, to be getting a cup of coffee with a script tucked under his arm, hearing people ask one another about their weekends. He didn't want to be cynical. He didn't want to feel like the weatherbeaten old gunfighter in a town full of well-meaning settlers. He wanted to work.

He found a seat at the table. A minute later the director of the day's episode, Gil Norway, took his place on the tall stool at the head of the table. He welcomed Alec, paying a brief tribute to his experience and his back-to-back Emmys. Then the day started.

The show was just coming off the climax of an extremely passionate love story. The dramatically beautiful, but married Lady Georgeanna Courtland had been desperately involved with Sir Peregrine Henslowe, a dashing young bankrupt gambler. Lady Georgeanna was now pregnant with her first child, whose father all polite society knew to be Sir Peregrine.

The story had been shifted to a side-burner—Peregrine was off on the Continent trying to rebuild his purse at the casino tables and Georgeanna was in the country, being pregnant in seclusion. In truth, the actor playing Peregrine was on a write-out to do an off-Broadway play and the actress was on her own maternity leave. Much of today's script was devoted to clearing up the loose ends from that story.

The first scene in the episode—Prologue A it was called—featured Karen Madrigal as the duchess and her maid, Molly, Trina Nelson's character. Alec leaned forward, listening, interested in Karen. He would be playing many scenes with her.

He knew from the episodes he had watched that she was very good. But he still had everything to learn about her process. Did she like to rehearse endlessly? Or did she sleepwalk through the day and burst into life when the taping started? Did she—

It was wonderful to be back. The voiceover

work he had been doing was all technique, no emotion. Until this moment he had not let himself admit how much he had missed being a part of a daytime cast. He could feel his foot jiggling. A light, jubilant, almost a fizzing sensation was spreading through his body. He could hardly wait for his turn.

Karen and Trina finished their scene. Scripts rustled as people turned the page. The door to the rehearsal hall opened.

Alec usually didn't notice interruptions like an opening door. People were always coming in and out of the rehearsal hall—production assistants with notes for the director, extras who wanted a cup of coffee. Actors learned how to block out such distractions.

But something stronger than this training nipped at Alec. He had noticed the door opening and he looked.

It was Jenny.

She pulled a chair away from the wall. The actors in Prologue B began to read. Alec watched Jenny. She didn't sit on the chair like a normal person. Instead she perched on its back, her feet on the seat. She leaned forward, her elbows on her knees, her hands clasped between her legs. Her white shirt fell open slightly.

Prologue B finished. The production assistant's stopwatch clicked off. While Gil was noting the scene's time, Trina turned her script over and wrote some big letters on the back. She held it up like a sign for Jenny to read. Alec leaned forward so he could read it too. "BELT!!" it said.

Startled, Jenny peered down at her waist and noticed the empty belt loops there. She stuck her thumbs through them and grinned at Trina, not in the least embarrassed.

A man's voice came from the other side of the table. "I have a problem with 2C—"

Alec dragged his eyes away from Jenny. It was Brian who was speaking, directing his words to Gil. Why was he talking about scene 2C? They had just finished with Prologue A.

"I don't get this business with Hastings taking a tip from Jaspar."

"What do you mean 'taking?' " demanded the young actor who played Jaspar. Alec wasn't quite sure how that character fit into things. "The way I read it, it's a shakedown. That's not nice." The actor was exaggerating, pretending to feel this outrage. "I'm dead broke."

"That's just it," agreed Brian. He wasn't exaggerating. "Do you really think a duke's butler would do something like that? Isn't there a question of dignity here?"

Whoa. Alec sat back. What was going on? Brian was quibbling about a little piece of business, nitpicking, holding everything up. This was the sort of thing that could turn daily life on a soap into a nightmare, an actor quibbling about every single detail. As bad as things had gotten during *Aspen,* Alec had never held up rehearsal. He had met privately with Paul, with the producers, even with the network, but once it became clear that he had lost, he had shut up and done his job.

He glanced around the table. How was rest of

the cast reacting? If this was an everyday occurrence, they would all automatically switch off. *Wake me up when this is over.* Some would get more coffee, others would draw close to their neighbors and start talking about the Mets.

But clearly Brian's objections were not a part of the routine. People were alert, looking at each other, puzzled and questioning. They didn't understand what was happening.

How important a scene was this? Alec supposed that having been in the cast for all of twenty-five minutes, he shouldn't judge, but it certainly didn't seem like it was worth wasting time on. Gil, the director, needed to take control here; he needed to cut off this discussion and get things moving.

Of course there was an interesting wrinkle. The actor complaining was the head writer's boyfriend, and the head writer was in the room.

Gil had been listening to the actors, looking at them over the tops of his half-glasses. Then he deferred to Jenny. "What do you think?" he asked her. "Is it going anywhere?"

"Actually it is. People did tip servants after house parties and such—it was called 'vails.' "

"But this has just been a dinner," Brian protested. He had pushed his chair back so he could look at Jenny directly.

This didn't make sense. Alec felt all his weatherbeaten old gunfighter suspicions reemerging. Brian had had this script for a week, and he lived with Jenny. Surely he could have discussed it with her privately. He must want to challenge her in public.

"I know." Jenny didn't seem the least upset. If Brian was challenging her, she wasn't taking up the gauntlet. "That's why Jaspar's surprised. He wasn't expecting it."

Maybe she was stupid. This was a complicated moment, an actor using his personal relationship with the writer to embarrass her and undermine the director's authority. She didn't seem to have a clue. She was breezy, unconcerned, unaware. The simplest explanation was that she was stupid.

No, she wasn't stupid, she wasn't unaware. A person didn't get to be head writer of a network show by being stupid. Little moments charged with greater significance were the heart's blood of a soap. Jenny wouldn't be able to write a soap if she didn't live and breathe in a world of nuances. Jenny had to understand absolutely everything that was happening. She probably was seeing a whole lot more than Alec was.

"Fine. I understand Jaspar's reaction," Brian said. "The problem is with Hastings. I can't see him doing this."

"It is a little out of character," Jenny admitted.

Oh, no. A little out of character. On daytime television? How could that be?

This was a soap opera. The story had to get told, and a rare week went by when someone didn't have to do something out of character. If you couldn't live with that, you shouldn't be working in daytime.

"If you're uncomfortable with it, it's not a problem." Jenny's voice was still as cheery, still as unconcerned. "Jaspar goes to Lady Varley's next week, and her footman's in the scene. I'm sure he won't mind another page or so." She hopped off her perch on the chair. "But I'd better go make a note of it. Otherwise I'll forget."

Alec kept his expression even, but silently he cheered. Jenny Cotton might be playing the blithe tomboy, but she had just made one clever move, the kind that does not happen by accident. *You don't have to say these lines. You don't have to do this business. We'll just give it to someone else.* No actor wanted to lose screen time. She had cut her boyfriend off at the knees.

Brian reddened. "That's way too much trouble for you. I'll do it." He spoke as if he were being magnanimous and accommodating, as if he were doing her a tremendous favor . . . which of course he was not.

Well, well. Alec picked up his styrofoam coffee cup. His interest was now thoroughly engaged. Here was a cast which needed to believe that they were happy, a head writer who was pretending that she was Huck Finn, a boyfriend who had something to prove to someone. This was going to be one interesting place to work.

Two

Alec let himself be swept up by the rhythm of the production day. After the table reading, the script was "put on its feet"—the director blocked each scene, showing the actors where and how to move, explaining the camera angles to them. Then the production moved to the studio floor, and all the scenes on one set were dress rehearsed and taped, followed by all the scenes on another set. So after the work in the rehearsal hall, the cast scattered. Those whose scenes were first on the schedule went straight to makeup; others went to their dressing rooms to work on their lines. Those who had little to do in the current episode went to the greenroom to drink coffee and play bridge.

On a badly run show, the pace of the day was sickening and unpredictable, a raging flood carrying tangles of snagged debris. On good shows, the day was a powerful river in whose current strong swimmers and expert boatsmen could move quickly toward the deep-water port ahead. Every day an episode was completed. Every day closure was reached. Alec had done film, he had done live theater, he had done commercials, he had done most everything an actor can do. He had yet to find anything that satisfied him as much as a good day on a good soap. Soaps weren't the right work for perfectionists, they weren't right for people who craved variety, but they were right for him.

He didn't have very much to do in this first episode, mostly stand around and let the viewers get used to looking at him instead of the actor who had originated the role. His scenes were all with Lord Robin—Lydgate's younger brother, Ray Bianchetti's role. Robin was telling Lydgate about the end of Georgeanna and Peregrine's affair. The scenes were "recaps," designed to tell the occasional viewer what happened in the shows he had missed.

Alec did not yet have a very strong sense of Lydgate. What he did know was brothers. And he guessed that when they were kids, Bruce, his oldest brother, wouldn't have much liked it if Gordon, Alec, or Ross had known something that Bruce hadn't.

So that was how he played it. Lydgate was interested in what Robin was telling him, but he pretended not to be. Not only was he ashamed of his interest in gossip—surely dukes were above gossip—but he was also irritated. A younger brother shouldn't know more than the older. It upset the normal line of power.

As they rehearsed their scenes, Ray picked up on what Alec was doing and came back with an element of irritation. *You know you're interested; why not admit it?* And this routine scene came to life. Lydgate and Lord Robin felt like brothers, an eyeblink away from rolling around on the nursery floor, scratching and biting.

"I'd heard you were good," Ray said. "But I had no idea. I am going to learn a lot from you."

The characters Alec had played in the past had not had particularly interesting wardrobes. In his first job as Chris, the brash young construction worker on *Day By Day,* he had spent most episodes shirtless and in jeans so tight that no real construction worker could have ever constructed anything. Dr. Robert Oldfield, on *To Have and to Hold,* had worn a white lab coat. On *Passions,* Derek—this was the part Alec was best known for, the one he had won his Emmys for—had worn repressed young lawyer's clothes. And Alan, his character on *Aspen,* had changed clothing styles as often as he had changed personalities, about once every three or four episodes.

But the costume that was waiting for the Duke of Lydgate was marvelous. The shirt was a finespun white linen with three neck buttons hidden under a narrow frill. The breeches rode low and tight. The dark dress coat was cut close to the chest. In front it was cropped to the waist, and in back it swept to long rounded tails. Superb fabrics caressed Alec's skin, and exquisite tailoring hugged his build. No wonder such cheap doughnuts were served with the morning coffee—this costume must have cost the earth.

"I like this," he said to Ray as they stood together in front of their dressing room mirror. "Are all the costumes this good?"

Ray nodded. "You and I are particularly

lucky." Ray was wearing a crisp, dark uniform, touched with gilt buttons and gold braid. He was a young, good-looking guy, in his early twenties with thick black hair. "The guys who play the fops and Dandys, their clothes are ridiculous. But the cravats do get a little tiresome."

Cravats were the neckcloths fashionable during the Regency, and no one expected a mere actor to be able to tie their intricate knots. A nimble-fingered girl from the wardrobe department, often with a Xeroxed sheet of directions tucked under his arm, would tie them right before a scene was taped.

"Don't even think of untying this yourself," the girl told Alec as she looped a length of carefully starched, white muslinlike fabric around his neck. "We'll do it for you. We caught Lord Varley cutting himself out of his and this fabric is a blend that we have specially woven for us. It's very expensive, so take good care of it."

"Yes, ma'am." It had been a long time since anyone in wardrobe had lectured Alec about anything. On *Aspen* he had been a star; the younger crew members never spoke to him.

"Now this is an Oriental. It's very stiff and rigid, there're no creases." The girl talked as she worked. "The Trône d'Amour has a collateral dent. The Ballroom had two collateral dents and a pair of angling creases. The Mailcoach is much looser. Sir Peregrine wears it, but you don't."

Alec had to smile. "You like working here, don't you?"

"Oh, yes. I worked on *Love Never Ends,* and I thought that was great, but this place, everything is so interesting." She stepped back to scrutinize her work. "Did you know that this really high neckware was developed because the Prince had swollen glands? There's a good chance he had prophyria, which was what was making the King insane."

"No, I guess I didn't know that." What was prophyria? Alec had no idea.

"You'll learn a lot working here. You'll love it," the girl assured him. "Feel free to ask anyone if you have questions. Any time."

"I will," he promised.

His three scenes were all set in the duke's library, a dark, richly paneled room with shelf after shelf of leather-and-gilt books. One of the young set dressers was concerned that Alec would think the set was anachronistic. "But it's supposed to be that way. It's supposed to look like your grandfather decorated it."

"Thank you for setting my mind at ease."

Alec's knowledge of the history of the decorative arts was not quite as comprehensive as this person believed.

"Wait until you see the Chinese room set," the kid went on. "It's gorgeous. And it would have been very fashionable. The Regent's palace down at Brighton had a lot of influence for a time."

"So I am au courrant about something?"

"You're no Sir Peregrine, but you aren't as out of it as Lord Courtland. His taste is almost Jacobean."

"No," Alec intoned in feigned disbelief. "Almost Jacobean? You can't be serious." What did "almost Jacobean" mean? He didn't have a clue. On *Aspen* half the crew had never bothered to figure out what state the show was set in, but here the crew members were all running around talking as if they had Ph.D.'s in nineteenth-century British history. He loved it.

He moved around the library set, pacing out the distances, wanting to become as comfortable in the space as his character would be. He ran his hand along the ornately carved back of the desk chair. How did Lydgate feel when he did that? Dukes were quite splendid chaps. Lydgate's land would have numbered in the tens of thousands of acres. Did he feel privileged? Or was he arrogant, feeling entitled to all this? Did his possessions and responsibilities feel like a heavy load? Alec didn't know yet. But he would eventually. Over time he would come to know everything there was to know about his character—how he got angry, how he showed impatience, what moved him. After that the fun began, pushing the character's edges, experimenting, exploring.

It was good to be back.

Within a week Alec was agreeing that working on *My Lady's Chamber* was as great as everyone had predicted. The cast was a gutsy, creative group of actors, full of talent and energy. No one played it safe, no one was faking a performance, no one was coasting. They all believed in the show; they were all determined to make it work.

It was a friendly place. Unlike on the hour-long shows where each episode was split into a morning and an afternoon cast, this cast met as a whole in the rehearsal hall every morning. Everyone knew everyone. Lunch was set out in the greenroom. The whole cast stopped work and watched the show while they ate. They were a team, a company, an ensemble. Alec had been working so hard during his time on *Aspen* that he hadn't see much of other people, and it felt good to be picking up some friends again.

As much as he liked everything about the production, his first week hadn't made him understand his character any better. It was strange. Everything else about the show was well written; the characters were interesting, clearly defined people. Even Lady Varley, the maternal confidante—usually one of the blandest parts on a soap—had a serious dislike of aging that came through in all her scenes. But Alec could not, for the life of him, figure himself out.

Lydgate had had only one story line. In the first year of the show, Amelia, well-born, beautiful, and immensely rich, had been in love with Sir Peregrine—the penniless gambler who later became the father of Lady Georgeanna's baby. Her guardians, Lord and Lady Varley, had been determined to keep her money out of his hands so they had engineered a match with the Duke of Lydgate. The duke, wealthy in his own right, did not need her money; what his advisors liked about her was that she was a competent, level-headed young lady. Managing a duchy is a great deal of work, and those who had the duchy's interests at heart thought that this particular duke needed an able wife.

So Lydgate wasn't smart. And he had a cold and formal manner. That was it. That was all Alec knew. He waited another week, then another. Everyone else seemed pleased with his work, but he wasn't.

This was the sort of problem that an actor should take to a director. *My Lady's Chamber* had two directors, Terence Malard and Gil Norway. They took turns. One would direct three episodes one week and then two the next. Their similarity of vision as well as their domestic arrangements—they were a longterm gay couple—gave *My Lady's Chamber* its unique, stylized look.

But they were both melancholy, withdrawn men, much more interested in the camera than in the characters. Whenever Alec tried to talk to them about a scene or about Lydgate's motivation, they would answer in terms of what kind of shots they were planning to set up. They were no help.

"Why don't you go talk to Jenny?" Ray, Alec's dressing roommate, suggested. "She's the one writing the part."

"I can't imagine that she wants that."

In Alec's experience, head writers shielded themselves from the actors. They claimed it was because they didn't want to start hearing the actors' voices in their heads; the characters' voices were what counted. That sounded good, and Alec had actually believed it for nearly a month when he had first started in daytime. Now he knew the truth—the writers avoided the actors because when given half a chance, an actor could consume vast quantities of a writer's time. Actors could be among the most self-centered creatures on earth, able to obsess endlessly on all matters relating to themselves.

"No, no." Ray was shaking his head. "Jenny's not like that. She hasn't been around as much as usual the last two weeks because she's been getting ready for the story conference." That was a two-day meeting that the writer and producer of a show had four times a year with the network people in order to review the writer's long-range story ideas. "But normally she's available. Her door is always open. She's one of us."

That sounded like a bad idea to Alec. A head writer shouldn't be buddies with the actors. He or she had to do what was right for the show, not what was right for the cast. Being friends could make it hard to let someone go when his or her story was over.

But if an open door was the policy around here, Alec wasn't going to be the only one too noble to take advantage of it. Jenny Cotton being so close to the cast might cause problems, but they wouldn't be his problems.

The next afternoon he went up to the third floor. He had stayed late to have some publicity stills taken, and it was well past five. Jenny's assistant was not at her desk, but the door to Jenny's office was indeed open. She was sitting at her computer. He knocked lightly and she looked up.

"What a nice surprise." She hopped out of her chair. "Come in."

"People tell me I can do this," Alec said to her now. "Barge in here without an appointment."

"Of course. Of course." She was as cheerful as always. "In fact, I'm usually around much more. The story conference was last week. I have to turn into the invisible woman to get through it."

"How did it go?" Alec asked. Those meetings could be a nightmare. The network executives sometimes had the story sense of an earthworm.

"I survived."

"What makes you think I was asking about you? It's Lydgate's survival I care about, not yours."

Her laugh was marvelous, clear and bell-like. "And here I was starting to think you weren't the typical self-centered actor."

"I don't know what would make you think that." Alec could feel himself smiling. "Do you really suppose I came in here to talk about world peace?"

She laughed again. "Would you rather hear how thrilled the network is with you? This business of Lydgate being envious of Robin—that's really interesting stuff, and it's mostly from you. I had never thought about it."

As critical as he was of his own performance, Alec was willing to concede that he was doing a good job with the relationship between the duke and his younger brother. True, Lydgate had inherited all the toys—the title, the money, Lydgate House, and Lydgate Abbey—but Ray's character was an active, vital man, full of gallantry and vitality. Details of his military career were vague, but clearly he had distinguished himself on the battlefield. He had considerable self-assurance; he was a young man who knew he had been tested. Of course the duke envied that. In fact Alec envied it too. He'd much rather have Ray's role than his own.

"Thank you," he acknowledged Jenny's compliment. "But beyond that, I don't really know what I am doing. I haven't figured this guy out yet."

"None of us can either," Jenny said promptly. "The whole writing staff, we all hate writing for him. No one has any sense of his voice." Jenny did the longterm story outlines; she also wrote the "breakdowns," detailed scene-by-scene summaries of each show. From those breakdowns her staff of five script writers—former Regency romance novelists, all of whom worked out of their homes—wrote the actual scripts.

"But we need him because he keeps Amelia from being happy," she continued, "and the viewers all love her. But he's like the Bermuda triangle. Whatever you throw in just disappears. The great disappearing character. That's why we hired you. If you can't do something with him, then no one can."

"You may think you're flattering me, but you're not. That's why characters die. Their writers don't understand them."

"Oh, come on. I just said that we need him."

"I have heard that before."

"You've been on four different shows. You must have heard everything before."

That was certainly true.

"So tell me," she went on. "I've been dying to ask you. What do you think of us? Are you happy here? Do you like being on a half-hour show?"

Alec found himself smiling again. It was usually actors who needed massive amounts of approval. But clearly Jenny did too. She wanted to have him like the show. She needed it. "It's certainly the warmest, friendliest place I've ever worked at. You know you can take risks without being shot down."

"I'm so glad you feel that way." She perched on the edge of her desk, obviously pleased. This was what she had wanted to hear.

So Alec kept his reservations to himself. "I do. I was told that you were the one who pleaded my case when the part was being recast. I appre—"

"Where did you hear that nonsense?" she interrupted. "The next thing you'll be saying is that I wanted to hire you just to remind the world that our show is doing great, and Paul Tomlin's is a big bomb."

Her smile had a mischievous, elfin edge to it. Apparently this was indeed part of why she had hired him. She was delighted that her show was beating the pants of *Aspen!!* She might seem like the chirpy kid next door, but she was competitive.

"I guess we shouldn't talk about that, should we?" She didn't wait for him to answer. "So what do you think of Colley Lightfield's story line? Do you think the viewers know that he's gay even though he's not admitting it to himself? We just can't decide how far to go with that since homosexual acts were illegal back then. It would be so interesting if—"

She wanted to talk about the show, the characters. It must consume all her time and thoughts. It was her life.

"I'm still too new to register an opinion," he answered. "I've only been around for three weeks."

"I know. I know." She made a face. "I suppose everyone still thinks of you as Derek."

He nodded. Yes, on the street, in the train, that's how people still recognized him, not as Lydgate, not as that idiot on *Aspen,* but as Derek, his old character on *Passions.*

"I'm starting to mind that," she said. "I'm getting very possessive of you. I want people to start thinking of you as the Duke of Lydgate. You're ours now. You should be—" She broke off as if she had just noticed something. Alec looked over his shoulder to see what she might have seen, but there was nothing there. When he looked back at her, she was on her feet, the color draining out of her face.

He rose instantly, putting out his hand. "Are you all right?"

"I'm sorry. I'm . . . Will you excuse me for a moment?"

"Of course. Of course."

She was out of the office before he was done speaking. He followed her into the hall, but by the time he was there, the door to the ladies' room was swinging shut behind her. There was nothing he could do.

His little sister Meg had been a sickly kid, and she was always disappearing like this. "I want to be alone for a while," she would say whenever someone called through a closed door, and Alec was never sure if she was being nice, wanting to spare other people, or if she really did want to be alone. He had hated that part of her being sick, the standing around, not being able to do something for her.

He put his hands in his pockets. The ladies' room door was wood-grained with a heavy chrome handle. He couldn't go in. Jenny wouldn't want him to. He looked at his watch. It was past six. The only people left in the building were the security guards. None of them were women he could send into the ladies' room to help her.

Of course maybe she didn't need help. He forced himself to go back to her office and sit down. Should he be worried or not? He didn't know. He got up to look at the crammed bookcase. There were diaries, volumes of letters, histories of every type, and paperback Regency romances packed into the shelves horizontally, two deep. He picked one up. Whoever painted the cover had gotten the cravat wrong.

Meg hadn't been a sickly kid. That had been the lie the family had told themselves for the first year. "When Meg gets well . . . when Meg feels a little stronger." The truth was that Meg had leukemia. It had killed her.

Alec picked up another book off Jenny's shelf. The guy on the cover of this one was wearing a colored neckcloth. The Duke of Lydgate would never wear one of those.

He had felt responsible for Meg. She had been a year younger than him. Surely keeping her alive had been his job, and he hadn't done it.

He heard footsteps. He put the book away and went into the hall. Jenny was a few yards away. She was walking slowly. Her arms folded across her stomach as if she were ill. She was ashen.

At the sight of him she blinked and halted. "Oh, you waited." She was surprised. She had forgotten about him. "Ah . . . do you mind if we finish this another time?"

She didn't look well. "Are you all right? Come sit down."

"I'm okay." She went into the office. "Really. Just go on. I'll be okay."

These were the shortest sentences he had ever heard her speak. When you were around a sick person a lot, you learned how to hear what she were really saying. Jenny was not okay.

Alec wasn't sure what to do. He knew what Jenny wanted him to do—disappear, leave her alone, let her deal with this in private. But if something were truly wrong, she might need help.

Be honest.

That was Meg talking. She had been the one who had broken the family silence. She had been the one who had made them all face what was happening. One night Alec had been helping her upstairs, because her joints were stiff and swollen. At the top of the stairs, she turned to him, her dark eyes wide in her pale face. "Could you say something to Mom and Dad, Alec? Could you tell them I want us to talk about this?"

About what? There's nothing to talk about. That's what he wanted to say, but her voice was so low and her grip on his arm so tight that he swallowed and nodded. "Yes, Meg, anything you want."

So he helped her to her room and went back downstairs. He dreaded going back to the kitchen. Being the first one to say it . . . it would be like he was the one who was making it come true.

He had been awkward, hesitant. He was only ten years old. But he had done it. He felt like she was his responsibility. So he waited until his parents were alone and then he spoke. "Meg knows she's really sick. She wants to talk about it."

His mother had gasped; his dad stared hard at his empty coffee cup. But they were good people, strong and courageous. They too knew what they had to do. "I'm sure she's right, son," his father had said.

So as a family they had faced the truth about Meg together. The next year wasn't easy, but the family grew closer and stronger . . . because they were telling each other the truth. And Alec swore after that he would always tell the truth.

Right now Jenny Cotton wasn't telling him the truth.

She was pale and worried. This was something serious. Female serious. He was sure of that. His character on *To Have and to Hold* had been an obstetrician.

There was nothing to do but blurt it out . . . just as he had done in his parents' kitchen twenty years before.

"Are you bleeding?" Maybe he shouldn't be so blunt, but he knew no other way.

"It's nothing . . . I'm sure it's nothing. It's not heavy or anything like that."

So she was bleeding. He couldn't stop now. He had to ask the rest. "Are you pregnant?"

She nodded.

"Then you need to talk to your doctor right away. Do you have the number? Do you want me to call?" He was eager to have something to do.

"Actually . . ." Jenny sat down and ran her hands through her hair. "I don't really have a doctor. It's been so recent . . . only a couple of weeks, and with the story conference, I haven't had time. But the hospital's so close, you know. I'll just call a car, or it might be as fast to walk over—"

She was at risk of a miscarriage, and she was thinking about walking to the hospital? "You are not walking anywhere."

"I suppose it's stupid, isn't it? But maybe there's no need to rush over there. Maybe if I wait here a while, it will stop. I don't know." She was sounding uncertain, not at all like herself. "I don't want to go sit there for hours and hours if it's nothing."

"No." Alec spoke firmly. Jenny was an adult. She had the right to make her own decisions, but there were times when you had to step in and take charge. "You're going to the hospital. The car service will probably get you there faster, but I can call an ambulance if you prefer."

That was her choice, a car or an ambulance. Whether or not to go to the hospital was not up for discussion. His tone made that clear.

"The car then. A car's fine. I don't need an ambulance. And you don't need to come. Really."

He could appreciate her position. She hardly knew him, she was embarrassed, she wanted to handle this herself, etc. etc. But he was not going to abandon a person, a woman, at a moment like this. He picked up the phone.

The show had a steady relationship with a nearby car service, and the dispatcher promised a car immediately.

Outside her office Jenny automatically turned left toward the staircase. Alec took her arm, directing her to the right. The freight-only policy about the elevator was strictly enforced, but surely no one would begrudge Jenny the use of it now. He put his hand over the rubber gasket of the elevator door, holding it open for her. The top of her head just barely came to his chin.

It was hard to think of her being pregnant. He had thought of her as a tomboy, a sprite, a tough little Tinkerbell. But she wasn't. She was a woman carrying a child. She might have been acting cheery and open, but all the while she had this secret.

The car was waiting. Alec opened the back door and then slid in beside her. He spoke a few words to the driver and the car pulled away from the curb. Jenny was stiff, staring down at her hands. She said nothing. She was silent, alone.

Alone. She wasn't alone. Alec cursed himself. "I'll call Brian the minute we get to the hospital." Why hadn't he done that right away? Brian was the father of this baby. He should be the one with her, not Alec. "I'm sorry. I should have—"

"No, no." She interrupted. "Really, no. It's okay. Brian's terrible at hospitals. He hates them."

She shifted uneasily. The idea of calling Brian made her nervous. Alec spoke calmly. "Fine. Whatever you say."

The car stopped at a light.

"It will just be another minute," he said.

She didn't answer. The light changed, and the car started forward again. Alec thought about taking her hand, but he suspected she wouldn't like it.

"I bet they can't do anything." She spoke without looking up.

"I don't know."

"Well, I do." Now she lifted her head. She stared forward, looking blankly through the thick plexiglass separating them from the driver. "I've been writing for soaps for ten years. I know miscarriages. At eight weeks there's nothing to do. Later there's medication for people actually having contractions. But at eight weeks there's nothing."

In the end there had been nothing more to do for Meg either. The family had tried everything. They had tremendous resources of energy and will. They were tireless; they were disciplined. But they hadn't been able to keep Meg alive.

"I hate this," Jenny was still talking. "I hate it—not being able to do anything. I don't mind working hard. Set me a goal and I'll meet it. I'll do whatever has to be done." Her hands were knotted into fists. She was a determined person. "But this doing nothing, I can't stand it."

Alec understood. His family had refused to admit that they were helpless against Meg's illness. Alec knew that was why he always struggled and persevered now, even through something as hopeless as *Aspen* . . . because he couldn't stand feeling helpless. He couldn't bear to watch Meg die again.

They had turned into the hospital; the car was pulling under the wide canopy of the emergency room entrance. "Stay there," he told Jenny.

He came around the back of the car and opened her door, holding out his hand to help her. Her lips were tight and she was even paler. Her freckles stood out, bright splotches mocking her misery. Her step faltered.

"What is it?"

"I don't know . . . nothing . . . I felt a little faint, that's all."

She didn't look well. Swiftly, instinctively, he put one arm around her shoulders and lowered the other to catch her at her knees. Just as Derek had done for Ginger back on *Passions,* he lifted her off her feet, carrying her toward the hospital entrance. He cradled her close, turning sideways as the automatic doors to the hospital whooshed open.

People rushed to help. An orderly appeared with a wheelchair. A white-capped nurse quickened her step. A woman with a clipboard hurried out from behind the registration counter.

"Can she sit in the chair?" the orderly was asking. "Do you need a gurney?"

Jenny was protesting. "I'm fine. Put me down." She didn't like being held, and she wasn't used to being carried. Alec lowered her into the chair.

And as he was straightening, he suddenly sensed the gasp, the sudden intake of breath, the questioning pause that every soap actor knows so well.

"Oh, my word,"—it was the lady with the clipboard—"I know you. You're Derek."

Jenny did indeed lose her baby. Alec called Brian while she was being examined. The two of them lived in Gourvent, a Brooklyn neighborhood not far from the studio. Brian was at the hospital within minutes. Looking gravely concerned, he shook Alec's hand and then a nurse's aide led him through the set of swinging double doors so he could see Jenny, something that had been forbidden to Alec. Later that night he called Alec to thank him again and to report that Jenny had been running a fever so she was being kept in the hospital overnight. But she didn't want people at the studio to know what had happened. Would Alec mind being a little vague?

No, of course, he wouldn't mind. He would do whatever she wanted.

He wasn't scheduled to work the next day, so he went to see her. Here in the hospital, unlike at her office, the door was closed. He knocked softly, not wanting to wake her if she was asleep.

"Come in." Her answer was immediate, but her voice sounded flat and weary.

He went in. The room was crammed with flowers. There was a green vase of long-stemmed roses on the windowsill, lilies and freesia on the nightstand, tulips on the bedside tray. Birds of paradise, ginger, and grapevine were lined up on the floor. It was no surprise. People in the soap world got up early and were used to doing things quickly. The show, the network, and people from other shows were weighing in with floral tributes.

Which was why Alec had brought her a bagel.

She was propped up in bed, wearing a pale, much laundered hospital gown. She didn't have any books or magazines, and the TV was not on. She must have just been sitting, doing nothing. He didn't imagine that that happened very often.

This wasn't what she wanted other people to see. Alec knew that. She wanted to be the cheery and lively kid sister. She didn't want people to think of her as having problems, but she did. Here was pain. She was suffering. Alec felt drawn to her.

He handed her the little white bag from the deli. "This is in case your breakfast was inedible."

She took it without saying anything. She reached inside and brought the bagel out, the little sheet of waxed paper falling open. She looked down at it and suddenly started to blink hard as if she were going to cry.

He didn't imagine that that happened very often either.

"Thank you for your help last night." She spoke without looking up. "I don't think of myself as a person who needs rescuing."

"You probably don't need it much," he said briskly. She wouldn't want sympathy. Warmth and tenderness would make her cry, and she didn't want to cry. "And you didn't really need it yesterday. I'm sure you would have managed fine on your own." Clearly she wanted to believe that. He pulled up a chair. "Tell me how you are doing. How's your temperature? I hear that's what's keeping you here."

She cleared her throat. "It's normal, and if it stays that way, I can go home this afternoon."

"Well, that's good."

Why had he said that? Why was he sounding hearty and consoling? Okay, she wanted to hold on to her composure, but that didn't mean they had to pretend she wasn't in pain. That was what he had liked about Dr. Robert Oldfield, his character on *To Have and to Hold.* In the end it turned out that the guy was practicing without a license, but his bedside manner had been great. He knew that there were times when a person just flat-out felt bad. "But I suppose you don't much care where you are."

She shrugged. "Being home will be a little better, but still—"

"A lousy thing happened to you. You've every right to feel bad."

"I don't know." She ran her finger around the bagel, smoothing the line of cream cheese oozing between the cut halves. "It doesn't seem fair. I never got to feel good about being pregnant, so why do I feel bad about not being pregnant?"

"The pregnancy wasn't planned?"

She shook her head. "No, and I think we were both still in denial about it. When I first thought it might be possible, we kept saying that we wouldn't discuss it until we knew for sure because why raise a big fuss over something that might not happen? And then when I knew, I don't know . . . we just didn't. I figured we had plenty of time to sort everything out, and now I suppose it's just as well that we didn't make any plans—"

She was rambling. Alec took her hand. "There's nothing like knowing that you're going to lose something to make you start wanting it."

Her hand didn't relax, didn't curve into his. She wasn't used to this, someone trying to comfort her. Alec kept his clasp light.

Even so she pulled herself free after a moment. "I've been lying here wondering if it was because of stress. I did just finish a story conference. My first boss used to say that story conferences made her hair fall out. Her hairbrush would be matted every day. I saw it. It was strictly stress. And"—Jenny's voice started to break—"I'd much rather have lost my hair than this."

Alec wished there was something he could say, something that would make her pain go away.

But there wasn't. "You're blaming yourself. Don't do that."

She didn't seem to hear. "I suppose I should have known this would happen." She ran a hand through her short hair. "I've never been very good at the girl stuff." She was tugging at the ends of her hair as if desperately, subconsciously, trying to get them to grow. Short hair was boyish. Long, flowing hair was womanly.

Alec started to protest. Surely she didn't think herself unattractive. Yes, her energy was tomboyish, but he liked that about her. He had been married to a professional beauty, and he had spent a long, long time standing at his old front door, looking at his watch, wondering when Chloe was going to be ready. She looked beautiful, absolutely exquisite, but neither she nor eventually he had found any joy in that beauty. Now he hated hearing women long to be beautiful.

But he kept his mouth shut. There was no point. If Jenny had always felt unfeminine, if that had been a life-long concern, a few words from him weren't going to do any good, especially now.

He was saved from saying anything by a knock which was immediately followed by the door opening and Brian coming in.

"Why, Alec!" Those were Brian's first words. That seemed strange to Alec. Surely Brian should have spoken to Jenny first. Oh well, maybe he was just surprised to see Alec. "You came to see Jenny. I'm sure she appreciates that."

Alec stood up to shake Brian's hand, but Brian was carrying flowers, and he didn't have a free hand. He had brought a dainty little arrangement, three blushing orchids nestled in moss, perfect for a hospital nightstand . . . or it would have been if Jenny's hadn't already been crowded with overblown arrangements.

"These are sort of redundant, aren't they?" Brian was speaking lightly, seeming to laugh at himself. "I could have been a little more original." He moved a basket of hyacinths and wedged his flowers next to her plastic water pitcher. Then he looked down at her. "How much longer will they entomb you here?"

"If my temperature doesn't go up, then maybe late this afternoon."

Alec was puzzled. If this had been a scene he was directing, he would have had Jenny dissolve at the sight of Brian. Here she had been doing her best to control herself in front of Alec, someone she barely knew, and at last comes the man she loves, the father of her lost child. Surely now the tears would come. Here was the person who would support her, comfort her. With him she would be safe; with him she could cry. But Jenny hadn't dissolved. She was as controlled and polite as she had been with Alec.

"I'm glad you're about to get out. This can't be any fun." Brian looked around the room. "I'd hate being in the hospital. It give me the willies just visiting."

For God's sake, man, she just lost your baby. Show her that you mind.

Brian went on talking. The room was small,

wasn't it? But at least she wasn't having to share it. Which flowers were from the network? Had they spent big bucks? His words seemed forced, his tone too bright.

Alec thought he understood. There had been a rule in his own marriage—Chloe was the only one who was entitled to get upset. Alec wasn't supposed to have any problems. His job in the relationship had been to solve the problems; her job was to have them. It had worked until they started having problems that he couldn't solve.

It must be like that with Brian and Jenny. Jenny was the problem solver. "I don't think of myself as a person who needs rescuing," she had told Alec. But here she was now, needy and distressed. She was having the troubles, and that broke the rules. Brian wasn't sure of what to do.

"So, Alec, tell me." Brian was waving Alec back into the room's one chair. He moved aside a vase of flowers so he could perch on the windowsill. "What was it like working with Steve Northland?"

Steve Northland? He had been the director of the movie Alec had done between *Aspen* and *My Lady's Chamber*. Why were they talking about *him*? "Fine."

"I had some conversations with him back when he was about to do *East Side*."

"Oh?" Alec's voice was careful. "Some conversations" could mean that two people really tried to work out a deal and then finally, reluctantly had to give up. Or it could refer to the director's assistant saying "Don't call us, we'll call you" at the end of a cattle-call audition. But, in truth, Alec didn't care what it meant. Jenny had had a miscarriage. Why talk about career stuff?

Of course maybe Brian was one of these men who couldn't show any genuine concern in front of an outsider. Just because he was glib didn't mean he was unfeeling. Alec supposed he himself should leave; that's probably how he could help Jenny the most, by leaving. So he stood up. Brian turned to him instantly, as if welcoming the distraction. Like the experienced actors they were, they ad-libbed farewells.

As Alec waited in front of the bank of cream-colored elevators, he wondered what was going on back in Jenny's room. What was the tone of their conversation? Was Brian sitting on the bed, his arms around Jenny, letting her cry against his chest? Or was he still perched on the windowsill, able to talk only about himself?

Three

Jenny knew all there was to know about hospital procedure. Every show she had worked on until her own had had a hospital in it, and her first boss had been a stickler for accurate research. But she had never been an actual patient before. She had never had the plastic-coated bracelet clamped on her arm. She had never been the one in the bed.

The solitude surprised her. She hadn't been prepared for that. On soap operas hospital rooms were always full of people—doctors, nurses, and visitors, tons and tons of visitors. If a patient woke up at three A.M., some faithful friend would be sitting in the chair, ready to play the scene. But last night when Jenny had awakened at three A.M., there hadn't been anyone in the chair. She had been alone.

The walls of the room had seemed gray when she had awoken last night. Now she knew that they were blue. It wasn't a pretty blue or an interesting blue, simply the sort of blue that when you woke up all alone seemed gray. Of course the room was now full of flowers, and that was nice, very nice, but it didn't change the fact that she was here alone. Alec had come, but he had left when Brian came. Brian hadn't been able to stay long—he was in today's cast—so now she was alone again.

She thought about calling her dad. She wouldn't feel so alone if she talked to him, but he hadn't known that she'd been pregnant. To tell him about the miscarriage would only worry him, and she'd spent most of her life trying not to worry him. It would have been different if she had had a mother, but everything about her life would have been different if she had had a mother.

"Oh, Jenny, Jenny. We're no good at this girl stuff, are we?"

She was eight, getting ready for her first ballet recital. Standing on a stool in front of the bathroom mirror, she was solemnly watching her father struggle with a wreath of artificial flowers. He was supposed to be putting it in her hair, bobby-pinning it around the scraggly, off-center bun. But her hair was thick and slippery. Her father was having trouble.

Tom Cotton was a young man. He had been a husband at eighteen, a father at nineteen, a widower at twenty. His wife had been young too. She had been named after a flower, Lily, and her death had been simple, a car accident, the other driver's fault.

Her parents had come and scooped up the baby. "You're in no situation to raise a child," they told Tom, and of course they were right. Tom was a wonderful guy—good looking, polite, and full of frank, honest charm—but he was a professional pool player. He went from one tournament to another, driving all night, showering at the truck stops, eating peanut butter crackers out of the vending machine. He and Lily had loved the life. After Jenny had been born, they had bundled her up in her little pink blanket and had gone everywhere, having fun.

But soon there was no Lily.

There was no way Tom could have managed Jenny alone, especially as she wasn't so much of a baby any more. When her mother had been alive, she had sat round-eyed in her car seat, quietly watching the world. But now she was crawling, and the knees of her little overalls would be dark and sticky from the floors in the pool halls. She was interested in cigarette butts and electrical outlets. She wanted to find out what pennies tasted like. On long car rides she thrashed and wailed, a prisoner of her car seat.

So Tom had let his in-laws take her, but after three months he had gone to get her back. He was only twenty years old, but he wasn't afraid of his responsibilities. Lily had hated her parents' home. What would make her daughter like it any better?

He gave up competition and opened up a pool hall in a dusty little town in eastern Oklahoma. He didn't like it as much as the traveling life—he missed the variety of the road and the sharp lilt of competition—but he did a good job with the pool hall. It was a clean, honest place. And he was raising his daughter to be clean and honest too.

He poked another bobby pin into Jenny's wreath. The little bun of hair slipped down over her left ear. He stuck a bobby pin on that side, pushing everything back in place.

Jenny looked at herself in the mirror. She could see her father's face too. His eyebrows were drawn close together. Clearly he had doubts. This was "girl stuff."

"I'm sure it will be okay now, Dad," she said.

"I don't know, sweetheart. Can you shake your head?"

"We aren't supposed to shake our heads. This is ballet."

Tom was willing to be persuaded. He held up a hand mirror so Jenny could look at the back of her head. There was a lot of stray hair everywhere, but the flowers looked nice. Jenny liked the idea of wearing flowers in her hair.

"These flowers, Dad . . . are any of them lilies?" That had been her mother's name, Lily.

"No, sweetheart, they're not."

The recital was being held in the junior high, and the little girls gathered in the gym. There were mothers in charge, and they had all come prepared with combs, brushes, even an ironing board. Jenny knew that she should go to one of them. "Please, Mrs. Pollard, could you help me with my hair?" They were all so nice. Any one of them would have done Jenny's hair for her. They would have taken the mass of bobby pins out of the clumsy bun and then brushed her hair until it shone, twisting it, pinning it, making it look like all the other girls' hair, the girls who had mothers.

But to ask would be admitting her dad hadn't done a good enough job. So Jenny didn't ask, and during the first pirouette the wreath fell out of her hair.

Jenny and Tom lived in a little house next to the pool hall. The two places were on the south side of town across the river from the churches and the schools, from Main Street and the nice houses. Tom kept up his property, but lots of people on the south side didn't. The houses were small and weathered with sagging porches and dirt yards. The roads were flat and narrow. There were no sidewalks, curbs, and gutters. After a heavy rain, big puddles collected in the shallow spots of the roads and yards.

Jenny was the only white child on the south side of the river. There were blacks and Indians, and in nice weather Jenny played with them. Her dad had put up a metal swing set for her at the back corner of the parking lot, and there were plenty of places to play along the river, under the bridge and in the broad shallows where the river bent.

But she played with those other children only in fine weather. This was a cautious time, a cautious place. "Don't be going into white folks' homes," black parents told their children. The Indian parents didn't have to say anything—their kids just knew.

So for much of her childhood Jenny was alone. She learned to read early. Every Saturday morning her father took her across the river to the Carnegie library and let her check out as many books as she wanted. When she wasn't reading, she made up stories of her own. She gave herself friends, brothers, and sisters. When she was an Indian princess guiding the lost pioneers, the wagon train would be full of other children. When she was a girl astronaut, a dozen or so other voyagers would be aboard the starship. She always had companions on her imaginary adventures.

Her father adored her imagination. He encouraged her to tell stories. "That billboard there, those two people on it, who do you think they are?"

Jenny would make up a story about them, sometimes two or three different stories. Her dad would listen and listen, maybe ask a few questions. When she was done, he would hug her. "You have your mother's imagination." Clearly he loved that about her.

Life would have been easier for Jenny if her father had let her stay on their side of the river, if they had crossed the bridge only for the library and the stores. But Tom knew that the other side of the river had Brownie troops and ballet lessons. He arranged for her to go to a grade school on the north side of town and he signed her up for all the things little white girls were supposed to sign up for.

The school was nice, and the activities were fun, but Jenny knew from the very beginning that she was different. Her Halloween costumes came from the dime store. One year she was a ghost, the next year a clown. The other girls were princesses, brides, or Gypsies. Tom sewed her Girl Scout patches on her sash with a man's big staggering stitches. The mothers used their machines, carefully threading the needle with one color of thread and the bobbin with another.

She never said anything to her father, but she would try on her own to be like the other girls. The Brownie troop would go on a hike, having packed their lunches in little knapsacks. Jenny would see the other girls' sandwiches—their mothers had cut the crusts off the bread. Secretly, glancing over her shoulder to be sure that no one was looking, Jenny would unwrap the wax paper on her own sandwich and would pinch the crusts off the bread, hurriedly swallowing the crusts so no one would see. But the sandwich never looked right; the edges were scraggly and compressed.

She wondered about her mother. Having been nine months old when Lily died, she remembered nothing about her. "Tell me about her," she would plead with her father. "What was she like? Did she dress nicely?"

"Sure, of course, sweetheart, of course."

"What were her clothes like? Describe them to me."

Her father would try. "Well, she had this green shirt."

"I know about that. She's wearing that in the pictures. What else? Did she wear dresses? Pretty dresses?" Jenny wanted, she needed, to know that her mother had worn pretty dresses.

"She must have, but sweetie, I don't really remember. You have her imagination, that's what counts."

"What about her hair?" Jenny knew that she

was badgering her father, but she couldn't help it. This was too important. "Could she do interesting things to her hair?"

"She wore it long, but sometimes on really hot days she would twist it up."

"So she was good with hair?"

"I guess so, but I'm not sure I know what you mean."

Would she have been able to do my hair? That's what Jenny meant. But of course she would have been able to. She was a mother. And her name was Lily. It was such a pretty name, so feminine. Someone named Lily would have to be good with hair.

A mother named Lily would have baked cupcakes for school parties, she would have bought Jenny the right clothes, she would have fixed her hair for the ballet recital. She would have cut the crusts off sandwich bread. Jenny believed that with all her heart. This wasn't another story she was making up. It was the truth.

It was awful growing up without a mother. Sometimes things would happen, embarrassing things. One time a part of her body that she didn't want to talk about started to itch. Night after night she couldn't fall asleep because of this horrible itching. It wouldn't stop and she was scared because it seemed wrong that she should itch there. She could have told her mother about it right away. She was sure of that. She could have taken her mother aside and told her in secret. Her mother would have taken care of it, and no one else would have ever known. But she couldn't tell her dad right away. She waited and waited until finally in the middle of the night she couldn't stand it any more.

He knew she didn't want him looking at her so he had taken her to the emergency room. Strange people had been there at that time of night, people who were drunk, people who smelled bad. Tom had kept his arm around her the whole time. Then it turned out to be a bug bite she had gotten while playing down by the river in a pair of loose shorts. The elastic of her underpants had chafed it and it had become infected.

If she had had a mother, she wouldn't have had to suffer for three nights, she wouldn't have had to go to the emergency room for a bug bite.

With time things got easier. Even though she was different, no one made fun of her. She was high-spirited and engaging; she kept her secrets to herself. She had a unique position at school, and she began to like that. She was not a part of a crowd, she did not have a best girlfriend, but she was the one kid in school everybody trusted. If an Indian kid needed to say something to a white kid, the message was sent through Jenny. During her freshman year in high school the drama teacher wanted to put on a play set in the civil war south, but needed to know how the blacks felt about it. She asked Jenny. Jenny didn't know, but it was easy enough for her for find out. She rode the bus across the river with these kids, and they told her what they thought. "No way we're playing slaves."

On the first day of Jenny's sophomore year, the school bus made its stops on the south side of the river and then rumbled across the potholes in the bridge. A loud whine of the brakes announced a stop at the base of Main Street.

The bus had never stopped here before. Not many people lived on Main Street. Most of the second-floor space above the stores was rented by insurance agents and realtors for their offices. There were a few apartments, but no one knew the people who lived in them. In the evening after the stores closed, the street was deserted. There were no kids playing ball or riding bikes. But clearly a high school student lived there now.

A boy got on the bus. Dark-haired, he was slender and tall. He looked at the faces before him—on one side of the bus were the bronzed Indians with their sleek black hair; the black kids were on the other side and there was one freckled white girl by herself in the front. This was clearly not the regular kids' bus.

September should come with cool, crisp wind, but it didn't, not in this part of the world. Early September in Oklahoma was as hot and yellow-hazed as August. The boy's mother might have called this move a fresh start, but he knew better. Looking at this bus full of outcasts told him what he already knew. Living downtown was odd, a mark of failure.

He slid into the seat across from the white girl. She was friendly, as she introduced herself.

"My name is Brian O'Neill," he answered.

Jenny would not learn his whole story for a year, and even then he concealed from her how much pain he felt. His mother had married young and wrong. The man drank, and she had finally left him, coming back to her hometown because she had nowhere else to go. Even here they could only afford the little apartment over the fabric store. Brian got the one little bedroom, Mrs. O'Neill slept on the fold-out davenport.

She had a mission, she needed to prove that she wasn't a failure, that she was just as good as people who weren't living over a fabric store. She expected Brian to accomplish this for her. He was going to be a success. He was to make them respectable.

Brian too wanted to succeed. He needed to have people know that he wasn't his father, even people who knew nothing about his father. But he didn't want to be respectable. That was his mother's goal, and all his life she had controlled and dominated him. He had an adolescent's dream—to be successful without being respectable. He wanted to be free.

A child of an alcoholic, he had a lightning-quick sense of situations, and as he got on the bus after school that first day, he was intrigued, even fascinated, by the one white girl on the bus.

She had no label. She wasn't one of the popular kids, she wasn't a greaser or a farm kid. She wasn't black, she wasn't Indian. She was just Jenny. Everyone knew her; everyone liked her. The popular girls all spoke to her. When a teacher asked her to help pass out the textbooks and she had picked up a stack of books too high for her, a black guy was out of his seat in a flash to help her.

But she had sat on the bus alone. She walked through the halls alone. None of the other sophomore girls could stand being alone, but she didn't seem to mind.

She seemed like the freest person he had ever met.

He walked across the bridge later that afternoon looking for her. She wasn't hard to find. As hot as it was, she was at the playground of the elementary school, shooting baskets with a couple of the Indian boys. They melted away at the sight of this strange white kid.

She was in cut-off jeans, and her sweat-dampened T-shirt was clinging to her newly developed frame. She tossed him the ball. He caught it, but instead of shooting a basket, he walked over to her, and handed it back. He was not athletic.

"But I'll watch you," he said.

"Oh, no." Jenny had felt perfectly at ease with him on the bus this morning, but now the way this boy was looking at her . . . she wasn't used to that. She shifted uneasily, holding the ball close to her body. "I've got to go in anyway. I promised I'd help my dad."

"Your dad's home?"

Brian was familiar with fathers who were home at three in the afternoon. He just wasn't used to this being something a person would admit to.

"Sort of," she answered. "He's probably not, but maybe. It doesn't matter. We live so close that it's hard to say."

She wasn't making any sense. She wanted him

to stop looking at her. But she didn't want him to go away. If he could stay and not look at her . . . "Why don't you come? You can meet my dad." That would be okay. Everyone liked her dad.

Jenny had never walked into the pool hall with a boy behind her. Tom Cotton had no idea what he was supposed to do. So he put out his hand and greeted Brian as if he were an adult. "We're cleaning filters today. It's gunky work, we'll be glad of the help."

Brian knew nothing about filters, overflow pipes, or drain cocks, but he liked a grown man speaking to him as an adult. And he had a feeling this was not what his mother would want him to be doing. This was a pool hall. It wasn't respectable. So he stayed all afternoon. And when the school bus came the next morning, he didn't sit across from Jenny. He sat next to her.

Sharing a seat on the bus and walking into school together are enough in a Midwestern high school to mark a boy and girl as a couple. That Jenny and Brian were boyfriend and girlfriend became an established fact long before either of them felt capable of addressing the issue.

The attraction between them was strong. Everything Brian felt he had to prove to the people in town, Jenny had already proven. So with her he could relax, with her he could be himself.

Jenny was already herself all the time. She had long ago given up pinching the crusts off her bread. It was hopeless. The remarkable thing about Brian—something so amazing as to be nearly incomprehensible—was that he *liked* that she was so different, he liked that she was bad at the girl stuff.

"What difference does it make?" he asked when she half-heartedly sighed about the fact that her blouses were all solid colors and seemingly every other girl in school had bought plaid blouses this year.

"How do they all know to wear the same thing? It's like they all subscribe to some newsletter that I don't get."

"And what an interesting newsletter that must be. Come on, Jen-O, those girls are so worried about how they look that they never have any fun. You have fun."

Brian liked that about her, and he adored her imagination. What freedom it gave her. She could take herself anywhere, she could be anyone. He knew that he wanted to be an actor. He had already discerned that talent in himself, and he loved losing himself in a script, becoming someone else. That was what made him feel free. But Jenny didn't need a script. She told her own stories.

The two of them wanted different things from their relationship. He wanted to feel independent, accountable to no one, and he believed he could learn that from her. For her part, she wanted a companion, a friend. She wanted to stop feeling alone. If she had been jealous or possessive, their friendship would have been over in weeks. But she didn't have any model for relationships. It never occurred to her to insist on knowing what he did when he wasn't with her—as his mother did. All she cared about was the closeness when they were together, and that they had.

By their junior year they were making plans.

They were going to go to New York. He would become an actor, and she would write. They spent long afternoons on the dusty levee or down among the shade of the cottonwoods, the pale brown river almost motionless in the summer heat. They talked and dreamed.

Jenny loved that Brian's dream had a geography, that he wanted to go somewhere. She was old enough now to understand the sacrifice her father had made for her. As conscientious a parent as he had been, Tom Cotton belonged on the road, playing tournaments in low-ceilinged, airless rooms, living in a world hazy with smoke, lit with neon VACANCY signs. Each year Jenny could feel the restlessness build in him.

She did as much work around the pool hall as she could. She kept the wire racks by the register stocked with candy and gum. She called the vending machine company when the pop machine wasn't working. She kept the books and cut all the checks. But that wasn't really what Tom needed from her. He needed her to get done growing up, so he could close the pool hall and go back on the road.

Throughout high school she and Brian worked, saving all that they could. They bought Greyhound tickets. They would be leaving a week after graduation. And the night before they went to New York, they made love for the first time.

For all that they had been together for three

years, there had been very little of the usual teenaged groping. Brian was the one who pulled back whenever curiosity started to build. "We don't want to start something we can't finish. We don't want to end up like my parents."

His parents had had to get married.

The novels Jenny read told her that something was wrong. She was the one who was supposed to be reluctant, not him. He was supposed to be gripped with uncontrollable passion. Unbridled urges, primitive lust, that's what the books said he was to feel for her, and apparently he did not.

She supposed that it was her fault. She wasn't pretty enough, she wasn't soft enough, she wasn't good enough at the girl stuff. And indeed when they finally did make love, it was nothing like the books. It was quick and it hurt. Brian's breath had come out in harsh gasps, and his body had jerked in hard spasms. He was like someone she didn't know.

They were in her bedroom. The little window air-conditioning unit whirred, blocking out all the other sounds. Jenny wished the window was open. She wanted to hear the crickets chirping, and the car doors slamming, the engines kicking into life, the low rumble of men's voices across the parking lot. She had grown up hearing those sounds. They might have comforted her now.

You shouldn't be surprised. Why should this be any different from the ballet recitals and home ec class?

At her side she felt Brian stir and raise himself up on his elbow. What was he going to say? He had to have been disappointed.

"We're going to New York." He sat up. "We're actually getting out of this place. This is the first time I've ever completely believed it."

He didn't mind. A lilting relief washed over Jenny. Of course he didn't mind. He knew her—he knew she wasn't like the other girls, that's what he loved about her.

So she was bad in bed. What difference did it make? It would be their secret, one more thing that bound them together.

The next morning Tom Cotton was sad. He was closing the pool hall, and as much as he was looking forward to the road again, he regretted that Jenny's childhood was over. "Why did you go and grow up?" He hugged her hard.

"But wasn't that the plan all along, Dad? For me to grow up?"

"Then it was a bad plan, Jenny. The worst plan we ever had."

Across the river, over the fabric store, Mrs. O'Neill was in shock. She had nothing to look forward to. Brian had been her life, everything that mattered to her, and now he was going. She was furious with him. This was just like his father. That's whose fault this was, his father's. Him and that Jenny Cotton.

That first year in New York wasn't easy, but it was fun. Brian and Jenny took strange little jobs, they lived in odd little places. And when they were down to their last dime, they would find an out-of-the-way pool hall. Jenny could play pool and she didn't look like she could. A person like that can always make the rent.

Things did happen for them. Brian got a small part on a soap. Jenny hung around enough that her cheerful ways got her a job as a production assistant. It was a tense show with bitter, unhappy stars, who were always insisting that the scripts be changed. Jenny's ear for dialogue became apparent to everyone, and soon she was hired to be on the writing staff. She was nineteen, she had never been to college, but that didn't matter. There is only one way to learn how to write daytime drama, and that is to do it.

She was a scriptwriter. She would be given a breakdown which summarized in prose the setup and purpose of each scene and she would write the dialogue for the scenes. Later she became a breakdown writer, helping the head writer divide up the story outline into individual episodes and scenes. On another show she was a "story consultant" responsible for developing the "short arc" stories, those that only lasted a couple of months. She did everything except the top job.

Brian kept encouraging her, and his vision was larger than hers had ever been. What about her own show? Why didn't she create her own world, her own stories, her own people? Surely her imagination was as good as anyone else's.

It was a ridiculous goal, a nearly impossible long shot. How often did the networks put on a new soap? Once every few years? This was even harder than selling a new prime-time show. So she wouldn't have done it . . . except that she had Brian and an idea that would not go away. She couldn't get the characters out of her head.

She couldn't get the time period—Regency England—out of her head. She tried writing her story as a novel. But she couldn't write a novel. A novel had to end, and she didn't believe that stories ever ended. A novel had one hero and one heroine, and Jenny wanted to make heroes and heroines of all her characters; everyone had an interesting life. She was a soap writer; this was her form. This was what she had been put on earth to do.

So she started writing the show's "bible"—character sketches of all the people, detailed descriptions of the settings, two years of story ideas, five sample scripts. It was a tremendous amount of work. At first she did it while doing breakdowns for *Love Never Ends,* but she would get the characters and the stories confused. By now Brian was doing well, he had a good contract and a front-burner story on *To Have and to Hold.* So he urged her to quit *Love Never Ends* and work full-time on *My Lady's Chamber.* He could support them both.

It was one of the best years of her life. She did nothing but work; she never left their little broom closet of an apartment; she never went anyplace or saw anyone. The characters she was writing about felt more real to her than anything on the noisy streets.

Brian cared as much about the show as she did. Jenny gave him full credit for finally selling it. "A historical soap"—it was such a new idea, it was such an expensive idea that no one even wanted to read the bible. But Brian persisted. The rejection didn't bother him. And finally all their efforts had paid off. It had all been so wonderful, the two of them with this ridiculous goal, this far-off dream that together they had made come true.

They had been in New York for ten years now. They weren't married. Jenny didn't care. She trusted Brian with all her heart. She understood he needed to preserve his symbols of freedom, signing only a short contract with the show, not getting married. That was fine. He had to make plenty of allowances for her. She still couldn't cook, she still couldn't keep a tidy house, she still couldn't dress, and she was still no great shakes in bed. He didn't care. The two of them were perfectly suited to each other.

Of course if she had had this baby, if she hadn't had the miscarriage, things would have changed. Brian could not have called himself free anymore.

To his credit, he had not mentioned freedom once. He had not whined or grown bitter and angry. In their few brief discussions of her pregnancy, he was rational. "You know I will support you in whatever decision you make."

That disappointed her. She had wanted him to be stupefied with joy. It wasn't fair to expect that, not when she was so ambivalent herself. But that's what she had needed from him: giddiness, rapture, star-spinning ecstasy. She wanted him to treasure her, to be devoted and protective.

You know I will support you in whatever decision you make.

Wasn't that what a woman of today should want? It was all very romantic when Rhett tells

Scarlett he will chain her to the bedpost to make sure that she has their baby, but in reality Jenny didn't want anyone chaining her to anything. She was glad to have a man who trusted her judgment.

Brian did. In fact he had trusted all her abilities long before she had. What was wrong with her, that that was suddenly feeling like not enough?

Four

Brian was back at the hospital when the doctor came to release Jenny.

"It would be a good idea to be quiet for the rest of the week," the doctor told her. "You can work at home, can't you?" He knew who she was.

She nodded, agreeing. She felt like staying in bed, like treating herself as an invalid, at least for another day or so.

"But she's been nominated for an Emmy," Brian protested. "The ceremony's tomorrow night. She has to go."

The doctor paused. He didn't like the idea, but the Emmys were television's highest awards. He turned to Brian. "Don't let her get knocked around."

"I won't," Brian promised. "I'll take good care of her."

Jenny liked that idea. She liked that he was going to take care of her.

For years they had lived in a very small apartment in Manhattan—the "Broom Closet" they called it. They hadn't minded the lack of space.

When Jenny was writing, she didn't care where she was, and Brian liked so much being in Manhattan with the theater, restaurants, shops, and gallerys, that he spent little of his leisure time at the apartment.

But once the network bought *My Lady's Chamber* and the show went into preproduction, the Broom Closet could no longer hold all that Jenny needed: the reference books, the audition scripts, the notes for future stories. She had to have an office. Since the network was sending the show out to Brooklyn to cut costs, Jenny looked for space out there, thinking she would rent a basement apartment in Gourvent, the gentrified neighborhood two subway stops away from the studio.

Instead she found a whole house for sale—a four-story brownstone with a deep backyard. And it certainly made sense to buy. The network had paid her a lot of money for the show, and the money was just sitting in a passbook account at the bank. Neither she nor Brian knew anything about investing.

She loved the house, and she honestly thought that they agreed about it, that everything was settled, when suddenly, sickeningly, she realized that he did not plan on going through with the purchase. Yes, yes, he said, the house was great, lots of possibilities, but it would tie them down so. What if something came up in California? Movies, prime-time television? It would be so much harder to move if they had a house to worry about. They wouldn't be free.

She had been shocked. Why hadn't he said

something earlier? Why hadn't he made his position clearer? She knew that he loathed confrontation, that he didn't like it when they disagreed, that he tended to gloss over his feelings, that he wouldn't talk about them even though he usually went ahead and acted on them. She knew such behavior was typical of adult children of alcoholics. She understood. She forgave him. But still . . . she had really started to love the idea of so much space, of being so close to the studio, of having a yard. She was disappointed.

As was the realtor. "It's your money," the other woman argued.

Technically that was true. The money was in Jenny's name, but that was just for tax purposes. She didn't feel like it was more hers than his. She couldn't buy a house on her own. "I'm sorry," she kept apologizing to the realtor.

She did tell Brian how disappointed she was. She wasn't trying to change the outcome; she simply thought he should know how much anguish a simple direct "no" would have saved her.

"Well, if you feel that strongly about it,"—Brian was not going to admit to being wrong—"then go ahead."

So she had.

They decided to hold on to the rent-controlled Broom Closet. They could stay in Brooklyn during the week and spend weekends in the city.

It sounded like a good idea, but it hadn't worked, at least not for Jenny. While she could keep track of every detail on the show, what every character drank, when each one's birthday was, she could never remember which borough her black sweater was in. So she gave up and moved everything out to Brooklyn. She was working so hard that she didn't have time to do anything else, even on weekends.

Brian continued to use both places. If he had a heavy week on the show, he did stay in Brooklyn. It was easier, more pleasant and spacious. But if he had a couple of consecutive days off or if he had an audition scheduled, he used the Broom Closet.

It was an ideal arrangement for him, and he rarely lost track of what was stored where. He had a meticulous sense for detail. He was, Jenny often thought, better at some of the girl stuff than she was.

He certainly was more interested in the decoration and remodeling of the house than she. On her own she would have painted all the walls off-white and bought some curtains from a catalogue. But he had a flair for the visual. They were currently remodeling the kitchen, and he was the one who cared about the floors and the countertops, not her.

But Thursday, the day of the Emmy ceremony, he called her from the studio. "I'm sorry, I just remembered. My tux is at the Broom Closet. I'll have to go pick it up as soon as I'm done here. Do you want me to come back to the house and get you?"

That made no sense. The ceremony was in midtown. "No, I'll stop and pick you up on the way."

"I'm really sorry," he repeated. "This isn't like me."

"It's okay." Jenny hadn't exactly been herself either this week. She was glad to see some sign that the miscarriage had upset him . . . if that was the reason for his mistake. "Anyway Trina's coming to help me dress."

Trina Nelson had all this girl stuff down cold. Within two months of being on the show, she had taken Jenny in hand, changing her overly severe ragmop hair into something that she described as "lively and spirited." She went shopping with Jenny when Jenny needed clothes to wear to story conferences. She told her what shoes and scarves to wear. Trina had presented Jenny's Emmy dress to her as a done deal.

"This is it. This is what you wearing. You better like it because you've already paid for it."

The dress was hunter green, a very unusual color in evening wear—or at least that's what Trina said, this not being the sort of information that Jenny possessed. It was floor-length, simple and sleeveless. Actually it was more than sleeveless. From collar to arm it was cut on a slashing diagonal, exposing Jenny's shoulders as well as her arms. The high collar was encrusted with Austrian crystal, the gown's only ornament.

Of course if she dropped her chin, she could feel the sharp points of the crystal bite into her neck. And, needless to say, the minute she realized this, Jenny kept dropping her chin to see how much it was going to bother her.

"Would you stop that?" Trina batted at Jenny's jaw to make her quit. "You look like you have Tourette's."

"But it scrapes me."

"For God's sake, Jenny, half the women there aren't going to be able to take a deep breath or their bosoms will fall out on national TV, and you're worried about a little scratching. If it's drawing blood, we'll talk, but not until then."

"I feel like an idiot."

"You don't look like one. You have such great arms."

Trina always said that, that Jenny's arms were her best feature. "That seems so pathetic," Jenny sighed. "I played pool all my life. That's not exactly sexy."

"It is to some men."

Jenny ignored her and turned to look at herself in the mirror. She supposed she did look okay. Short people were supposed to wear one color, weren't they? She had read that somewhere. Even so, she hated evenings like this. She hated being judged on her appearance. Tonight was supposed to be about work, who had done the best work, but much of it would instead be about clothes. Sure, Jenny might look all right now, but sooner or later something was bound to unravel, pop out, turn under or suffer some clothing calamity that she didn't even know about.

She wished Brian were here. He liked her the way she was. He didn't mind that she was so bad at all this.

"Money, some I.D., a lipstick." Trina was checking the contents of Jenny's evening bag, a little fringed, mesh flapper bag that Brian had found in an antique store. Trina approved of Brian's taste. "That should do it. You don't need a comb. If you touch your hair, I'll kill you."

Jenny's hair was fluffed and moussed to within an inch of its life . . . or to be literal, to all three inches of its life. Jenny had always thought that one advantage of short hair was that people couldn't do weird things to it when you got dressed up.

She had been wrong.

Trina clipped some crystal earrings onto Jenny's ears. Jenny shook her head. The earrings were heavy, but they didn't fall off. The collar still bit into her neck.

Trina stepped back. "I think you're ready. Now promise me that you will not touch your face, you will not touch your hair, and you will stop impaling yourself on your collar."

Trina herself was not going to the ceremony. Tickets were expensive, and the network paid only for people who were nominated. In Jenny's case, the network was also springing for a limo. The plan was for Jenny to drop Trina off before picking up Brian.

Brian was waiting out in front of the Broom Closet's building.

"I *am* sorry about being so disorganized." He waved his fingers near her cheek, showing that he would have kissed her but he didn't want to disturb her makeup. "Now that is one gorgeous dress. Do you know where Trina found it?"

Jenny shook her head. "The collar bites into my neck."

"I don't think this evening is supposed to be about comfort, Jen-O."

"I suppose not."

He looked great, all elegant and assured, his lean, carefully shaven features slightly saturnine over the crisp white front of his pleated evening shirt. Jenny wanted to lean against him, have him put his arm around her. She wanted to feel the satin of his lapel against her cheek. But she supposed that that would ruin her hair.

He adjusted his shirt cuffs. "I do hate these things."

"You? Hate a publicity event?"

Jenny meant to sound light and teasing. She had a feeling she just sounded cross.

"Well"—he was defensive—"it is a little strange to come when you haven't been nominated." He must have heard the tone of his voice for he immediately let it lighten. "I guess I'm one actor who can't blame the writers for not being nominated."

"That's for sure."

There was nothing light or teasing about that remark. It was flat-out bitchy.

But he did only have himself to blame. For a year and a half now, she had had an idea for a great story line for him. A viscount would come to London, looking a great deal like the butler Hastings, Brian's character. They would turn out to be half-brothers, Hastings being the illegitimate son of the viscount's noble father. Brian would play both parts. Dual roles like that were challenging, attention getting, and lucrative.

But the network had refused to let her do the story unless Brian signed at least a two-year contract. And he refused. Six months was all he would tie himself up for. He wanted to be free.

And he wanted to be out of soaps. He never said it, but she knew. It was hard for some soap actors to maintain their self-respect when so many others thought they were talentless hacks. Jenny thought it was probably like being a housewife during the early days of the feminist movement. Everything such a woman read said that what she were doing was easy, mind numbing, and pointless. It took a lot of strength to ignore that message.

Many women had had that strength, and many daytime actors did too. Brian should have it. He was good at his job. He gave Hastings an air of firm authority. Hastings was seasoned and trustworthy, he had a presence that radiated far beyond his routine "dinner is served" lines. Brian should be proud of what he was doing. He shouldn't worry about what people who never saw his work thought of him.

But he did.

The state of his career hadn't bothered him when they were working so hard getting the show off the ground. But he had changed agents twice in the last six months, and he still wasn't getting the kind of response that he was hoping for.

So she shouldn't be surprised that things hadn't be so great between the two of them recently, that they were communicating less well, that they never seemed to be playing on the same team anymore. Brian was unhappy with his career; that was bound to affect how he felt about everything, including his relationship with her. This was just a rocky patch. They would get through it. She was sure of that. In this business one audition can change your life.

When his life changed, when it got better, hers would too.

The first time Jenny went to the daytime Emmy Award ceremony she had been a small-town-kid amazed. It was exactly like the opening of the Academy Awards that she had been watching on TV for years—a wide red carpet sweeping up to the entrance of the hotel, yellow police barricades holding back the crowds of fans who were calling out names, taking pictures, waving autograph books. And she had been one of the people getting out of a limo. She had always felt a little unreal, as if this couldn't be happening to her, as if it were one more of her wonderful daydreams.

That's how she had felt in previous years. This year she wished it wasn't happening to her. She wished she were back home in bed.

Brian got out of the limo first and raised his hand, acknowledging the crowd. The roar diminished slightly; he was not one of the major stars—something Jenny's viscount-brother story line would have taken care of. Jenny thanked the driver and by the time she was out of the car, Brian was at the barricades, signing autographs. The next limo drew up to discharge its passengers. Jenny moved out of the way.

"Excuse me, excuse me," a young voice called

to her from the other side of the barricades. "Are you somebody?"

Jenny shook her head.

Brian didn't linger. There was a fine line here—an actor wanted to seem gracious and obliging, but God forbid he should look like he *needed* to have the crowd fawning over him. He touched Jenny's arm—she had no makeup to ruin there, and they went inside. The first five floors of the hotel were shops and offices. A guard was stationed at the base of the escalators to check tickets. As she glided up the moving stairs, Jenny peered down through the atrium to the ground floor. More and more people were streaming in. The women's dresses were gorgeous; the beads and sequins glittered, the crinolines rustled.

In the sweeping semicircular foyer outside the ballroom portable bars had been set up, and people were drinking, glad-handing, networking. The place was jammed. The noise was almost overwhelming. People had to speak very loud or draw almost threateningly close.

Up here Jenny couldn't pretend that she wasn't somebody. She was, and everyone knew it. She had power. She could make someone a star. Every actor she had ever worked with wanted to speak to her; every actor she hadn't worked with wanted to speak to her. She quickly lost track of Brian.

She wasn't shy, she liked people, but she didn't like this kind of socializing, this generalized sucking up. If a person wanted a job, she'd rather that he ask, turn in a résumé, have an agent call, whatever, not spend his time telling her how great she looked. What did that have to do with casting the show? Her feet started to hurt.

I just had a miscarriage. I shouldn't be here. People should be worrying about me, patting my arm, putting cold compresses on my forehead. Someone should be taking care of me.

Brian was supposed to be taking care of her. He had promised the doctor.

The doors to the ballroom opened. Feeling a little like she was sneaking out of school, Jenny slipped in. The vaulting gold-and-white room was still cool and quiet. The tables were draped with white linen and set with high-pedestaled flower arrangements. She found the tables assigned to the *My Lady's Chamber* crowd. They were empty. Jenny sat down anyway. Under the cover of the tablecloth she kicked her shoes off. She ran a finger under her collar. She wondered if the crystals were giving her a red mark that would show up on TV. Cameras would be trained on her as the names for the writing nominees were read out. They would keep a camera on her while the winner was announced so that all of America could see her reaction. What would make her look like more of an idiot, winning or losing? The actors were all good at this business of listening for their names with a camera in their faces, but she wasn't.

"Jenny." Someone spoke. She looked up. The crystals bit into the back of her neck.

It was Alec Cameron. That was a surprise. She

hadn't seen his name on any of the lists. The show hadn't paid for his ticket.

"I saw you come in." His voice was low, nearly gentle. "Are you all right?"

That wasn't an idle query. He knew about her miscarriage. He was worried about her. He would be nice to her. He would take care of her. Jenny wanted someone to take care of her. Except that she would never, not in a million years, let him. He had already done too much for her. She wasn't used to that, and she felt at a disadvantage. "I'm okay. My feet hurt a lot, and I'm afraid of my dress, but otherwise I'm fine."

He laughed. "I can understand your feet hurting, but why are you afraid of your dress?"

"It's not exactly me, is it?" She plucked at the dark green crepe.

"I don't agree," he said instantly. "I saw you when you came in. You looked great . . . and like yourself."

Those weren't two ideas she often heard in the same sentence—"looking great" and "herself." "Trina picked out the dress," she muttered, embarrassed.

"But she's not wearing it."

He had a point there. She shrugged, not sure what to say. Then she noticed his eyes dropping down to her arms—her supposedly sexy arms.

Suddenly Jenny felt better. She wasn't a kid at her first dance. She was the head writer of a network show, and this man liked her arms. She motioned for him to sit down. She couldn't talk with her head tilted back, not when her dress had been designed by an acupuncturist. "Why did you come? To root for your dear friends from *Aspen*?"

Aspen!! had been nominated for nothing, not for lighting, editing, costume design, music, nothing. It had been a source of great satisfaction to the *My Lady's Chamber* crowd.

"I came for my ex. One husband paying court isn't enough for her. She needs two."

"Oh, yes. Your ex-wife, she has been nominated, hasn't she?"

Alec had the ex-wife to end all ex-wives. Up until the time he had started on *Aspen,* he had been married to Chloe Spencer, America's daytime sweetheart.

They had been Derek and Ginger together on *Passions*, and their story line had had audience ratings that were legendary. Derek had been an overworked, exhausted young associate at a big law firm. Ginger had been the hormone-stuffed, yet naive daughter of the firm's managing partner. He considered her absolutely forbidden; she therefore felt safe with him, she could test out her sexuality on him. He became a challenge, almost a symbol of her father, and her flirting became openly alluring. Then—in a segment that Jenny knew Alec had intensely fought, that he had almost quit over—Derek raped Ginger. The rape was supposed to evince his true love for her. Eventually the characters got married in one of the decade's most gorgeous weddings, but a perfectly happy couple is useless to a show. By then the couple's own marriage was wavering and the network wanted Alec to star in *Aspen,* so a few months after the wedding Derek's plane crashed in the Great Smokies.

"Chloe says she would like to meet you," he was saying. "If that's all right with you, I'll go get her."

"You'll go get Chloe Spencer?" Jenny reached under the table for her shoes. "You're going to try to get Chloe Spencer through a room like that?"

"I would have done my best." Alec grinned, acknowledging the difficulty of moving Chloe Spencer from one place to the next. She had charisma, star power, a Q rating that was through the roof. Even in a crowd of pros like this, everyone wanted to speak to her, be seen with her.

He pulled out Jenny's chair, and a moment later they were crossing back into the crowded foyer. Alec apparently knew where Chloe was holding court and he skirted around the crowd, ducking under a couple of potted trees and coming up behind a pillar.

Chloe's back was turned toward them, and it was, without a doubt, one spectacular back. It was quite bare, framed only in a drift of sea-green chiffon. The skin was flawless and pale, the shoulder blades were perfectly formed, lightly curving; the spine was fine and straight. Chloe's silvery blonde hair was swept up, and even her hairline was lovely, two symmetrical wings on either side of an inverted. "V."

Alec said her name, and she turned instantly. She was delicate and fair-skinned with wide-set green eyes and the best cheekbones in daytime.

"Oh, Alec." Her face brightened with a smile. "Come look at Noah's picture."

She held out a photograph. It was of a smiling Asian baby, a chubby-cheeked little fellow with narrow, upswept eyes and a wispy mass of straight black hair.

Jenny glanced down at Chloe's left hand. The actress was wearing a wide gold band and an enormous diamond. Jenny vaguelly remembered reading in the fan magazines that the actress had remarried and she and her new husband had adopted a baby.

"Isn't he gorgeous?" Chloe was gushing. "And this picture is two weeks old. He's much cuter now." She was crowding close to Alec, looking at the picture along with him. She was so close to him that their arms were touching and one of the airy chiffon panels of her dress had drifted over his dark sleeve. Jenny never stood that close to men.

"He looks great. Is he sleeping any better?" Clearly Alec already knew a lot about this baby.

"No." Chloe laughed. "He isn't. And everyone says that sooner or later I'm going to have to let him cry, but I don't think I'll be very good at that." She tilted her head, admiring the picture again. She really was extraordinarily lovely. Everything about her, the line of her jaw, the curving shell of her ear, was perfect. Jenny had believed herself immune to the pain of meeting beautiful actresses. She thought she could look at them without feeling overwhelmingly inferior. But Chloe Spencer was unique.

Alec had been married to her. This exquisite,

delicate person had been his wife, had slept in his bed. No wonder he had never remarried.

She felt a light touch on her arm, drawing her forward. Then Alec spoke. "Jenny, you'll have to forgive this woman; motherhood seems to have done something to her manners."

"Oh, I am sorry." Chloe put out a slim, perfectly manicured hand. "I do hope you understand. Do you have children?"

"Ah . . . no."

Alec spoke quickly. "Chloe has been telling me how much she likes the show."

Chloe's transformation was almost instant. The mother disappeared. The actress, out to charm a head writer, took over. "Oh, yes, I do," she gushed. "The writing is marvelous. I'm so envious. We have this new team of writers, and they can't—"

"Chloe." Alec's voice was cautioning.

"But it's true," she protested. "You wouldn't believe how bad—"

"Chloe." He interrupted again. "This isn't the place."

He was right. Even if *Passions'* new writing team did have the creative finesse of a backhoe—something Jenny believed—the Emmy Awards was not the place for an actress, even as established a star as Chloe Spencer, to openly complain about her show's writers.

"Oh, all right," she sighed. "But you know I'm no good at keeping my feelings to myself."

Alec smiled as if he had known that for a long time. Was that part of why he had come, to watch out for her, to protect her? People like

Chloe Spencer never had trouble getting other people to take care of them.

More people were waiting to speak to Chloe, so Alec and Jenny stepped back. The crowd was heading into the ballroom. They moved in that direction. A bottleneck near the door forced them to stop, close to each other, but Jenny's dress didn't have any chiffon panels to float over his arm.

"I take it that Chloe and her second husband adopted the baby?"

Alec nodded. "I think it's working really well for her."

"Did you and she want children?" Jenny supposed that technically this wasn't any of her business, but she was curious.

"I did."

An interesting pronoun. *I,* not *we.* "Then why does she have one, and you don't?"

"Because she's the one who remarried."

Not for one instant did Jenny think that that was the whole story. "Who's her new husband?"

"He's an older guy, in his late fifties, I think. He's good for her."

"So your ex-wife is now someone else's trophy wife?"

He grimaced. "I suppose."

The crowd was pressing in, forcing them closer. "Do you still want children?"

"It's not an active and immediate source of pain."

But yes, I do. Jenny could hear the words he hadn't said. She waited a moment, hoping he would go on, but he didn't. Clearly he did not plan on saying anything more.

She let the crowd carry her inch by inch toward the door. Someone knocked against her, jostling her. She wasn't used to wearing high heels. She lost her balance. She felt her hair brush against Alec's chest. He steadied her, two warm, firm hands closing over her upper arms. Then he moved her to stand in front of him so his body was blocking the worst of the crush.

He was bigger than Brian. He was taller, his shoulders were broader. She couldn't help noticing that. And this sort of effortless gallantry . . . Brian never did anything like that. Of course, Brian hadn't had much in the way of role models, showing him how adult men should behave toward adult women. Apparently Alec had.

He had carried her into the hospital. She didn't remember exactly how it had happened. She had felt dizzy, faint, and then suddenly she was off her feet, in his arms. She remembered one arm closing around her shoulders, but nothing else. His other arm must have been beneath her knees. She didn't remember how that felt. And she didn't remember what she had done. Had she put her arm around his neck? Had she been able to hear his heart beat?

They were through the door and in the ballroom. Alec let go of her. The two places on her arms where his hands had been suddenly felt cold and naked. She turned to look at him.

She was surprised at how well he looked in evening clothes. He had such a fresh, outdoorsy, vigorous presence. Men like that often looked awkward in formal garb. But Alec didn't. His tuxedo jacket rode across his broad shoulders easily and naturally.

Of course, the Duke of Lydgate had a very formal wardrobe, and Alec looked great in his costumes.

"Why are you looking at me like that?" His voice intruded into her thoughts. "What are you thinking about?"

"Lydgate."

"That guy?" Alec made a face. "Can't we leave him at home?"

She ignored him. "I was just thinking—we don't know much about his sex life, do we?"

Jenny won. How she got herself up onto the stage, she didn't know. Brian had probably pulled her out of her chair. Once she was there, she could see the director silently pleading with her to keep it short, so she simply stepped up to the mike and said, "Thank you."

She carried the graceful statuette—an angel shooting basketball was how the industry described it—back to her seat. All along the row Brian, George, and the others were twisted forward in their seats, leaning toward the aisle. They wanted to look at the Emmy, touch it, hold it. The nominating process was structured so that the half-hour shows had virtually no chance. But *My Lady's Chamber*—their own little, underbudgeted outsider—had bagged one of the big ones. They felt vindicated, triumphant. Brian put his arm around her, hugging her tight and hard.

After the telecast George, the executive producer of *My Lady's Chamber,* waved everyone into the bar. The party would continue. Brian was as attentive as he had ever been, keeping his arm around her all the time. Even when Alec came over to congratulate her, leaning forward to brush a kiss against her cheek, Brian kept hold of her.

Now he was remembering to take care of her, now that she had won.

His hand was moving along her back. She hoped he remembered what else the doctor had said. They weren't supposed to have sex for a while. That shouldn't have been a problem. They hadn't made love since she had first suspected that she was pregnant.

But tonight might have been different. Would her Emmy have attracted him more than her supposedly sexy arms?

Five

Friday, the morning after the Emmys, Jenny woke up feeling awful. Her mouth was dusty, and something thick and heavy was pushing against her eyes. She sat on the edge of the bed. Why didn't they have these ceremonies on Saturday night so people didn't have to go to work the next morning? Because the prime-time viewing audience was bigger during the week. She knew that.

She went down to the kitchen. Brian was sitting at the long pine table, his script open. He was working on his lines. His black hair was still damp from the shower. His shirt had fresh creases in the sleeves. He was ready for work.

She wasn't. She dropped into a chair. "Are any of the workmen coming today?" This kitchen remodeling was taking forever.

"No," Brian answered. "The backsplash tile isn't in yet."

Why did they need to tile the backsplash? What was wrong with plain old wall? Tile was easier to clean, but she never cooked and Brian never spilled.

"Then I think I'll work at home today," she said. "I'm not going into the studio. I'm beat."

"Don't you want to celebrate with everyone?"

"We celebrated last night. That's my problem." A person who went from one month to the next without touching a drop of alcohol shouldn't have champagne before dinner, wine with dinner, and then more champagne afterward. Brian hadn't had a thing to drink, and he was doing fine, creases in his shirt sleeves and everything.

Of course, he hadn't had a miscarriage three days ago.

She glared at him resentfully.

He got up to make her a cup of coffee.

"But no one from the cast was there last night." He had to speak up over the whir of the electric coffee grinder. "They'll be so happy for you. The answering machine was full of messages this morning. I'm sure someone will be planning some kind of party."

Brian made wonderful coffee, strong, fresh, and fragrant. He always emptied out the kettle and started with clean, cold water. He used an European-style coffee maker, a glass beaker with a stainless steel plunger. It wasn't a speedy operation.

Jenny put her head down on the table. So she owed it to everyone else to go in today, did she? She was getting tired of this business of always being the cheerful one, good old perky-and-bouncy Jenny. Why was that her job? She and George, the show's executive producer, would have awful stomach-churning meetings with the network. Everyone who knew about the meetings would be scared and depressed, and they all always expected Jenny to cheer them up. Why couldn't she be the one who got cheered up?

Last night she had been the one who had been nominated. She should have been the one running to the bathroom to throw up. But throughout dinner George had been nervous, Brian had been nervous, the whole table had been nervous. So she'd felt like she had to calm everyone down. It was as if the seats at the table had place cards. *This chair has the right to be anxious. This chair has the right to be hysterical.* By the time Jenny had sat down, all the good ones had been taken, and she was left with *Calm and sane.*

Why did she have to get stuck with that chair? Why did she have to be a good sport all the time? No one expected Chloe Spencer to be a good sport.

Brian had finished the coffee. Jenny took a sip and set her cup down with a sharp click. Coffee sloshed over onto the pine. He wasn't going to like that. The table was new. No, it wasn't. That was the problem. It was almost a hundred-and-fifty-years old, having started life in a Swedish homestead. They had paid the earth for it, and Brian kept talking about how soft pine was, how careful they needed to be. But Jenny had to believe that those good Swedish farmers stumbling around on dark mornings occasionally had spilled their coffee on the table.

She moved her cup around, making little rings in the spilled coffee. It was very satisfying. "I got out of the hospital two days ago. I won an

Emmy. I think I'm entitled to do whatever I want."

Brian was crossing the kitchen with a wet rag. No, no, it wouldn't be a wet rag. People in Oklahoma used wet rags. No doubt farmers in Sweden used wet rags. Brian would be using a cloth, lightly moistened.

What a bitch she was being. This wasn't like her. She didn't want to feel this way about him. He was her partner, her friend. It must be the miscarriage.

You've read all about miscarriages, there's grief afterward, grief and pain. Why did you think that wouldn't apply to you?

Because it was girl stuff.

She stayed home and spent the day thinking about Lydgate. Her instinct told her that there was a story in his sex life. She had had such a strong response to Alec last night. His body, his presence, his movements, his touch—she had been aware of everything about him. Surely that was telling her something about the character he played.

But what? She stared at the blank computer screen for twenty minutes.

He had put his hands on her arms last night. His hands had been browner than her arms. He was coppery tan, she was almond.

Brian's skin tones were fairer than her own. How was a person supposed to play the magnolia-skinned belle when your coloring was more salt-of-the-earth than your boyfriend's?

Now why was she thinking about that? She was supposed to be working on Lydgate. Alec protecting her from the crowd—what did that say about Lydgate? Nothing. If he had noticed Amelia being jostled—and that was a big *if*—he would have signaled for a footman.

She wasn't making any progress. Lydgate and Amelia in bed. There had to be something to this. She turned from the computer and picked up a pad and pencil. It didn't help. She wasn't coming up with anything. Lydgate and Amelia. Alec and Karen. She kept seeing Alec and Chloe.

Alec's first daytime job had been as a construction worker. It was one of those young beefcake parts—the writers put a character in a blue-collar job so he never has to wear a shirt. Bare skin and muscles was often all there was to such parts, but Alec had given his character an alert animal quality. The man was always touching something, the back of a chair, a piece of lumber. He was very rooted to the physical world. It made sense that he would be half-clad so often. The man lived through his body. Sensuality wasn't something that was turned on for the love scenes. It was how he lived. Scenes that weren't supposed to be about sex, Alec had made to be about sex. And that had only been his first job. During the Derek-and-Ginger story, he had managed to make even fatigue sexually interesting.

This was embarrassing. Here Jenny—now Emmy-winning Jenny—had an actor who was great at subtle sexual tension and she could not think of anything to do with his character.

She worried about it all weekend, and on Sunday night she finally gave up. She wrote a couple of scenes and threw them into an episode. Let Alec and Karen see what they could do.

On Monday she worked at home again—that was her day to concentrate on the long-term story outline, and she couldn't risk any of her notes being seen by anyone. Even the actors weren't supposed to know what lay in store for the characters. So she wasn't back in the studio until Tuesday. Because of the days she had missed after the miscarriage, she had been away for nearly a week. It seemed like an age.

She arrived later than usual. It was seven o'clock and the day had started. One of the girls from wardrobe was wheeling a big rack of costumes down the first-floor hall. Every so often she peered around the clothes to be sure the path ahead was clear. The minute she saw Jenny, she abandoned her rack.

"Now I want you to take note of this," she announced to Jenny. She was clearly proud of something. "We're clearing out some space. We figure Lydgate will be getting a bunch of new costumes. Makeup claims they know everything first, but we're miles ahead of them on this one."

On what one? Jenny watched as the girl retrieved her cart and maneuvered it onto the elevator, presumably to take it down to the basement storage area. What had that been about? Why would Alec be getting new costumes? Jenny had spent the weekend trying to get him *out* of his costume. Shaking her head, she headed down the hall. She pulled open the door to the stairwell.

Frank, who played Jaspar, and Jill, a production assistant, were on the landing. At the sound of the opening door, Frank turned. He saw Jenny and instantly dropped to his knees.

"I offer my apologies." He clasped his hands in melodramatic pleading. "You have my deepest apologies, my maximum apologies, my maximum deepest apologies."

Jenny stared at him. "What are you talking about?"

He got up, brushing the dust off his knees. "Alec. You might not have known, but when I started here, I was a total snob about soap veterans."

"Were you really? I don't believe it."

She was being ironic. Frank had trained at Yale, and he did not let anyone forget that.

"It's the truth," he said, proud to be so humble. "But Alec has made me change my tune. The last couple of days he's been unbelievable, hasn't he?"

"What's he done?"

Frank drew back, puzzled. "Surely Brian told you. Lydgate's all anyone is talking about."

Brian hadn't said anything about Alec or Lydgate.

Frank went on. "His performance has been eye-opening, revelatory. I can't believe how good he is."

Eye-opening? Revelatory? What was going on? She had been watching the show at home, but an episode was taped a week before it aired. Any changes Alec had made in his performance last week she wouldn't have seen yet.

She went up to the director's office. Terence was directing today's episode. He was gathering up his script and notes, getting ready to go into the rehearsal hall. He stopped and waved Jenny into a chair. "So have you heard about our amazing duke?"

Amazing? Terence was not one to exaggerate—or even necessarily notice—what an actor was doing. "I keep getting bits of the story. You tell me."

"He found his character. Totally, out of the blue, wham-o, one day there the guy was. Gil says it started last Thursday." Thursday had been the Emmy ceremony; Wednesday Alec had come to see her in the hospital. "Then I saw it Friday, and Gil said yesterday was even better. We can hardly keep the camera off him."

Terence and Gil occasionally felt that way about a prop—that they couldn't keep the camera off it. There had been a teacup last summer that Gil had been fascinated with and finally Francine Kenny, the actress who played Lady Varley, had dropped it. She said it was an accident, but everyone knew that she was tired of the china getting more close-ups than she was. And no one blamed her. So for the two directors to be stirred by an actor . . . something must be happening indeed.

"I'm not taking any credit for it," Terence continued, "and neither is Gil. We knew when you hired him that he was good, but I didn't know how good."

"What's he doing?"

"I don't want to intellectualize it. You come see for yourself."

Jenny would have liked to follow Terence into the rehearsal hall, but it was only fair to wait until at least dress. And after a week away, she had plenty to do. She looked at some audition tapes, returned about forty million phone calls, and edited some scripts. At one-thirty she went down to the floor.

The studio floor was a large vaulting space with room for eight sets. The show had more than fifty. One way a writer could save money was by managing the story so that sets were used for several days in a row. To have union labor breaking down a set on Monday afternoon and then putting it up again on Wednesday was expensive. Money was so tight on *My Lady's Chamber* that Jenny did a lot of strange things to the story in order to keep the sets as "stand ups."

Everyone was clustered around the large Almack's Assembly Room set. Makeup, wardrobe, and prop people were all there, waiting in case they were needed. Jenny didn't join the crowd. As interesting as it was to watch a scene as if it were a staged play, what mattered was how it came across on video. She went into the glass-walled control room, a spaceshiplike booth off in the corner. From here the director called the shots, the sound engineer monitored the sound levels, and so forth.

Jenny watched on the monitors as Colley Lightfield, the extravagantly foppish, effeminate baron, had a scene with his mother, Lady

Lightfield. She was whispering furiously to him about his need to marry for money. In a moment, Jenny remembered from the script, Lydgate would enter, and Lady Lightfield would—for about the seventieth time—talk about her six unmarried daughters.

It was not the sort of scene you rushed out and submitted to the Emmys. Quite contrary. You passed it along to the actors with rolled eyes and apologies. Why Lady Lightfield would ever, in the middle of Almack's, explain primogeniture and entailment to a duke who had to have understood this since the cradle made no sense even to Jenny, and she had been the one who had written it. But scenes like this were necessary. All soaps had to recap their own stories, but *My Lady's Chamber* had to give history lessons as well. Viewer mail made that clear. So Jenny put them wherever she could. Lady Lightfield was the one to give the lesson because she had other scenes in today's show. It was happening at Almack's because the set was up, and Lydgate had to listen to it because Alec's contract guaranteed him three appearances a week.

The Almack's set was near the control booth. Jenny could look up through the glass and see Alec waiting for his entrance. He was in Lydgate's most formal garb: black velvet knee breeches and a black coat, with diamonds on his fingers and in his neckcloth. He was in character. His shoulders were stiffer, the line of his mouth narrower. His own careless masculine charm had become the duke's austere handsomeness. His easy confident sexuality had become magisterial and cold. He stepped forward to make his entrance. Jenny turned back to the monitors to watch the scene.

Colley twitched his lace at his strong-minded mother and flounced off almost charging into Lydgate. Jenny could hear Terence calling for camera three.

Lydgate was irritated and impatient with the near collision. The camera remained on him during much of Lady Lightfield's explanations.

The previous actor had always played these scenes as if Lydgate was stupid, as if he really did need to have this stuff explained to him again and again. But Alec's duke wasn't stupid. He was bored and distracted. He didn't want to be bothered with this. It was tedious. It was about other people. Why should he care?

So that was it. Jenny suddenly saw a different dimension in the character she had created. The man didn't like things that were complex—not because he was stupid, but because he was too self-centered, too caught up with his own interests, to want to hear from the outside world.

His replies were crisp, curt enough to make Lady Lightfield uneasy; she started rushing her lines. Jenny noticed a production assistant showing the stopwatch to Terence. The scene was running short. Terence murmured a word into his headset. And through the glass of the control room, Jenny saw a stage manager signaling to the actors to stretch, pulling his hands apart as if pulling taffy. Alec responded by having Lydgate stop listening. So after each of Lady

Lightfield's speeches, there was a pause while he recollected himself and deigned to reply.

It was chilling, this complete disinterest in other people. *I'm all that matters.*

This was interesting, very interesting. An accident of birth had made this man a duke. He controlled a vast estate. The lives of hundreds of tenants depended on him. He had a voice in the House of Lords, he controlled several seats in the House of Commons, and church positions were within his patronage. And he didn't care about anyone. Everyone else bored him.

"And . . . we're clear." The stage manager waved his script, and the actors relaxed.

"Nice work, people," Terence spoke through the intercom and then leaned back in his secretarial chair and spoke to Jenny. "So?"

"He understands the character better than I do."

"Do you remember the stuff you had in the bible about him being a collector?"

"Yes." When she was first thinking about the show, Jenny had imagined the duke as a art collector, interested in paintings, porcelain, and old manuscripts. But the character had always seemed too cold and stupid for even that kind of a passion, and she had let it drop. It was just as well. Terence and Gil's cameras would have fallen in love with the objects in the collections, and all the actors would have quit.

"Did you tell Alec about that?" Terence asked.

"No. There wouldn't have been any reason to. I gave up on it."

"Well, you might want to rethink that," he suggested. "Because Alec got there on his own. Last Friday he had this amazing scene—actually I'm surprised Brian didn't tell you about it—it was with Amelia, and he did not look at her once, spent the whole time with the things in the room, touching them, ignoring her. Wait till you see it. He has the best-shaped hands in the cast."

Alec would probably never see his face on camera again. "What did Karen say?" When an actor changed what he was doing, sometimes it was the other actors who had the best sense of whether the change would work in the long run.

"She hated it. But that was Amelia talking, not her."

"Amelia's supposed to hate him," Jenny answered.

But the minute she said it, she realized that that was not true. Amelia had hated much about her life, but she hadn't really hated Lydgate. He was inconvenient, tedious, a rock in the road that she had to plan around, but there hadn't been enough there for her to hate. She hadn't been afraid of him. He hadn't been dangerous.

He was now.

The assistant director was on the intercom, calling for people to take their places for Prologue C. Jenny looked over Terence's shoulder at the script. Prologue C, the last little snippet before the opening credits, showed the duke and duchess entering Almack's.

Nothing was happening in the scene. Its sole purpose was to show off Amelia's gown. This was another thing that viewer mail made clear—

people wanted to get a good look at the clothes. The actors didn't like it, but it was fine with everyone else, even Jenny. So blinking much money was spent on these stupid costumes that they might as well get their own screen time.

Jenny had seen a sketch of the dress, but this was her first view of the actual thing. Shimmering lilac silk fell in slim, fluid folds from a high waist. A deep pleated frill stiffened with silver embroidery was gathered into a flounce at the hem of the skirt, and twists of amethyst ribbons adorned the sleeves and the bodice.

The camera was going to be on the dress, and Jenny was interested in Lydgate. She left the control room and went out onto the floor, crossing through the tangle of cables. She nodded to Trina who was perched on a packing crate, running lines with Pam Register. Pam played Amelia's impoverished cousin Susan. Jenny joined the group around the Almack's set.

The stage manager called for quiet, and Lydgate and Amelia made their entrance, pausing at what appeared to be the top of the stairs, waiting a moment before entering the Assembly Rooms. Amelia was lovely and resigned. Lydgate was upright and distant, barely aware of her.

Karen turned to ad-lib a silent word to Alec, her movement stirring the silken folds of the dress. Alec mouthed a response and even though the camera was not on him, he took the smallest step backward.

It was a good touch, that withdrawing. It was the sort of thing some men did, the desire to distance themselves welling up even when they were unaware of it. Jenny hated it when Brian—

When Brian did it. That was Brian's gesture. Brian took that little step backward all the time.

She had hardly completed that thought when the stage manager called that they were clear. Prologue scenes were always short. Alec moved off the set and a girl from wardrobe hovered around Karen, wanting to protect the dress. Then a voice came over the intercom. Something had gone wrong with a light. They needed another take. Alec and Karen moved back to their places. They repeated the scene note for note, beat for beat, Karen appearing resigned, Alec distant. She turned to ad-lib. He took that small step back. And suddenly everything about Lydgate seemed like Brian.

What a stupid thought. Why should Lydgate remind her of Brian?

But suddenly the set blurred. She had to grip the back of a chair. Everyone was clustering around her—"Are you okay . . . She's faint . . . Maybe her meridians are out of line . . . it's her planets . . ."

She brushed everyone off. "I'm fine. I'm okay, really. I just didn't have a chance to eat lunch, that's all."

A tunafish sandwich was thrust in her hand, and people were urging her to eat it. The tuna had a strong fishy odor, she could smell the sharpness of the pickle, the yeastiness of the bread. A sick uneasiness churned through her. The Almack's set went dark. The grips were wheeling the cameras away.

She was overreacting. Alec had picked up on one mannerism. It wasn't an unusual gesture. It didn't have anything to do with Brian. It was nothing.

So why was her heart pounding? Why did she feel faint?

She thought about Lydgate's first scene of the day. What did Brian do when people bored him? He didn't interrupt, he didn't walk away—children of alcoholics avoid confrontation—he instead went glassy, just as Lydgate had. Lydgate had been looking at Lady Lightfield with the same expression Brian often wore.

Her eyes searched the studio floor. She need to find Brian. She needed to see his familiar face, needed to see him looking like himself, not like Lydgate. Then she remembered. Brian wasn't in today. He was at the house, supervising the tile contractor's last work on the kitchen.

The kitchen. The antique farm table. The endless pursuit of the perfect tile, the exact finial. A collector. Lydgate was a collector. He cared more about objects than people.

Did Brian?

Jenny was up in her office. She hardly remembered how she had gotten there. She sat at her desk. She knew she would get nothing more done today.

It was crazy to be this upset. So what if she had used a thing or two from Brian's personality to develop one of her characters? That's what writers do. It was no big deal. The first time you felt guilty, you felt like you were betraying your friends, violating their privacy, but then you got used to it.

This was more than that. Something within her was shrieking. This wasn't a minor offense, an everyday transgression of privacy. She felt feverish, her arms ached. Her body, her instincts, were pounding a drum, sending her a message.

But she already had used Brian on the show. Knowingly and deliberately she had paid tribute to their relationship. Lord Courtland and Lady Varley had grown up together and had loved each other since they had been children. Their parents had arranged marriages for them to other people, and they had both been loyal and faithful spouses to those people, but even after all these years they still loved each other . . . because they had grown up together.

That was how she had used Brian. That was all.

She switched on the video monitor and the intercom and sat with her elbows on her desk, her hands pressed to her eyes, listening as scenes were called over the intercom. Occasionally she would look up and watch on the monitor. Her recall of this script was suddenly complete—she knew precisely which scenes the duke was in, and when they were finished, she waited ten minutes and then went down to the second floor, pass the guard's desk and the mail cubbies, past the closed door of Brian's empty dressing room. She knocked on Alec's door.

"Come in, come in." It was Ray Bianchetti's voice, deep and friendly.

She had forgotten that Ray would be there.

She opened the door. The two men were standing in front of the counter, removing their makeup. Ray was bare-chested, a pair of sweat pants riding low on his lean hips. Alec was in jeans and his shirt was unbuttoned, the tails hanging loose. Their coloring was different, but they had the same broad-shouldered build, and they were both leaning toward the mirror with the same easy masculine grace. They did seem like a pair of brothers.

They straightened when they saw her. Ray wiped his face with a towel. "I suppose you've come to praise our young friend because he's finally figured out how to do his job."

"Yes, as a matter of fact, I have."

Alec turned toward her, buttoning up his shirt. "It took me a while," he said, as if he were apologizing for not having achieved this instantly. "But I think I've got the guy more or less pegged."

He gestured for her to sit down. The dressing room was long and narrow. The cinderblock walls were painted ivory. It was crowded. Ray's former roommate had left behind a suite of cheap living room furniture, a wood-armed sofa in a nubby fabric with a pair of matching chairs. She took one of the chairs. The furniture was crammed so close together that to reach the sofa, Alec had to step over the coffee table.

On the left thigh of his jeans there was a lighter patch, the denim almost frayed. He must have been wearing a tool belt at some point.

He sat back on the sofa, one foot propped

up on the coffee table. Lydgate would never sit like that.

What exactly had she come here to say? *Please tell me that this isn't happening. Please tell me that I didn't base this character on Brian.*

She took a breath and looked straight at Alec. "You are doing a fabulous job." That was very hard to say. The last thing she felt like was praising him for the quality of his work. "What can you tell me about the character?" She was speaking too formally, but she couldn't help herself. "You know I have trouble writing for him. I'd appreciate your insights."

Alec didn't say anything for a moment. And a sharp pain shot along the undersides of Jenny's arms. It was as if he understood everything. But he couldn't. That wasn't possible.

"I don't know how well I can articulate this," he said at last, "but I see him as a man who was raised by women—"

Yes, Brian had been raised almost entirely by his mother.

"—and by women who did not particularly like men."

Oh, yes, that too.

"On one hand," Alec continued, "that made him feel like the center of the universe, but he also knew that it wasn't supposed to be this way. That there was supposed to be someone else in the center—his father. I guess he would have been a duke too."

"The old duke," Jenny murmured. "That's what we call him." Was this at the center of Brian's soul, the absence of a father?

Tucked into the chrome frame that held the mirror to the wall were more than a dozen snapshots. They ran all the way up one side of the mirror and partway across the top. They were pictures of a baby, a black-haired little fellow in a blue blanket. He was Tony Bianchetti, Ray's son. As young as he was, Ray was the only person in the cast with a conventional life—a wife, a house, a child. He was a father.

Alec was still speaking. "My brothers and I always spent a lot of time with our dad. You do on a farm. You'd see him kicking and cussing a big piece of machinery and then settling down to fix it. You look at him and you know what you're going to be like. And in my case, that always felt okay."

"That's how it was for me too." Ray had sat down in the other chair to tie his shoes. "My father and uncle have an auto body shop, and we were down there all the time. My brother still is."

Ray brought an effortless masculinity to his character, something that he had off camera as well. Alec had it too. Jenny remembered how the pair of them had looked when she had come into the room, so thoroughly comfortable with themselves as men. Was Brian like that? Did he have that certainty at the core of his soul?

No.

She had to face it. This wasn't a case of copying a few mannerisms, an occasional quirk of personality. Fourteen years of knowing Brian had gone into the creation of this character. That's why she had never felt comfortable writing for him, because she hadn't been willing to face that she had based him so closely on Brian. Lydgate was Brian.

And Lydgate was an awful person.

She would get rid of Lydgate, that's what she would do. She would kill him so she never had to think about this again. She could do that. She was head writer. The network wouldn't like it, but if she fought, if she held fast, she would get her way.

Or she could rewrite the character, make him nice. The cast would be bewildered; the fan magazines would jeer at her, but she could do it. This was her show. The network might own it, but it was hers. She could do whatever she wanted. It was hers.

So she wasn't going to ruin it. She would do what was right for the show. Alec Cameron's performance was right for the show, and she would give him what he needed.

The day was over. The cast and crew were leaving. They were all going home. She dreaded going home. Brian would be there. He was an expert at conciliation. He could smooth anything over. But what did that solve?

She put her key slowly into the lock. The front door to the house opened into a little enclosed foyer. Beyond the inner door were the narrow stairs and a passageway that led back to the kitchen—Brian's perfect blue-granite, bleached-pine kitchen. Jenny could smell the slight vinegary scent of fresh paint.

He had been so supportive when she had been

developing the show. He had encouraged her ambitions. But what about after the miscarriage when she had again needed support and encouragement? He hadn't known what to do or say. Ambition was fine—she was allowed to be ambitious. Misery was a no go. He couldn't handle misery.

He was at the kitchen counter, making dinner, a lean, willowy man in trim jeans. He looked up from the chopping block. "Hi." His voice was pleasant. His voice was almost always pleasant. "We're doing vegetarian tonight, all sorts of eggplant things. Is that okay?"

"Sure."

"The tile turned out well, didn't it?" He used the butcher knife to point to the new backsplash. "I think we made the right choice on the grout color."

"It looks great." Why hadn't he asked her about her first day back at work? Why wasn't he looking at her? How important was the color of the grout?

She sat at the kitchen table, listening to the sounds of him work—the quick, soft rush of water in the faucet, the muffled thud of cabinets opening and closing, the sharp clicking of the electronic pilot light on the burners.

Lydgate was incapable of intimacy. Behind his magisterial facade was a black-ice selfishness. Brian didn't have the duke's grandeur. In its place was his placating, surface charm. What lay beneath was the same. Her fictional creation forced her to acknowledge the truth about him.

She had been hoping that when he felt better

about his career, their relationship would be more satisfying. But that wasn't going to happen. He would never comfort her, he would never take care of her, he would never speak openly to her about his feelings. He didn't know how. Brian would never be completely honest with her because he didn't know how to be honest with himself. It would always be like this.

My Lady's Chamber
Script Episode #96

SUSAN: But Amelia, my dear cousin, you don't love Lydgate. To spend your whole life with someone you don't love . . .

AMELIA: What else can I do? This is what Aunt Emily and Uncle Varley think is best. I must trust their judgment. They are the only family I've known.

SUSAN: I can believe this of Uncle Varley, but Aunt Emily . . . she and Lord Courtland—

AMELIA: (SHARPLY) Susan! (THIS IS FORBIDDEN GROUND) Our aunt has the finest character in England.

SUSAN: I know she does. Of course she does. I'm not saying . . . but she can't help who she loves.

Six

The actors had their dressing rooms on the second floor. Two corridors were set at right angles to each other. The shorter one had the men's dressing rooms, the longer one had makeup and the women's dressing rooms. The two halls met at the stairwell where a security guard sat at a desk opposite from the fire door. Along the wall beside him were a couple of pay phones and a row of mail cubbies where the contract players picked up their fan mail, memos, schedules, and the scripts. The scripts usually arrived a week or so ahead of the taping date.

The first page of the script listed all the basics—the names of the producers, directors, and writers, a list of the characters involved in that episode, and a list of the sets required. The second page had a prose summary of each act—acts being separated from each other by the commercial breaks. The summaries let an actor get a quick sense of what scenes he was in, what his character was doing.

One afternoon a couple of weeks after the Emmys, Alec was in his dressing room, lying on the sofa, his head and feet propped up against the furniture's wood-trimmed arms, when Ray came in and dropped a script on his chest.

"Wake up, son. You're about to get a sex life."

Alec grabbed the script so it wouldn't slide to the floor. "Who's the lucky lady? It is a lady, isn't it?"

"Do you mean 'lady' as opposed to 'serving maid?' Or do you mean 'lady' as opposed to 'plump young footman?' "

"Either."

"It's both. Her Grace the Duchess of Lydgate, she's the lucky bird."

"I suppose that makes sense." Alec sat up and opened the script to the second page.

The summaries told him nothing. In 1C—the third scene of the first act—Lydgate was in his library working on estate papers. In 4C, he entered Amelia's bedchamber and made love to her.

The scripts were fastened in the upper left-hand corner with a single industrial-sized staple. Other shows used costly binders; *My Lady's Chamber* had a stapler. Alec flipped to 4C, the show's final scene.

CUT TO: (ACT 4 C. AMELIA'S BED-CHAMBER. AMELIA ALONE AT DRESSING TABLE, LOST IN THOUGHT. LYDGATE KNOCKS, ENTERS BEFORE REPLY.)

LYDGATE: Madam.

Well, that was great dialogue. Nothing like having an Emmy-winning writer on the show.

AMELIA: (RISING) Lydgate.

Could these people communicate or what?

(LYDGATE APPROACHES HER. AWKWARD BEAT. BEGINS TO UNTIE CRAVAT.)

Now that was going to be tricky. Untying cravats was not nearly as hard as tying them, but it wasn't something you could do in the dark either. Even the wardrobe girls sometimes had trouble. Now Alec was going to get to untie his own on camera.

(CAMERA ON AMELIA, DISTASTE, RESIGNATION. LYDGATE INITIATES SEX. FADE OUT.)

BRIDGE TO:
COMMERCIAL:

Lydgate initiates sex? Was that it? Alec had read some unhelpful scripts in his day, but there had to be some sort of prize for this one. There were only about forty jillion ways to "initiate sex." Which one did His Grace favor?

And the script was two pages short. Whoever had written it—and this was the sort of thing that wouldn't have been done without the approval of Miss Jenny Cotton—was expecting him to do that initiating for two pages' worth of time.

Didn't Amelia have a really great silver brush on her dressing table? Gil could focus the camera on that for two pages, and everyone would be happy. Everyone except the viewers.

Ray had been reading the scene over his arm. "Is my inexperience showing, or is this sort of underwritten?"

It certainly was. "They do have me untying my cravat. That could take me hours. Of course then I'd be too exhausted to perform my conjugal duty."

"If you're really lucky, it will be one of those knots that goes around the neck three times first, and you'll be waving your arms over your head like a windmill trying to get out of it." Ray demonstrated. "Isn't this a nice piece of business?"

"No," Alec said bluntly. "Especially when you consider that these people probably didn't wear deodorant."

This wasn't a joking matter. Alec had been playing romantic leads for nearly ten years now, and one of the first things he had learned was sex scenes themselves were largely technical. The director told you to kiss right, kiss left; you had to keep the actress's hair from obscuring close-ups. Both you and she would have lots of body makeup on, and under the heat of the lights that's what you'd smell.

But in every other show he had done, the sex scenes came at the end of a steadily building romance, and that's where the emotion was. He had known how each character made love. Chris, the brash young shirtless construction worker on *Day by Day,* had been athletic and physically exuberant, given to as large a movement as the camera could handle. Robert, the unlicensed doctor on *To Have and to Hold,* had been the opposite: all sensitive, delicate moves, a hand slowly opening on a woman's back. Derek, as distasteful as the idea of rape had been to Alec, had been smoldering repression, polite formal gestures suddenly growing sexual and intense.

But Lydgate? Alec didn't even know how Lydgate would kiss. Or if he did.

He looked up at Ray. "If you're about to have sex with a woman you have absolutely no interest in, do you kiss her first?"

"Beats me. I've only had sex with my wife and I'm interested in her."

"That's no help." Alec started to read the scene again.

"You're stumped, aren't you?" Ray was surprised at the thought.

"For the moment, yes."

"What are you going to do?"

Alec put down the script. He was increasingly aware that the younger actors on the show were hungry for guidance. Ray was a very talented actor, but he was weak on the long close-ups that many scenes ended with and he tended to go wooden during the recapping scenes. They were the sort of things a daytime actor picked up from watching other people work. As experienced as some of the others were at acting in general, no one on the show really had solid daytime skills. Except Brian, of course.

"I'm going to go talk to Karen," he told Ray. "When you're stuck, go talk to your partner. When you're in a movie or a play, take your questions to the director. Here, work with the other actors. Especially in the sex scenes. The actress has to be comfortable with whatever you're going to do to her." Alec got up and stepped over the coffee table. "Or at least she should be prepared to forgive you."

Slapping the script against his leg, he rounded past the guard's desk and went down the women's hall. He knocked on the door of the dressing room Karen and Trina shared. "Are you decent?"

"Close enough," Trina called out.

They were already out of costume. Trina was in a bra and a half-slip, which was decent for her. Karen was wearing a pale blue crossover kimono. Her dark hair was still in Amelia's soft Regency knot, so the gorgeous length of her swanlike neck was fully exposed. Alec supposed he was going to be doing weird and wet things to that neck next week.

Karen was an excellent actress. Alec had nothing but respect for her abilities and her dedication. But she was one of the most unhappy people he had ever met. She was nervous and high-strung; she was incapable of finding joy in anything. Her performance—even her creation of the calm, accepting Amelia—came out of nervous tension. She was willing to take great risks on camera because she believed that she had nothing to lose. She played every episode as if it were going to be her last.

"Have you picked up the new script?" he asked.

Both women shook their heads.

He laid the script on the counter in front of Karen. "Check out Four C."

She turned to the summary and found 4C. "Make love?" She was suspicious. "You and me?"

Alec trusted that the distaste in her voice was for Lydgate, not for himself. "The script calls it 'initiating sex.' "

"But why?" she protested. "We don't like each other. Why are we going to bed together?"

"Maybe I have an excruciatingly painful hard-on."

"Then masturbate," she suggested. "Leave me out of it." She turned to the end of the script to read the scene.

"Or grab one of the maids." Trina was looking at the script over Karen's shoulder. "You could bop me. I'd love a story. I'd even put up with your excruciatingly painful hard-on."

Karen looked up from the script. "This doesn't exactly help. What's the point?"

"Ratings." Trina was blunt. "*Destiny's Journey* has a trial going on. Our boys upstairs must remember what happened to *Passions*' ratings during Derek and Ginger. So they want Alec to do his stuff again. Although watch yourself, Karen"—her voice grew teasing—"you have to have heard what the tabloids said his stuff entailed."

Karen ignored her. "And the thing is short. Who's directing?" She flipped back to the front of the script. "Not that it matters. Let's go talk to Jenny. This is her fault." She rose, put her character's jewelry into a little plastic bag, and clipped it to the hanger her costume was on.

As soon as the door to the dressing room shut behind them, Alec glanced up and down the hall to be sure that no one was around. Pam and Francine were at the phones, but they were absorbed in their conversations. He took Karen by the arm.

He was still in costume, his calf-length, black-leather Hessian boots adding to his height. Her thin satin kimono made her seem small and vulnerable in contrast. He supposed the sexual chemistry was going to have to come out of that somehow, the fact that men are simply taller, stronger, more powerful than women. Amelia was smarter, better read, more sensitive than Lydgate, an all-around better human being. The only thing he had going for him was economic power and biological size.

What a great guy.

Alec spoke. "You know that rumor Trina was referring to?" He was glad that Trina had brought it up. It had to be dealt with. "About Chloe and me on *Passions.* Does that worry you? It's not true."

"Oh, I know that." Karen was quick to answer. "How could it be?"

Six months after the airing of Derek's rape of Ginger, a month or so after Alec and Chloe themselves had married, a rumor had swept through the fan world and then finally appeared in print in one of the tabloids—that during the rape scene, Alec had actually had sex with Chloe.

It was absurd. There were far too many people hanging around the set, to say nothing of the fact that Chloe had been encased in a body stocking that was none too easy to get her out of. And even though everyone in the business knew that it couldn't be true, the rumor had yet to die. Every year or so it would resurface, dogging Alec, embarrassing him.

The trouble was that while it was untrue, it was only untrue by ten minutes. As soon as the scene was over, he had gone to Chloe's dressing room, locked the door and had, for the first time, made love to her.

"You did not have to say anything," Karen continued. "It wasn't necessary. I trust you."

There were indeed actors who took advantage of love scenes, sticking their tongues down a woman's throat or grinding their erections up against her. Alec was not one of them.

"And anyway"—Karen tightened the sash of her kimono—"I know you don't feel about me the way you did about Chloe Spencer."

Alec shut his eyes and gave into a moment's exasperation. Trust an actress to make everything about herself. Now if Alec didn't exploit the situation, it would be a judgment on Karen's powers of attraction.

Times like this he thought he should have stayed in Canada.

Jenny was in her office. When she saw Alec and Karen, she pushed back from the computer. "Now what can I do for you two lovebirds?"

She was pleased to see them. Obviously they

had come in to talk about a script, and there was nothing Jenny liked more than talking about the show's stories.

"You can tell me," Alec said, "why I am inflicting my animal self on this delicate lady."

"It's simple. You need an heir."

Oh, of course. An heir. A son. Alec sat down. He understood that.

Really little kids, the toddlers, don't weigh enough to keep their seats down at a movie theater. They would sit there so proud of themselves, their chubby little legs sticking straight out, their feet barely clearing the edge of the seat. Then gradually the seat would start to rise, closing up on them. It was adorable.

He had married Chloe for a swirling blur of reasons. She had seemed delicate and fragile, so like his little sister Meg. She had been lovely and elegant, the gleaming American trophy a boy can't get if he stays home in Canada. And she had been Ginger. Day after day he had gone to work and pretended to fall in love with her. After a while it stopped feeling like pretend anymore.

He wanted children. He never expected Chloe to give up her career or turn into the farmer's wife that his mother had been. Of all acting careers, daytime allows a person to have a family life. Chloe had agreed with that. She said she wanted children too. If she was lying to him, she was lying to herself even more.

Slowly the truth came out. This was a woman who had always had total control of her beauty. Maintaining that beauty, the perfection of her figure, her skin, her hair, her nails, was a tremendous amount of work. The weight gain, the swelling, and the nausea of pregnancy repelled her. Childbirth terrified her. The pain, the sweating, the matted hair, the coarse breathing . . . it all seemed like a nightmarish, loathsome loss of control. She couldn't even look at pregnant women on the street. They seemed pathetic to her, even elephantine.

When the depth of her anxiety became clear, she wanted Alec to say that it was all right, that there was nothing wrong with her, that this was how she was supposed to feel. She wanted to be told that she was so talented, so uniquely lovely, that she was entitled to these fears.

He couldn't do that. He couldn't say that he thought this was normal. He thought she needed therapy.

He didn't mean that she should have to go alone. Counseling was something that the two of them could undertake together. They would meet this problem with the same determination that his family had faced Meg's illness.

But Chloe refused to acknowledge that there was a problem, that there was any reason for her to change. She was willing to adopt a child . . . if, and only if, Alec acknowledged that there was nothing wrong with her. As much as he hated dishonesty, he had considered lying to her so she would consider adoption, but that hardly seemed like a good foundation upon which to build a family.

So he didn't lie, and she found that she

couldn't tolerate being married to someone who didn't think she was utterly perfect.

Karen and Jenny were talking. Their voices seemed to be coming from a long way off. Alec forced himself to pay attention.

"I suppose I hate it." Karen was saying. "What do I do, close my eyes and think of England? Or Sir Peregrine?" He was the bankrupt gambler Amelia had loved before her marriage. "Should I be thinking of him?"

"Oh, no." Jenny answered. "Don't do that. Don't think about Peregrine. Don't think about anyone. That's how lonely you are, you can't even think of anyone to think about."

"I can relate to that," Karen said glumly.

"You just want a baby."

"I can relate to that too."

Alec listened to them. Karen's role in this wasn't the problem. It was his. He needed to be involved in this discussion. "Here's my question," he said. "I can't help but think that sex between these two would be pretty boring. Lydgate doesn't care about being a good lover. Wouldn't he just come in the room after she's in bed, blow out the candles, and get under the blankets, and it would all be over in a couple of minutes?"

"That thought had crossed my mind," Jenny admitted.

Then why had she let the thought keep going? Why hadn't she held on to it?

"That may be the most easily believable scenario," she continued. "But it's boring."

He knew that. "I thought we prided ourselves on believability and historical accuracy."

"I let you keep all your teeth, didn't I?"

He didn't mean to be quarreling with her. He knew that they were presenting a fantasy. Everyone in *My Lady's Chamber* was well-nourished and scrupulously clean. That hadn't been so in the nineteenth century.

But he still wanted to make the scene as consistent as possible. Here you've got a guy who's not very interested in sex—Alec believed that about Lydgate. How do you make his scenes erotically charged?

"What's he doing in the rest of the episode?" Alec flipped back to the summary. "He's in the library. Why's he in the library?"

"Because the set was up," Jenny volunteered.

What a cheesy show. "Okay, he's probably not going to get turned on by working on estate papers." Derek, the compulsive young lawyer, might have been, but not the duke.

"And I thought I did all the estate work," Karen said.

"He would have to sign stuff," Jenny answered.

Alec pressed his fingers to his forehead, trying to visualize the scene. Lydgate was at his desk. Papers were in neat stacks, little notes from Amelia and the lawyers telling him what to change, where to sign. How did that make him feel?

Impatient. Resentful. Angry.

He let his hands drop. "I probably hate you," he said to Karen, but he wasn't seeing Karen and all her high-strung fever—he was seeing Amelia, cool, unshakable. "I hate you for being smarter than me, I hate you for thinking so little of me, I hate you because I need you."

Jenny did something, stirred, made a motion, something, but Alec didn't look. He was focused, concentrating on Amelia. Karen was in character too, entirely Amelia.

"That's how the two scenes fit." Alec knew he had it. "I'm in the library, I'm thinking more and more about what a pain it is to be married to someone so perfect, someone everyone else thinks is so wonderful. So I want to take you down a peg or two. What better place than in bed? This isn't about making a baby, it's not about desire. It's about power. The old I've-got-a-dick-and-you-don't."

This was going to work. He turned to Jenny. She would—

She was white. Her eyes filled her face, they were wide and startled.

What on earth had he said? She was truly distressed. He had just been talking about his character. He hadn't said anything personal.

Oh, God, of course. His character was personal for her. She was basing Lydgate on Brian. He hadn't been thinking about that.

He had first realized it in a flash-flood instinct, the kind that he had built his career on. He had been riding down the elevator from Jenny's hospital room, thinking about the way Brian had been perched on the window ledge, how uneasy Brian was with Jenny's pain, how distasteful he found it. That was all Alec had been thinking about, how he didn't particularly like or respect Brian. Then somewhere between the fourth and third floor he suddenly knew he was also thinking about Lydgate.

Until this moment he hadn't known for sure if Jenny was aware of what she had been doing. But it was clear now. She knew.

I hate you for being smarter than me. He had said that. That wouldn't be easy for her to hear.

But it was true. Brian must resent her. He was less talented than she was, he made less money than she did, his job depended on her. What man wouldn't hate being in that position?

Why did some women do this? Good, strong, intelligent women, energetic and accomplished, kept falling in love with men who didn't deserve them.

And nine times out of ten they paid for it in bed.

He couldn't say anything about Brian, not with Karen here. He spoke carefully. "What we have to remember is that Lydgate isn't very interested in sex." Did she know this about Brian? Surely she did. "These distancers usually aren't."

Her head was up, her eyes were wide. No, she hadn't known.

No wonder she had underwritten the scene. She hadn't wanted to face the truth behind it, the truth about herself and the man she thought she would spend her life with.

Your sex life stinks, doesn't it? And he has you believing that it's all your fault.

Was that what had Brian told her, or at least

allowed her to believe? That she wasn't alluring enough, feminine enough?

Hadn't it ever occurred to her to blame him?

Brian wasn't gay. Alec felt sure of that. When you were a male working in this field, you quickly learned how to identify other men's sexual orientation. But Brian did not relate to other people physically. He was made out of air, not earth. There was something asexual about him. It was as if—to use Jenny's language—he had no gender.

So he must have made Jenny feel as if she didn't either. But she did. She wasn't made of air. She was the earth, a magnet, made of iron, nickel, and cobalt. She turned the air around her into a powerful magnetic field, capable of attracting anything. Her mind was silvery-quick, and the muscles of her arms were as sleek as a pool cue.

Alec suddenly felt lightheaded, his body curious and afire. This was no eleven-year-old tomboy peering down from the tree. She was a woman, and he was drawn to her as a woman. *Let me show you.* It was an arrogant thought, but he couldn't help it. *There is a quickness to your hands, a liveliness to your step. You believe in your mind, you must learn to believe in your body too.* He had seen tapes of the fiery scenes she had written for Georgeanna and Peregrine. She could fantasize about passion. She could imagine it. She needed to learn to live it.

Two days later new pages were circulated for both 1B and 4C. In the earlier scene Amelia was now in the library with Lydgate, and Alec's ideas provided the motivation. Jenny was facing the truth of what she had written. Lydgate was impatient with the estate papers and resentful of Amelia. She was exasperated and despairing. Here she was, trapped in a marriage with a man whom she couldn't respect, who resented her. Unlike a modern woman, she had no way to escape. All her money was his to control; divorce took an act of Parliament.

Four C was now shorter and much more menacing. Amelia was in her nightdress, brushing her hair, and when she rose at Lydgate's entrance, she clutched the brush to her, almost as if it were a weapon. Lydgate extended his hand. "Your brush, madam." The scene ended there with a close-up of Amelia laying her brush in Lydgate's hand.

For the next two weeks, the scripts were late and full of revisions. Soap fans might be stirred by the phallic imagery of a hairbrush, but they weren't going to be satisfied with it for long. A scene between Amelia and Lady Varley established clearly for the viewers how essential it was for Lydgate to have an heir. Lady Varley had raised Amelia, she loved her dearly. She spoke with her face tight, her eyes soft with pain. "You must endure it, child. You must."

Alec made no effort to make Lydgate sympathetic. The character had repressed all his guilt and self-doubt, the things that might make him appealing to viewers. He was simply a cold, oppressive force, a modern woman's nightmare of what the boys in power can do, how they will let her go so far and then the gate slams shut and she can travel no further. No one will listen to her, no one will believe her, she has no money, no rights.

It was a powerful story.

The first episode was aired two weeks after Alec had gotten the script, one week after it had been taped. Most daytime dramas taped an episode three weeks before it aired. *My Lady's Chamber* worked on a one-week delay. Alec thought that was an invitation to disaster—what if a contagious flu ran through the whole cast?—but Jenny claimed it made the show more responsive to the audience.

So it was almost immediately clear that the viewers loved this story. The show's ratings took a nice little hop, and Karen's fan mail tripled. Amelia was trapped, she had almost no chance of personal happiness; she instead had to find solace in dignity and duty. People admired her for it.

Alec's mail was taking a strange turn, women describing their fantasies of meeting him. A different sort of person was now stopping him on the street, strange women dressed in leather and dog collars or in business suits so severe that they might have been prison uniforms. They were women who wanted Lydgate's anger, felt the need for his coldness.

Alec was repelled by them. He wanted to ease up on the scenes, make Lydgate more sympathetic, but he couldn't justify it to himself. He had fought against Derek raping Ginger because he had thought it was out of character and because he objected to the idea that Ginger had enjoyed it. But this was in character, and it had never been suggested that Amelia liked one thing about it.

He wished that he were involved with someone. He needed to be reassured about his capacity for tenderness.

July 16
Dear Mr. Cameron,
I've never before written what I suppose must be called a fan letter. But I want to convey the extent of my appreciation for you. You are an actor of stature . . .

July 18
Dear Mr. Lydgate,

Please don't think I am crazy because I know this to be true. In a past life you and I had a strong sensual and passionate relationship. We were nothing as mundane as husband and wife. Our love towered over other people's notions of right and wrong. We were beyond society's contentions, we were . . .

July 16

I must meet you. It is urgent. I need. At 7:30 P.M. next Thursday I will be at the corner of Garfield and Seventh Avenue in Park Slope. Friday at the same time I will be at Grand and Clinton in the Lower East Side. I have keys to apartments near both spots. We will not be interrupted.

I'll be wearing a red flower. Red for passion.

Seven

My Lady's Chamber
Script, Episode #603

(PROLOGUE B: LYDGATE IN LIBRARY. HE IS AT THE DESK WHICH IS COVERED WITH PAPERS. A CLOSE-UP SHOWS HIM BORED AND IMPATIENT. WE HEAR)

AMELIA: Lydgate, this question of Rose Hill Farm must be settled. The tenants have had the use of that field for ten years. We cannot take it from them without compensation.

LYDGATE: Crawford tells me that the matter is settled. I have no further interest in it.

AMELIA: He let the field to his nephew. That's how he settled it. He took it from people who had been farming it for ten years and gave it to his sister's son.

LYDGATE: I repeat, the matter is settled.

AMELIA: (VERY FRUSTRATED) Then at least you must address the situation in Cornwall. You know what has been happening to the price of tin.

LYDGATE: (GLARES AT HER. HE HAS NO IDEA WHAT HAS HAPPENED TO PRICE OF TIN.) You take too much upon yourself, madam.

AMELIA: (STRUGGLING TO CONTROL HERSELF) I do not mean to offend you.

Week by week the ratings kept inching up. The number one show was in the middle of an explosive trial, but it didn't matter. Each week George, the show's executive producer, would come into Jenny's office with a fax of the latest numbers. He'd be shaking his head. "This is unbelievable. We're actually pulling this off. I never thought we would."

Jenny could feel the difference on the street. Neighbors who used to only nod pleasantly now spoke to her, having learned who she was. She overheard people on the subway discussing the characters. The clerks in the bookstore wanted to know what was going to happen next. The girl behind the register at the deli kept wishing for the show to be an hour long. "I really hate it," she said as she wrapped Jenny's sandwich. "It's over so fast."

Jenny loved it. All these people were watching her show, following her stories, caring about her characters. She was making their day brighter. If they were busy, she gave them an excuse for sitting down for thirty minutes. If they were lonely, she gave them companions. If they were curious, she gave them information, she taught them history. It was almost as if she were their mother, taking care of them

Why couldn't Brian feel the joy that she did? He deserved to. He had worked as hard as she had to get the show started. But the show's success wasn't making him happy. He didn't seem to care. He wasn't happy. And she wanted him to be happy. She would have done anything to make him so.

At least one of us should be happy.

My Lady's Chamber
Script, Episode #501

AMELIA: (STARTLED) You cannot be thinking of leaving your husband. (THIS NEVER OCCURRED TO HER.)

GEORGEANNA: I thought you understood. Phillip is so cold. He cares nothing about me.

AMELIA: But he is your husband.

GEORGEANNA: So am I doomed? (A WILD, FRANTIC GESTURE) I have the right to be loved, don't I? Peregrine loves me. Are you telling me I should turn my back on that? Are you telling me that love doesn't count?

AMELIA: I'm saying that—

GEORGEANNA: (DESPAIRING) I thought you were on my side. I thought you understood.

Francine Kenny, the elegant and distinguished-looking actress who played Lady Varley, the show's maternal confidante, stopped by Jenny's office. "Murr and I have been wondering about something." Murrfield Thomas played Lord Courtland. "There hasn't been anything in the scripts all summer about us being in love with one another."

"There hasn't?" Jenny stared at her. "Are you sure? That can't be right." Lord Courtland and Lady Varley were the characters who had loved each other since childhood; their devotion was a steady contrast to the other characters' flighty passions or rigid coldness. Their love had never been an urgent front-burner story, but it was a "tent pole," something that held the other stories up. There was no way Jenny could have gone three months without mentioning it.

"I'm positive, Jenny. Trust me. I'm right."

Of course she was. The actors kept close track of exactly how many pages they were getting in each script.

Jenny tugged at her hair. "I'm sorry. It just fell through the cracks. We have so much material right now, I made a mistake. It doesn't mean anything. We aren't trying to get rid of that element. Honestly we aren't."

Francine looked relieved. Actresses in their fifties did not find other work easily. "We were worried about that."

"Don't be. And thanks for coming in. I should have noticed it myself."

Francine left, and Jenny jerked angrily at the papers on her desk. *It doesn't mean anything.*

Had she said that? Of course it meant something. It meant everything.

She had modeled that love on Brian and herself. She had done so consciously and deliberately. *I thought that's what love was, growing up with someone, sharing your past with him.* But she didn't believe that anymore and so unconsciously, unaware, she had stopped writing about that love.

My Lady's Chamber
Story Outline,
Episodes #455-520

Georgeanna and Amelia are in the same boat—married to men they have no affection for. Georgeanna's response is stormy, passionate, and rebellious, and she ends up pregnant and exiled. But as much as we disapprove of Georgeanna's wild behavior, we don't want anyone wholeheartedly applauding Amelia's stoic acceptance. There's a cost to making her decision, a narrowing of herself.

When Georgeanna is determined to run off with Peregrine, Amelia withdraws her support. She is not cold-hearted, but her imagination cannot encompass an alternative to marriage.

George appeared in the door of Jenny's office. She spoke first. "Did you realize we haven't said anything all summer about Lady Varley and Lord Courtland?" He had probably come to talk about the latest ratings, but this was more important than the numbers. She had made a mistake with the story. That was awful.

He thought for a moment. "You're right. I guess we haven't. Is it a problem?"

She sighed. "No, I suppose not." At least not a problem with the show. And she just wasn't going to think about what it said about her own life.

"I have some other news," he said. "You know who Edgar Delaney is, don't you?"

"Of course." He was a well-respected Broadway comedian with several Tonys to his credit.

"He loves the show. He wants to join the cast."

Jenny drew back. "Come on, George, you know we don't do celebrity walk-ons."

They had had these requests before—big-time stars who, as a lark, a publicity stunt, wanted to be on the show for a few days. But Jenny felt that those appearances were like winking at the audience; they undercut a show's illusion of reality.

"It isn't like that. He wants to sign a contract."

"He does?" Edgar Delaney wanted to join the cast? This was a different story. People like Edgar Delaney were so often snobs about daytime. The whole soap community loved it when an actor with a solid theatrical reputation joined a soap. "What's the catch?" She could tell by George's face that there was one.

"He wants to start September first, and his agent has declared that that's non-negotiable."

"September *first*?" It was August seventh.

September first was three weeks away. She couldn't introduce a new character on three weeks notice. It would mean reworking the entire fall outline and revising many of already completed August scripts as well. It wasn't possible.

And she had meant it when she had told Francine that they had too much material right now. Tricia Steckler, who played Georgeanna, was due back from her maternity leave in September. David Roxbury, who played Peregrine, would be back then too. Jenny was going to be underutilizing them. It was no time to add a new character.

But Edgar Delaney? He wasn't knocking on Paul Tomlin's door wanting to join *Aspen!!* "What did you tell them?"

"That it was absolutely ridiculous, and you were the only writer in the business who would even consider it."

Jenny liked hearing that. She liked what people said about her—that she was the most flexible, most responsive writer in the business. Having that reputation was important to her. "I guess I can think about it."

Edgar Delaney's interest was not public information, but that night Jenny told Brian. He had always known everything about the show. She had told him automatically. It wouldn't have occurred to her not to. But as she told him about this, she felt uneasy. He was, after all, a member of the cast. One actor shouldn't know about another's contract negotiations.

He listened to her stiffly. "So it's your decision," he said.

"It is, and I don't know what to do. It will be so much work, and we have so many wonderful stories coming up. I already let something slip without noticing."

"Then don't do it."

"But this is Edgar Delaney. What a coup. I almost feel like I owe it to all of daytime to do it."

"Then do."

A lot of help he was.

By the end of the next day she knew that she had no choice. This was an opportunity *My Lady's Chamber* was going to have to pass on. It just didn't make sense. It would involve too much upheaval, too much change.

The decision depressed her. It was the right thing to do, but it was so adult. Having her own show had always been such fun. "Hey, kids, let's put on a show"—that's what it felt like sometimes, she and all the kids in the neighborhood putting on a play in someone's backyard. Of course, the network often tried to spoil her fun, telling her she couldn't go on location, she couldn't build new sets, but the network was the grown-up, everyone out in Brooklyn were the kids, and kids always have to work around grown-ups' rules.

Now she was turning into one of the grown-ups. *This wasn't supposed to happen to us, Brian. We were going to remain kids forever.*

Late that afternoon she went down to the studio floor. She liked being alone on the sets, sitting where the characters sat, touching the things that they touched.

The studio was cool. Once the lights went off for the day, the heat in the room rose into the darkness above the catwalks and the electric cables. Jenny turned on a few floor lights and began to pick her way through the trail of cables, ladders, and discarded styrofoam cups that surrounded the pristine sets.

She stopped at Amelia's bedchamber. She did like this set—it was one of the loveliest. The walls were a quiet green with delicate, intricate moldings detailed in ivory. The furniture's scrolling curves were painted ivory and trimmed in gold. The bedhangings were a pale primrose with a soft pattern of green vines. Jenny sat down on the bed, leaning back against the headboard, imagining Amelia here.

Amelia was married to a man she didn't love. As were Georgeanna and Lady Varley. Jenny hadn't noticed how often she was using that device. At least Georgeanna and Lady Varley loved other people. Would Amelia fall in love again?

Would Jenny?

She heard footsteps. It was a heavy tread. She guessed it was one of the security guards wondering who had turned the lights on. She called out.

The footsteps quickened, and a moment later Alec Cameron came around the walls of the set.

"That didn't sound like you." Her voice inflected upward, an unconscious note of pleasure. "I thought you had a lighter step."

She had no idea that she knew what Alec's footsteps sounded like, but apparently she did.

"I might," he said. "But His Grace of Lydgate doesn't. I'm tromping the halls, breaking in a new pair of his boots." He stepped onto the set so she could see.

He had on his own shirt, a loose, faded blue polo shirt. Beneath it he was wearing the duke's cream pantaloons and a pair of Hussars. The pantaloons were knit, fitting over his thighs with the closeness of tights. The gleaming black leather of the boots came up to his calves, rising to a slight point in front. Handsewn seams molded the boots to his legs.

"They're nice," she said.

"Thanks."

His answer was brief, and he started to move away. Clearly he did not intend to interrupt her.

"No, no. Don't go," she said. "Do you want to sit down? Take a break from your breaking in?"

"If you are sure I'm not bothering you."

As an answer Jenny waved her hand toward the one seat on the set, Amelia's delicate vanity stool. But Alec paid no attention to her gesture. A moment later his weight was pressing the mattress down, and his blue polo shirt was brushing against her arm. He was on the bed with her.

Jenny shifted uneasily. Why had he sat on the bed? It was too familiar, too intimate.

But it wouldn't feel intimate to him. He was at home on this set. He played scenes here two, three times a week. This bed was where he worked. It would feel no more intimate to him than her office sofa did to her.

She folded her arms so they weren't touching his and tried to think of something to say.

"I saw a copy of the press release from the leukemia people." She hardly knew what she was saying. "You do a lot of work for charity, don't you?"

His hair was rumpled—he had long since brushed out Lydgate's artfully windswept style. His shirt strained just a bit at his shoulders and then fell in loose folds over his torso.

"A fair amount, I guess," he answered. "But it's mostly for the leukemia foundation."

Actresses, especially daytime actresses, were used to this business of sitting right on top of other people. The sets were so narrow, the shots were so tight that the actors all stood closer together than people did in real life, and they got used to it. Karen, Trina, or Pam would think nothing of sitting so close to Alec.

"Why leukemia?"

"My little sister had it."

Jenny winced. All thoughts of herself and proximity vanished. "What happened? Is she okay?"

"No. She died."

"Oh, Alec." Jenny turned, propping her elbow against the headboard, wanting to see him better. "I am sorry. How awful."

"It was, but it was also a long time ago."

"When was it? How old was she? How old were you?"

"She was nine when she got sick, twelve when

she died. I was a year older. She would have a much better chance now. Survival rates have improved a lot. The technology is remarkable."

His voice was even. He must be used to talking about this. He undoubtedly had a set spiel that was part of his pitch at fund-raisers. Jenny knew that she was supposed to talk about treatment and technology. But she wasn't interested in treatment and technology. She cared about people. "What was she like? What kind of girl was she?"

Alec had been prepared for the treatment-and-technology question. It was a moment before he spoke. "What was she like?" He stared up at the dark tangle of overhead lights. "She was a great kid, but funny, full of contrasts. Even before she got sick, she looked fragile, and I guess she was. She was always pale and slight, and she never seemed to have much muscle. But she was tough. She had this fabulous sense of balance which made her fearless. She'd walk across any beam in the barn. If we needed to reach something, we'd throw her up on Bruce's shoulders, and she'd go up on tiptoe to—"

He broke off, rubbing one hand across the back of his neck. "I'm not sure I'm going to do a very good job of talking about this . . . but it probably does explain why I tend to be drawn to women who have a lot of contrast in them."

"Like Chloe Spencer?"

That just popped out. Jenny knew she shouldn't have said it. But when she had imagined the frail little girl standing tiptoe on her big brother's shoulders, the girl had had Chloe's delicate features.

"Chloe didn't have as much contrast to her as I first thought," he replied.

Jenny waited for him to go on, but he didn't. He wasn't going to talk about Chloe.

"So what happened after your sister died?" she asked instead. "What happened to your family?"

"That's a real soap writer's question."

He was right. It was the sort of question writers of soap operas asked. No story was ever completely over in such a writer's mind. The end of one caused another to start. That was how soaps worked and, Jenny believed, that's how life worked. "Some families fall apart after a child dies."

"I think that might have been a danger for us," he admitted. "For two years everything had been about Meg. We had all organized ourselves around what she needed. That's what we understood family life to be about, working together for something. I suppose we would have fallen apart if we hadn't found something else to focus on."

"What was that? If you don't mind my asking, that is."

"Actually it was me. No, no"—he held up his hand, cutting off her surprise—"I wasn't sick. I had Talent." His voice put a capital letter on the word. "During the last six months or so Meg liked people to read aloud to her. Everyone did it, but I was the one who enjoyed it, and soon it became clear that I was good at it. By then my teachers had noticed and they started pushing my parents, 'You have to do something with this boy's talent.' "

So there had been lessons and opportunities. "Prince Edward Island has a lot of tourists in the summer, and there are all sorts of little recitations and theater performances for them. You know *Anne of Green Gables*? I was Gilbert from one end of the island to the other."

The lessons had had to be paid for. Someone had to drive him to auditions. If a production was too far from home, living arrangements for him had to be worked out. Even as his older brothers and his one surviving sister married, they still helped out.

"That's a big responsibility, being the focus of the family's energy," Jenny said. "How did you feel about it?"

"Ambivalent, I guess. I loved performing, I liked all those opportunities. And since there were six kids in the family—five by then—who wouldn't want to feel special? But I was fifteen when I went off to Ontario to spend the summer with a repertory company, and I did feel like my talent was taking me away from the family just as surely as Meg's leukemia had taken her away. But I don't know why you called it a responsibility. I didn't see it as that."

"Could you have quit?"

"Oh." He saw her point. "Fortunately I didn't want to."

"What reconciled you to being the one with Talent?"

"It was when I was—" He stopped. "Oh, I

suppose it was just growing up, getting used to it, that sort of thing."

"That's not what you were going to say."

"No, it isn't."

"Why not? Was it about sex?"

He looked down at her again. "How did you know?"

"I know stories."

He smiled. "And if I don't tell you, you'll imagine something much more dramatic and lurid, won't you?"

"Of course."

He had been sixteen. "Which might not be early in New York but it certainly was early on Prince Edward Island." He was a good-looking kid, and the lady in question had been the sister of his high school drama coach. She was divorced and had come back home to live with her brother's family. She had sewn the costumes for the school play.

"Measuring your inseam and all?"

"Don't make a joke of it. This is my life."

But Jenny was right; that had been how it had started.

"So what did this have to do with going to New York and becoming an actor? Did you think that actors have sex all the time?"

"Yes, I did. Don't laugh. I was only sixteen. And I did know that things like this were not happening to my brothers. If this was what having talent meant, then I was glad that I had signed up. But what about you? I take it you didn't come to New York just to have sex all the time?"

She shook her head. "Actually it was Brian's

dream that brought us here more than mine. We've been together since almost before we could walk." He must already know how long she had been with Brian. It was common knowledge around the studio. "I knew I wanted to write. I didn't at that time know that I belonged in television."

"What did you think you would be doing?"

Clearly Alec wanted her to talk about herself. He had one arm crooked behind his head, his face turned toward her. His raised arm pulled his shirt close to his chest. Jenny wondered what he had looked like at sixteen.

I tend to be drawn to women with a lot of contrast in them.

She was tempted. Contrast? Did he want contrast? She could make herself sound chock-full of contrasts. *I may look short, but I have the wristbones of a very tall person . . . I may be a writer, but boy, do I know my multiplication tables . . . I may look married, but I am not.*

What was she thinking of? She wasn't the sort of person who needed every man on earth to be attracted to her. She didn't flirt, she didn't cast lures. Why had she even thought about it for one minute? *I may not be married, but I feel like I am.*

At home she found a note from Brian. He had an early audition in Manhattan tomorrow. He was spending the night at the Broom Closet. He had been planning a cauliflower curry for dinner. The recipe was in—

Jenny dropped the note. She wasn't making

cauliflower curry. She would eat an apple and some microwave popcorn.

Why was Brian going to an audition? Why wasn't *My Lady's Chamber* enough for him? Here she was, writing the best show on daytime, and it wasn't enough for the man she was supposed to love. He could have a gigantic story, the best story on the best show. All he had to do was sign a longer contract.

She had originally intended Sir Peregrine for him. He would have been perfect in the part, but the network wouldn't accept someone in that important a role without a multiyear contract. David Roxbury, who had been cast in the role, was now flooded with opportunities while Brian was still signing his daytime contracts six months at a time.

Was it going to be like this for the rest of their lives? Would he spend his entire adult life as restless and dissatisfied as he had been as a kid?

Their whole lives. Forever. Like this. But what was she going to do? *Sorry, bro, you've been a bit of a downer lately. I'm out of here. Sweat it out on your own.* She wasn't like that. Alec Cameron wasn't the only one with a sense of responsibility.

Alec . . . with one arm crooked behind his head, he had gestured with his other hand, letting it rest on his leg when he wasn't talking. Terence had said that he had the best-shaped hands in the cast. That had surprised her. She had always thought that Brian had elegant hands with his fingers so tapering and long. But she could see Terence's point. There was a power and a strength in Alec's hands, a sureness, a—

She had to stop thinking this way. She had to. Brian was her life. She loved him.

She picked up a magazine. All the women in the ads were so graceful and feminine, so completely unlike her. She turned on the TV. The news was on—the local weather. But what was the point in listening? It was August. It was going to be hot.

This wasn't working. Her thoughts were still churning. Only one thing could stop her from thinking.

She went up to her third-floor study and turned on the computer.

MY LADY'S CHAMBER

MEMO

DATE: August 8
TO: George
FROM: Jenn-Jenn the Revision Queen

I know Sept. 1 is only three weeks away, but let's go for it. Tell Edgar Delaney that he can join our happy band. I'm totally psyched. Read the attached, and if you think it's as wonderful as I do, take it to the network boys. I'm assuming that they will shriek no more than usual so I have already started monkeying with the finished scripts.

MY LADY'S CHAMBER

MEMO

DATE: August 16
TO: All Cast Members
FROM: Miss Royall

Please disregard memo dated August 14 and be advised of the following script changes:

#614 act 1B becomes #615 act 1C
#614 act 2A " #615 act 2B

The attached salmon-colored pages are revisions for #613 act 1A. The attached cherry-colored pages are revisions for #613 act 3A.

Delete #614 act 1C and expect new pages for #615 act 3A.

Those of you who wish for complete, clean scripts, please address your concerns to our Xerox repairman.

A level of chaos that hit *My Lady's Chamber* was nothing like Alec had ever seen before. Sometimes the cast would go three days without getting new scripts, and revised pages were constantly being added to the scripts that they already had. Each new set of revisions came on a different color of paper, and the scripts began looking like rainbows—pink paper, lavender paper, pumpkin paper, goldenrod, blue. The associate producer was having to plead with people to change their days-off schedules. Everyone was keyed up and jumpy.

Alec had heard of films going through this kind of revision, but never television, especially daytime television. They had to complete an episode every single day. And this show had only one week between the day they taped a show and its air date. That wasn't much margin for error. What on earth was Jenny thinking of?

Wardrobe said that they were getting two new characters. The actors had been in for fittings. "An old, kind of fat guy," the people from wardrobe said, "and a girl with a major pair of boobs."

"What kind of parts do they have?" That's what the cast cared about. "How do they fit in?"

The girls in wardrobe didn't know. "But whatever it is, it's going to be wonderful," one answered. "Jenny would only do this to make the show better."

People were starting to make mistakes. Lady Courtland's props were put in Lady Varley's chamber. Jaspar wore Colley Lightfield's stickpin. Wardrobe sent Alec a pair of pantaloons to wear at Almack's. By now even he knew that men had to wear breeches to Almack's.

Jenny might be making the show better, but the show was already good enough. These last-minute ideas might be great, but they were too disruptive. Alec was convinced of that.

Somebody needed to stop her. Somebody needed to warn her how thin the ice was. That was the executive producer's job. But of course George wasn't going to stop her. Neither would Terence or Gil. None of them were leaders. George hated confrontation, and Terence and Gil only thought about their camera work. This little ship was sailing straight toward the edge of the map because no one was bothering to navigate. Did anyone else see how close they were to running out of ocean?

He jammed the last round of script revisions back into his mail box. He would deal with them later. He took what he hoped was today's script and went up into the rehearsal hall.

It was still early. A couple of people were getting coffee. Trina Nelson and BarbEllen Garrett were sitting at the table, taking off their nail polish, a bag of cotton balls and a bottle of polish remover between them. Colored fingernails would have been historically incorrect.

Alec greeted them. "So you two got moved back into today's lineup?" According to his latest set of revisions, their scenes had been cut out of this episode and moved to tomorrow's.

"What do you mean?" Trina held up her hand, checking for stray traces of polish. "Were we ever out of it?"

Alec didn't like the sound of that, and two minutes later Terence confirmed his suspicions. Trina and BarbEllen were needed tomorrow, not today.

"Why didn't anyone tell us about this?" BarbEllen dropped a red-soaked cotton ball in disgust.

"We did hand out revised pages," Terence said. "And I told Jill"—she was one of the production assistants—"to be sure and talk to you. At least I think it was Jill."

Trina slowly placed the cap back on the polish remover bottle. Clearly she did not remember any conversation with Jill.

She wasn't happy. An actor was paid for each episode he appeared in. BarbEllen and Trina had dragged themselves out of bed, coming out to Brooklyn, and spoiled their manicures for nothing. They would not be paid for the day.

"We'll call a car right away," Terence offered. "We'll take care of getting you home."

"Thanks," BarbEllen said. She did not sound overwhelmed with gratitude.

Along the table people were looking at each other. There was whispering over by the coffee trolley. The mood in the room was uncertain. Whose fault was this? BarbEllen and Trina's for not paying enough attention to the piles of multicolored revisions that were appearing in the mail cubbies every day? Jill for not talking to them? Terence for not being clear enough in his directions? No one knew whom to blame.

Alec knew the answer. You didn't blame anyone. The show might be badly run, the cast and crew might be crazy, but they worked as a team. They were united, they were comrades. They shouldn't jeopardize that.

Alec grabbed his script and flipped to the second-page summaries. Terence was passing behind him to get a cup of coffee. Alec leaned back in his chair and gestured for Terence to come closer. "Amelia has tea with Lady Varley in 2B." He kept his voice low. "How strange would it be to have their maids with them at the start of the scene?"

"Only mildly," Terence answered. "But they wouldn't be doing anything, they wouldn't have any lines."

This tightwad of a show couldn't stand to pay people who didn't have anything to do in an episode. Alec got out of his chair and drew Terence to a corner. "You've got two cast members who are pissed off and they have every right to be so." He was speaking firmly. Terence had to do something. "A little money will take care of it. Pay Trina and BarbEllen for the day, and they will feel fine. The show isn't going to be canceled because the network has to pay two actresses for an extra day."

Terence picked a bit of fluff off the sleeve of his black shirt. He was thinking. Then he made a decision. "You're right. Of course you are." He went back to his place and made a note on his script. He rapped on the table, calling the cast to sit down. "A few more changes, people. Please bear with us. In 2B, Trina, you'll follow Amelia into the room. BarbEllen, you'll take her wrap. Then you both leave. If you want copies of the show for your Emmy reels, please let us know."

The tension in the room eased instantly. People smiled at Terence's little joke. The show was being generous. The family was looking after its own. Everyone felt better.

"Then I'll need a wrap," Karen said. "I've already got my costume and it didn't have one."

"Fine." Terence made another note on his script. "Will someone tell wardrobe that Amelia will need a wrap?"

No. Don't say "someone." Make it one particular person's responsibility. Otherwise it may not get done. That's why we're in this mess in the first place. Alec leaned forward and caught the eye of Steve, one of the production assistants. He pointed to him, and Steve nodded. Yes, he would take care of it.

Alec settled back in his seat and picked up his coffee cup. Over the rim he saw Brian giving him a good, hard stare. Brian had noticed Alec assigning the task to Steve. And Brian didn't like it.

Fine. Don't like it. But if you don't want me doing it, start doing it yourself.

If this thing blew up, it would be right smack in Jenny's face. Surely Brian had every responsibility, both professional and personal, to try to defuse the explosive. He had as much daytime experience as Alec did. He had to know that this wasn't right. He had to know what should be done to fix it. But he wasn't doing a goddamn thing.

Alec could feel his impatience with Brian hardening into contempt. He found it hard to be around the other actor. Then it occurred to him that there was no reason to keep those feelings out of his performance. How much compassion would Lydgate feel for a servant?

He waited for the right script. One day Amelia, in her distress and anxiety, returned home very late. Dinner was delayed. The incident was supposed to be about her unhappiness, but when Hastings came to tell Lydgate, Alec let his character go harsh and blaming

The contempt in Alec's performance left Brian blinking. Alec didn't care. *Imagine Jenny every single day that she lives with you. This is what it's like to be on the other end of total self-centeredness.*

Alec moved off the set quickly, but he had to stop and wait for the girl from wardrobe to untie his cravat. Brian "moved in," as one of the scripts would say.

"Hastings is a nice guy," he said pleasantly. "Why are you treating him this way?"

Alec wanted to smash his face in. Brian didn't even have the courage for a confrontation. *Why are you acting as if we like each other?*

Brian didn't like him, Alec was starting to see that. Until Alec had come, Brian had been the most established actor on the show. He had some of the perks that came with experience and success. He was the only actor who didn't have to share a dressing room, and it was the largest one in the building, the only one with a phone. But he hadn't been given that dressing room because he was a success. He had it because he was the head writer's boyfriend. Production on the show had started before Jenny's office had been finished. She needed somewhere to work. That's why a phone had been put in—for her, not him. He had just held on to it after she had moved upstairs.

You like the perks of being important, of being a star—the phone, the private dressing room. But you don't want any of the responsibilities. And you aren't important. You aren't a star.

But he *was* the head writer's boyfriend, and Alec happened to think that said head writer was one terrific person who was making some big mistakes. He forced himself to speak calmly, softly. There was no point in getting angry.

And there was also no point in talking about the characters. They weren't the issue. "How's Jenny doing?"

"Who, Jenny?" Brian was surprised by the change in subject. He drew back, a little wary. "Why do you ask?"

"All these changes in the scripts. Something's going on."

"Of course, but you're going to have to get used to that." Brian's tone was patronizing. "If she gets a good idea, she runs with it. That's the price we pay for having such a good show."

The price *we* pay? Alec didn't give a damn about the price *we* paid. What about Jenny? What price was she paying? This had to be a phenomenal amount of work. "Is she holding up okay?"

"She's fine. Jenny's always fine."

Alec wanted to rip off his cravat and throttle the man. No one was always fine. How could you be married to a woman—or nearly married—and think she was always fine? Well, why not think that? Then you never had to do anything for her.

This was what Chloe would have been like if they had still been married during *Aspen.* She might have fretted a little about what Alec was going through, but she would not have been genuinely worried. Alec would be able to cope with anything. She believed that with all her heart. Her faith in him was touching, but it also excused her from doing anything to help him.

Had there been some kind of sign-up sheet at

birth that he had missed? Sign here if you never want to be accountable for anything or anyone. Why did life let some people get away with this?

He lowered his voice. "How can she really be fine? She did have a miscarriage a couple of months ago."

Brian stopped dead. His face went expressionless. He had been playing a butler for two years; he had expressionless down cold. "Ah, but that isn't any of your concern, is it?"

That goddamn son of a bitch. Forget the cravat. It would take too long. Alec would use his hands, his own two hands. Get them around that pale throat and squeeze. Grow up working on a farm and you had strong hands.

This stupid costume. Why didn't it have any pockets? What were you supposed to do with your hands? How were you to keep from killing your fellow actors if you didn't have any pockets?

"Alec, wait up."

It was Jenny's voice, calling out to him as he was leaving the building. He turned to wait for her. She was sprinting down the hall, wearing a baggy sweatshirt and a pair of black cotton shorts. They were good shorts, cuffed and pleated, but clearly the manufacturer had intended them to be ironed, and that Jenny had not done.

"I hear you saved us last week," she called out. "The business with Trina and BarbEllen showing up on the wrong day." She was at his side now. "Thanks. We need all the help we can get. We are sort of making this up as we go along."

Alec opened the door for her. She looked tired, but she was smiling. There was a relaxed, impish glow about her. The kid in the tree house was back.

He loved seeing her like this. It was great to be around people who were still having fun.

But fun could be dangerous. Tree limbs could break. Tree houses could fall. Someone had to warn her.

"What's going on, Jenny? All those changes in the scripts. What are you up to?"

She looked at him sideways; her eyes were dancing. "Can you keep a secret?"

"Of course."

"You know who Edgar Delaney is, don't you?"

"Sure." Alec broke off. "Wait a minute. He's not the 'old, kind of fat guy' wardrobe's making costumes for, is he?"

Jenny nodded.

"That's incredible." Alec forgot everything he had wanted to speak to her about. Edgar Delaney joining the cast? All of daytime would be thrilled. "Is that what this has been about, making room for him?"

"Do I hear astonishment in your voice?" She flicked her hand close to her ear as if she was listening to a tuning fork. "What is surprising about a fine actor wanting to join a fine show?"

"Oh, shut up," Alec told her. This was remarkable news. "Tell me the deal."

"He loves the show. But it was September first

or nothing. So I needed to lay some groundwork for the character, and of course once I got going, I just kept thinking of all these cool things, and I couldn't stop myself. The story is going to be so great. Can I tell you about it? You can keep a secret, can't you?"

She had already asked that. "Of course I can."

She went over to the loading dock. It was high, hitting her just below her shoulder blades. But she put the heels of her hands on the dock and hitched herself up. Not many women could do that. She was strong.

Alec didn't know exactly what he had in mind when this conversation had started—probably to try to get her to understand the possible consequences of so many last-minute changes. *What matters on a soap,* he would have said with deep-voiced pomposity, *is consistency. We cannot come in day after day and do our jobs if we aren't sure whether or not we're going to have the right scripts.*

But instead he was leaning against the loading dock, listening to her tell the new story. She was laughing, swinging her legs, banging her heels against the cement riser. Her hands were moving wildly. It was a good story. She had such terrific ideas, she was so fresh and creative. He had to approve of what she was doing. Of course he did.

It was hot outside, hotter than it had been in the air-conditioned building, and she pulled off her sweatshirt. Her T-shirt was sleeveless, and when she waved her arms, the clear, clean muscles of her arms moved beneath her skin.

She was amazing. He had to ask, "Did you

worry that you might not be able to make it work?"

She shook her head. The sun cast a golden highlight in her hair. "No, I don't worry about that. I never know how hard it will be to do something, but I always know that I'll be able to do it. I trust my imagination."

"Why?"

She looked puzzled. "What do you mean, why?"

"I told you all about my past. Now you can tell me about yours, why you trust your imagination."

"I don't know." Her answer was bright and cheery. "I suppose it's never let me down before. Why should it now?"

That couldn't be the whole story. Who had let her down? Why had she needed to depend on her imagination?

"Do you know what interests me about you?" he asked.

"That I can take the next three years of your career and turn them into the theatrical equivalent of the Bermuda Triangle?"

"No, that's what terrifies me about you. What interests me is how you always seem so open, so simple and uncomplicated, and you aren't."

Lots of actresses tried to cultivate a Greta Garbo-like air of reclusive mystery when, in truth, they would tell anyone anything if it would bring them publicity. Jenny was the opposite. She acted as though she was telling you everything, her manner made it seem like she had nothing to hide. But she did.

"So I am a woman of contrasts?"

Why had she said that? It seemed like an odd phrase. He didn't answer, and when he looked back at her again, the imp was gone. She was watching him silently, seriously, with some kind of question in her eyes.

This was exactly what he had meant. Here was the other side of her, here was—

Oh, Lord. Alec stopped breathing. The world was spinning. Here on the concrete apron of the loading dock, here in the hot late afternoon August sun, he was riveted, disbelieving. This couldn't be happening. Not to him. He was sensible, he was down-to-earth, he was Canadian. But it was happening. He had never been more sure of anything in his life.

He was in love with her.

Eight

Goddamn. He hadn't asked for this. He didn't want this. She was as good as married. She had been with Brian since she had been fourteen. Half of her life she'd been with him. No sane man would fall in love with a woman with a commitment like that.

But he had.

He knew what he should do. Pick up his hat, cane, snuff box, calling cards, whatever, and get the hell out of there. He was at the fork in the road, and one fork was labeled "Life As We Know It." An okay road that looked to be—a few hills, a couple of boring flat lands, nothing to get worried about. The other fork was "Life While Being In Love With Someone Else's Woman," and who knew what that road was like, because you couldn't see any of it. It plunged straight downward into steaming darkness.

He should step back, turn away while there was still time.

But he couldn't. That would mean turning away from her.

He didn't move from the edge of the loading

dock. The shadows lengthened and the evening cooled. But he stayed there with Jenny. This was danger, being here with her, but it was a irresistible, velvety danger. She softened under his interest, she blossomed and melted. She told him about her childhood, about Oklahoma, the Indians, the river, and Brian. She told him about her first year in New York, about her first writing job, how ecstatic she had been that she had found her place in life. And of course, she talked about the show, how she loved the characters and the stories, how she couldn't imagine any job on earth being more wonderful than the one she had. She talked and talked. It was as if no one had ever listened to her before.

He began to understand much. She had grown up in a flat, dusty world where the sun had had a silent white-hot glare and the night had brought the noise of the pool room. No wonder the world she had created was cool, ordered, and elegant. As a child she had been judged by standards she didn't understand; on her show she had created a class system that she could control.

She had grown up an outsider. Now she was the heart and the life of *My Lady's Chamber.* She was at last at the center of everything. No wonder she wanted the show to stay at half an hour. A thirty-minute show was small enough that it could feel like a family, and she had never had a family before. The show gave her sisters, brothers, a swim team, a prom committee, a Junior League, a bridge club, a congregation, all the collections and gatherings of people she and her father had been excluded from.

He forgave her. Oh God, yes, of course he did. So what if the place was badly run? So what if it was an unprofessional mess? So what if enormous risks were being taken with the network's money and people's livelihoods? It was making Jenny happy, keeping her from being lonely. That's all that mattered—her well-being.

So what if this was a dark rocky road he was on? So what if no traveler would ever choose such a journey? The road had her name on it. How could he be anywhere else?

At the end of August Edgar Delaney's contract was officially announced, and indeed all of daytime was thrilled. Jenny even got a falsely polite congratulatory note from Paul Tomlin, the head writer of *Aspen!!*, and she had just enough nastiness in her soul to pin it to the rehearsal hall bulletin board. Ray brought in darts.

Edgar was playing James Marble, a very wealthy, middle-class merchant who wanted to establish his daughter in society. "I stole the character straight out of Georgette's *A Civil Contract.*" Jenny considered herself on a first name basis with the late, legendary Regency novelist Georgette Heyer. "But the daughter's completely different."

My Lady's Chamber
Script, Episode #609

(ACT TWO B. LYDGATE MORNING ROOM. AMELIA AT TABLE, PAPERS IN FRONT OF

HER. HASTINGS MOVES IN WITH A TRAY. AMELIA LOOKS UP.)

AMELIA: His Grace and I are most grateful to you, Hastings. (SHE IS SPEAKING WARMLY, SINCERELY.) I do not know how the Rose Hill Farm matter would have been settled if you had not intervened.

HASTINGS: I was glad to be of service.

AMELIA: It was not your responsibility. It was generous of you to trouble yourself.

HASTINGS: It was nothing. I was a child on His Grace's estates. I know the tenants. A few words in young Tim's ear made him see the folly of taking a field from a family that has had it for ten years—even if he is the steward's nephew.

AMELIA: You risked making an enemy of Mr. Crawford.

HASTINGS: (SETS DOWN THE TRAY AND WOULD HAVE SHRUGGED IF HE WEREN'T SO WELL-TRAINED. HE'S NOT AFRAID OF ANY STEWARD.) Mrs. Buck—the Bucks are the Rose Hill Farm tenants—she is saying that she always knew that Your Grace would never let this happen, that you have the tenants' interest at heart.

AMELIA: How nice of her. (SHE IS PLEASED, THEN RECOLLECTS HERSELF.) His Grace and I care about all the people on the estates. (A BIG LIE. LYDGATE COULDN'T CARE LESS.)

The casts of some shows were difficult to join. No one made newcomers feel welcome. The longtime stars swept grandly into their dressing rooms, never speaking to anyone, while everyone else was split into factions, the knives always out. *My Lady's Chamber* was nothing like that. Everyone always tried to make new people feel at home. On Edgar Delaney's first day there was a partylike atmosphere in the rehearsal hall with more expensive pastries on the trolley and more interesting fruits in the basket. The napkins, usually the cheapest possible paper, were brightly colored—periwinkle, tangerine, and lime. The conversation was just as it had been on Alec's first day, people talking about the "big, happy family," all of them telling Edgar how much he would like it here.

What Alec would have said to Edgar Delaney was too complex for pre-rehearsal chat. *This is a good place to work; it is the most exciting, creative, flexible show on daytime. But there's danger. The place is not well-run. We are flying without a safety net beneath us, and if one of us crashes, we will all go down together.*

But Alec kept his mouth shut. A warning was pointless. The issues were too complex. No one new to daytime would understand.

Jenny was in the rehearsal hall just as she had been on Alec's first day, and she was unusually well-dressed. Trina must have put her together. She was in a pair of white knee-length city walking shorts with a white long-sleeved Oxford cloth blouse. The shorts had neat creases running down the leg, the blouse had neat creases running down the arm. She had on a thin oxblood leather belt and matching oxblood loafers. Her socks were thin white knee highs. It was all Alec could do to keep away from her.

He went instead to introduce himself to Rita Harber, the nineteen-year-old actress who would be playing Isabella, Edgar Delaney's daughter. The girl was at the trolley, getting herself a cup of coffee. Her long black hair was swept over one shoulder, and a pair of lavender Lycra jeans cupped and defined her bottom as intimately as a leotard. The matching Western-cut jacket stopped at her waist so it didn't block any of the view.

Alec spoke to her. She turned and acknowledged his greeting, smiling politely. She was a striking girl with clear features and dramatic eyebrows. Then she leaned across the trolley to get one of the new carnivallike napkins. Her jacket fell open.

Alec blinked. Wardrobe had said something about her figure, but he had not been prepared. Here was a bosom to be reckoned with. Not just a pair of breasts packed into a black tank top, these were genuine, world-class hooters, jugs, garbonzos, marachis. Rita straightened, and then they were pointing straight at him, a pair of cone-shaped missile launchers. These things could have lead the charge of the Light Brigade. They could have sunk the Titantic.

Any other place, any other time, Alec would have found this display of flesh funny. It was, after all, seven-fifteen in the morning. Half the people in the room were women. Half of the other half were gay. The remaining few were half-asleep. No one was going to appreciate the fireworks.

But the girl was flaunting her body so aggressively that instead of finding it funny, he felt uneasy. She seemed almost menacing. The weatherbeaten gunslinger checked his holster. He had a feeling he was going to need his gun.

"So is this your first show?" he asked her, although he knew the answer. An experienced actress would not have come dressed like this.

She nodded. "I never planned on working in daytime, but then I realized that it could be an important training ground—"

The flesh above her ribbed top was vibrating. Alec forced himself to pay attention to what she was saying. Her voice was full of earnest confidence. "I can see that this is a real opportunity to learn one's craft," she continued. "It doesn't have to be something you're ashamed of, not if you view it as a learning experience."

A learning experience? Was this offensive or what? A nineteen-year-old kid was telling him that he didn't have to be ashamed of his profession, at least not as long as he thought of daytime as the bunny slopes, the kindergarten of acting. It would take a bigger bosom than even hers to excuse that.

"I think we'll learn a lot from Edgar," he said tactfully.

As he suspected it would, her pretty face went blank. She didn't know anything about Edgar Delaney's theatrical reputation. Like many of her generation, she probably only knew film and television stars. Theater—getting up on the boards and going it live in front of an audience—didn't count.

Her next day on the set she was again in form-fitting clothes and they were again anything but childlike. Her leggings were pale green Lycra and instead of seams running down the outside of her legs, the front and back of the pants were held together by little bands of the pale green fabric and between each band was a square of naked skin. The bands went from the hem to the waistline. There was no way she could be wearing underpants.

Day after day she came to the studio dressed like that. She did not seem to own any normal garments. Everything had cut-outs, chains, or the most extreme decollages. The other actresses came to work in jeans or sweats, their hair wet, no makeup on. Rita Haber was always meticulously turned out in Frederick's-of-Hollywood-hooker garb. It became a game among the rest of the cast, both male and female, straight and gay, to guess which body part she would expose next.

She shared a cramped dressing room with two of the other younger actresses, BarbEllen Garrett who played Lady Varley's maid and Pam Register who played Susan, her ladyship's shy and impoverished niece, Amelia's cousin. They kept everyone else apprised of Rita's underwear—the open-nipple bras she wore under clinging knits for "that more natural look" and the frequent absence of panties.

One day Alec, Brian, and Ray were lounging

on the set of the duke's library waiting for their scene to be called. Pam and BarbEllen tiptoed over. They gestured for the men to come closer.

"You have to hear this," BarbEllen whispered. "She has a girdle with the cheeks cut out."

None of the men understood.

"It's your normal girdle, just like my mother wore," Pam explained, "except that across the butt where my mother wanted plates of steel, there are two oval cutouts." Pam turned around and demonstrated on the back of her demure white frock.

"I don't get it." Ray looked interestedly at the spot on Pam's dress that she had been using to explain this phenomenon. "Why bother with the rest of the girdle if you're just going to let the flab hang out in back? What's the point?"

"It's a curve, not a point," Alec said. "The bras give her points, the girdle curves."

Brian cleared his throat. "This isn't right. She's our colleague. We shouldn't sneak around talking about her like this."

Alec grimaced. Brian was right. Alec didn't want Brian to be right. He wanted Brian to be an idiot, a fool, incompetent, boorish, swinish, bird-witted, and vicious.

But that was nuts. Jenny wouldn't have loved someone like that.

"Why shouldn't we talk about her?" Ray demanded. He didn't like Brian lecturing him any more than Alec did. "You don't wear clothes like that unless you want to be talked about."

"That's like blaming women for being raped," Brian argued.

Alec was determined not to agree with Brian. Brian could have recited the Ten Commandments and Alec would find a way to disagree with him. "We aren't saying that she's asking to be raped, and no one in Dressing Room Six"—the one he and Ray shared—"intends to rape her. But dressing like that, she does want to be talked about, and we're simply complying with her wishes. We're helpless little pawns in a well-planned publicity campaign. Wait until she hires Margaret Carmen or Tami Balken."

Those were the soap world's two most active publicists, people stars hired to flack their careers, to get them on talk shows and on the cover of *Soap Times.*

"Actually," Brian said, "she's gone with Dennis Cointreaux."

"What?" Alec had been joking about Rita hiring a publicist. Dennis Cointreaux was another publicist, less established than Margaret or Tami, reportedly less ethical.

"She's hired Dennis Cointreaux?" Ray scoffed. "That's ridiculous. I don't have a publicist. Do you, Alec?"

"No, but I think my ex-wife does."

"Your ex-wife is Chloe Spencer. Don't you think there's a little difference between what's appropriate for a Chloe Spencer and a Rita Haber?"

"But how do you get to be a Chloe Spencer?" Brian was defending Rita. "You want to build a name for yourself, you want to—"

Alec interrupted. Chloe was not a creation of her publicist. "You get to be Chloe Spencer by being Chloe Spencer. She had an acting coach long before she had a publicist."

"But it's a different game than when you and Chloe got started. The fan magazines are a lot more important now, and unless you're going to rely on your show's publicist"—

Which Alec had always done, and so had Chloe for the longest time. What was Brian doing defending a little tart like Rita Haber when he had Jenny?

—"you've got to hire your own."

"Fine. Fine." Alec was finished with this conversation. "You all claim you're running a free country here. She can do whatever she wants." He turned away

Brian spoke to his back. "It's a shame that people are so hard on women who are ambitious or determined.

"Jenny's ambitious," Alec snapped. He was facing Brian again. "She's as determined as they come. I do not disapprove of her."

"We aren't talking about Jenny. We're talking about a motivated, talented young woman"—

Jenny wasn't motivated? Jenny wasn't talented?

—"who's not going to spend the rest of her career in daytime."

"So daytime's not good enough for Rita Haber?" Now Ray was mad too. "Gee, Brian, it has been good enough for you the last ten years."

Ray was a street kid. He knew how to fight.

"It can be harder for a man to turn his back on a steady paycheck," Brian answered. He didn't want to fight. He was trying to be conciliatory, trying to make sure that everyone was agreeing. "You have domestic responsibilities," he said to Ray, "and so do I."

So did he what? Have domestic responsibilities? He must mean Jenny. Now Alec was truly incensed. Was that Brian's new excuse? That he had stayed in daytime for Jenny? That Jenny had been holding him back? What a load of crap that was. Did she have to live with this every day? Brian blaming her because he wasn't writing, directing, and starring in his own box-office smash?

All those meetings with Paul Tomlin during *Aspen* had been frustrating and embittering, but Alec had been determined not to get angry. *It's a difference of opinion* had been his mantra. *We view soaps differently. That he doesn't know his head from a brick wall is no reason to get angry.*

But now Alec was angry. Brian was being so falsely mild, pretending that they weren't quarreling. It drove Alec nuts. There wasn't anything in his speech you could pick as offensive, as worth ramming his teeth down his throat. He pushed your buttons, made you livid, and then slithered off.

And he didn't appreciate Jenny. The goddamn son of a bitch didn't appreciate Jenny.

If you want out of daytime, then leave. Walk. The network won't care. The viewers won't care. And I sure as hell won't.

Alec knew that wasn't going to happen. Brian

would never leave daytime. He was one of these "I could have been a contender" types; he'd spend his whole career blaming someone else that he hadn't taken any risks.

My Lady's Chamber
Script, Episode #100

PEREGRINE: It's all the Varleys' fault. Amelia loved me. I know that. She would have married me. We talked of Gretna Green, but she wanted their blessing.
GEORGEANNA: Amelia? Elope? I hardly think that too likely.
PEREGRINE: (PAYS NO ATTENTION) My family's manor, it needs a new roof. The facade is Elizabethan. I could have improved it, made it much more pleasing to the eye. And the land. Other people are draining their land. I could have drained more land.
GEORGEANNA: (LAUGHS) Oh, Perry, what do you know about drains?
PEREGRINE: I would have learned.
GEORGEANNA: You still could.
PEREGRINE: There's no point now. Not without the money. (HE CROSSES TO THE SIDEBOARD, POURS HIMSELF A DRINK.) I could have done anything if I had had that money. It's all the Varleys' fault.

"So what do you think of Rita?"
Alec's heart gave a little skip. He had been in

the green room finishing up a phone call when Jenny had walked in. There were other people in the room—people she particularly liked, Trina, Francine—but she had come to sit next to him.

You wouldn't have if you knew. If she had any idea how he felt about her, she would never seek him out in a crowded room, she would never drop down on a sofa next to him. His feelings for her would embarrass her: she would feel guilty and awkward.

"Rita seems fine," He kept his voice mild. "She hasn't had anything hard to do yet, but she's very committed to learning how to work with the camera."

"I wasn't quite sure about hiring her. It does seem like if you're going to cast someone with boobs like that, you need to do something with them, make them a part of the story." So far Rita's figure had been concealed beneath high-necked gowns and shawls. "But George and Thomas were both wild about her audition tape." Thomas was their casting director. "Brian was too."

Brian? Brian had seen the audition tapes? Alec stirred uneasily. Why the hell was she still listening to that jerk?

Because she was living with him. Because she was more or less in love with him.

Well, shit. There it was, on the line. Alec had to face it. When you grow up on Prince Edward Island, you live and breathe Anne of Green Gables. "Think of Anne of Green Gables," he had said when he had told his family about Chloe. "Then don't. The 'don't' part will be her."

But Jenny . . . she didn't have red hair, she didn't wear braids, but she had the freckles, the imagination, the spirit, and the chatter. She was Anne, his own dear Anne, everything he would ever want in a woman.

The trouble was this Anne had already found her Gilbert.

And you're never going to leave him, are you?

She probably knew the guy was a jerk. She might not even love him very much anymore. But she had made a promise. She had given her word. She would never go back on it. She would never leave him. Maybe if Brian were doing great, Jenny could ease herself out of his life, but Brian would never be doing great—Alec was sure of that. To be as successful as Brian wanted to be, a person had to take risks, and Brian couldn't do that.

So Jenny was stuck.

Nine

For someone who wasn't doing much on the show yet, Rita Haber was getting quite a bit of fan mail. The magazines were full of little mentions of her—"What hot new young actress is bringing a youthful zest to *My Lady's Chamber*?" Alec wasn't convinced about how many actual viewers were involved. A good publicist could get anyone coverage in the fan magazines, and mail campaigns could be orchestrated.

He soon played his first scene with her. It wasn't much. Amelia had invited Isabella to call, and Lydgate happened into the room—something that didn't seem too likely to Alec. He would have thought Lydgate would have steered well clear of Amelia and her friends whenever he could. Nonetheless he turned up. Amelia and Isabella rose; Amelia murmured Isabella's name. He bowed with his usual cold graciousness. She was sweet, shy, and extremely intimidated about meeting a duke. Alec wasn't sure what the point of the scene was, and Gil, Terence, whichever one was directing, didn't know either.

Rita proved easy enough to work with. She

hit her marks, remembered her lines, and kept track of where the camera was. Dress went smoothly, no props fell on anyone, no one got tangled up in a costume. Alec went back through the set's door to prepare for taping.

But when the cameras were rolling, instead of dropping her eyes demurely, Rita sent Lydgate a challenging flirtatious look. Her greeting, halting and timid in rehearsal, came out saucy and teasing.

This wasn't in the script. And it wasn't an accident, a mistake. She must have been planning it all day.

Acting is a team effort. On a soap you set your performance early in the day so your fellows could build on it. You didn't pull little stunts like this. You didn't make your character look great and leave everyone else looking like a blinking fool.

Rita Haber had no business changing something this important during taping. In film or even prime-time television, the director would have stopped the scene, but in daytime you did your best to make the first take work. Rita knew that. She had been counting on it.

Alec stepped back in cold outrage and directed the sternest possible look at the impudent girl. She blinked. She hadn't been expecting him to be so withering. She drew back, confused and speechless.

Amelia instantly, instinctively, put her hand on Isabella's arm. She knew Lydgate's stern wrath, and she hated to see it directed on this innocent, fun-loving girl.

The three of them, Amelia, Lydgate, and Isabella—Alec, Karen, and Rita—held their positions. The final close-up was supposed to be on Rita, but in this case it was now on him. Alec kept the duke locked in his cold distaste. A moment later the stage manager waved his script. "And we're clear."

Rita clapped her hands. "Wasn't that great?" She was gleeful. "Alec, your look. I was terrified. It was wonderful."

The sympathy Amelia had for Isabella drained out of Karen. Her lips tightened, she gave Rita a hard look and left the set.

Rita flicked a hand in her direction. "Some women don't like other women to succeed, do they?"

Alec would have left if he could, but he had to wait for wardrobe to untie his cravat. "I'm sure she just feels like you have a lot to learn."

Rita started to bristle. Alec tilted back his chin for the wardrobe girl. "But isn't that what you've been saying, that you're here to learn your craft?"

"Grading The Writers"
Soap Times, October 6

This one is hard. But we wouldn't be doing our jobs if we didn't find something wrong with the writing on *My Lady's Chamber.*

The women all like each other too much. There are no glorious catfights, there is no splendid bitchiness. Lady Varley has been in love with Lady Courtland's husband for years,

> but the old girls are great buddies. Why isn't Susan aching to scratch her cousin Amelia's eyes out because Amelia has all that glorious money and Susan has so little dowry that no one will dance with her? Georgeanna must want to murder Amelia because Amelia caved in on her when Georgeanna decided to elope with Sir Peregrine. But what do you want to bet that when Tricia Steckler returns from her maternity leave, Amelia and Georgeanna will make up immediately?
>
> This sisterly solidarity is all very politically correct, but this is make-believe, a chance to do the things we're too nice to do in real life. What gives, Jenny Cotton? Why are you afraid to make your women bitches?

Within days Rita was announcing that she had found her character. Alec supposed that he should be sympathetic, having struggled so hard to find his own. But he wasn't convinced that Isabella's character had ever been missing. She had been a shy, timid girl, awed at the circles she was moving in. The new Isabella was spunky and confident, looking at the upper reaches of society with a skeptical eye.

No one in the cast liked it. "You never know what she's going to do," groused Murrfield Thomas, Lord Courtland, who had not yet played a scene with her. "It's so disruptive."

"What would happen to the show if we all created our own characters?" someone else grumbled. "Why is Jenny letting her get away with it?"

"Because it's a cute characterization," Alec

said. Whatever he thought privately, he wasn't going to listen to public criticism of Jenny. "Come on, this is part of what we love about the show, that the people upstairs are so willing to listen to us. Jenny has let Karen and me run with our story. Why are we complaining when she does the same for Rita?"

"Because we don't like Rita," Trina said bluntly. "And you and Karen aren't hurting the rest of us. Rita's starting to get as saucy as me." Trina's character had heretofore had the monopoly on pertness. "I can live with not having a story as long as I'm doing all the female comedy. But if I'm not the funny one, I'd better fall in love with someone fast."

On Friday Rita ad-libbed a witty little farewell line. It was good, and Terence let it stand.

During the table reading Monday morning, Trina read the exact same line. The people who had been in Friday's cast stirred, remembering. "Wait a minute," Karen said. "Didn't Isabella say that last week?"

"What do you mean?" Trina hadn't been in Friday's cast. Otherwise she would have noticed Rita stealing her line. "Did Jenny make a mistake? Did she use the same line twice?"

"No, no." Rita rushed to answer. Everyone in Friday's cast knew that she had pretended to ad-lib the line. She couldn't blame it on Jenny. "It was all my fault. Really it was. I read the scripts the minute I get them, I love them so." She sounded more triumphant than contrite. "And that line—it must have struck me, and then I forgot where I heard it. Oh, Trina, I'm so sorry. You must just hate me."

You bet I do, said Trina's look.

Retaping Friday's scene was out of the question. "I'm sorry, Trina," Gil said. "We'll have to cut that bit."

Pencils rattled. Scripts were rifled. No one liked this. Brian spoke up. "Let's work something out." He turned to Trina. "We can call Jenny, ask her to come up with another line."

Oh, wonderful. Alec dropped his script in disgust. What a great idea that was. Call Jenny at home—Monday was her day to immerse herself in the longterm story projections—ask her to stop thinking about that and come up with something clever. What a great guy Brian was. Here he was, finally exerting some leadership, and it was all at Jenny's expense.

"We're not going to do that," Alec said firmly—although it was not in the least his decision. "It's a bitch, Trina. You've been screwed. There's no question about it. But we're not going to disturb Jenny."

At lunch he went up to Trina.

"I'm not mad at you," she said before he could speak. "It's her." She slapped a slice of turkey on some whole-grain bread. "My mother said I should never call anyone a bitch, but that cookie, she's a bitch."

"She is indeed."

"And she's getting away with it." Trina picked up the squeeze bottle of mustard. "That's what makes me so goddamn mad. She's getting away with it."

Alec moved out of firing range of the mustard. He was in costume. "It does seem like it."

"Are you talking about Rita?" Karen came up and joined them. She too was in costume, her white lace-edged night rail. Her beautiful dark hair floated around her shoulders.

"I've been calling her a bitch," Trina replied.

"Oh, she's worse than that. She's evil."

"Evil?" Alec asked. "Come on, Karen, don't you think evil's going too far?"

"No, I don't." Karen was serious, her voice was urgent. "She's dangerous. She could do a lot of damage."

Alec listened politely, but discounted everything she said. This was Karen being Karen. She needed to see everything at its darkest and most dramatic, she loved having things to worry about.

And in truth, they did have something to worry about. During the morning rehearsal Gil had cautioned the two of them that their bedroom scenes were starting to get repetitive. They were hitting the same notes again and again.

Alec reminded her of it now, hoping to channel some of her tense energy in that direction. It worked. During dress she played Amelia with such desperate emptiness that even as Lydgate, Alec felt a spurt of tenderness for her unhappiness.

"You blew it," Karen said as soon as they finished the rehearsal.

"I have to agree," Gil's disembodied voice floated over the intercom. "You do not have our permission to start making Lydgate a sympathetic character."

"But she's so miserable," Alec groaned. "How can I not notice?"

"Then notice," came the unhelpful response. "Just don't care."

Karen could see what Alec thought of that advice. "I'll tone it down," she said. She might be crazy, but she was a good team player. She wanted to help.

Alec waved a hand. "No, don't. I'll figure something out. I'll be impatient with you for being so emotional." He would be good at that. He had experience. Chloe's extreme emotions had turned the least bit difficult into the downright impossible. "I'll be pissed at you because you can't be as coldblooded as I am."

"Do you want to run through it again before we tape?" Gill asked over the loudspeaker.

"No." He and Karen were pros. They could get it right without rehearsal.

The scene opened with a fancy mirror shot—Amelia reflected in the mirror over her dressing table. The stage manager called for quiet. A props person quickly lit the candles on the dressing table. The cameras started to roll. Alec waited two beats, then moved in, careful to hit his mark so that he would be reflected in the mirror. Karen leaned forward to blow out the candles.

The second candlestick was out of position. As she blew out the first candle, Karen's hair brushed against the one still lit. Alec saw a tiny blaze.

He reacted instantly, crossing the set to catch her hair between his palms, clapping the flame out.

"My God, what are you doing?" Karen jerked away from him. She hadn't known that her hair was on fire.

"Your hair, madam," he replied. He stayed in character. Surely even Lydgate wouldn't let his wife burn up in front of him—she might take some valuable tapestries with her. "It was smouldering from the flame."

"It was?" She took a step back. Her reaction was stronger than Alec thought it should be, but there was nothing he could do about that. She was off her mark so he moved closer. She retreated again, this time backing into her dressing table. It crashed to the floor. Silver-topped perfume bottles rolled across the carpet. Amelia's jewels—her topaz armlets, the Lydgate emeralds, her pearl collar—cascaded into a heap. The water from the flower vase pooled into a dark puddle.

Gil called for the cameras to cut.

"Your hair was on fire," Alec explained to Karen. He wasn't sure she had understood. "I put it out."

The prop people were already at work, turning the dressing table back up, replacing the duchess's jewel case and silver brushes, checking the carpet. A hairdresser was approaching Karen with a pair of scissors and a brush, wanting to snip off the burned ends of her hair.

She was paying no attention. Her hand was at

her throat, her eyes were wide. "I'm in love with my butler."

"What?" Alec drew back. Where had that come from? Everyone close enough to have heard her was staring.

"It's true. I know it." Karen's voice was high, her breath was coming out in gasps. "I saw Lydgate in the mirror ... coming across the set, I thought he was going to beat me."

"No." Alec shook his head. Even Lydgate would not do that.

Karen hardly heard. "And I felt so alone. I mean, she is so alone. Who would protect her? Who would stop him? And across my mind flashed a face. Hastings. The butler." She sank down onto the bed. "I don't believe it. I'm in love with my butler. Oh, my God ... I'm in love with my butler."

Her butler . . . that was Hastings, that was Brian. Alec's eyes shot to the servants' hall. Brian was there, waiting for his scene. He was coming forward, stunned. "What? You're in love with me?"

"Yes, yes. I suddenly felt it, I knew. I'm sure." Karen's ivory skin was flushed. "It makes sense, doesn't it? Don't you all see? He and I, we run Lydgate Abbey and Lydgate House, the whole estate. He's smart, I'm smart. He's organized, I'm organized. I totally depend on him. I must love him. Would someone call Jenny? Would someone please call Jenny? I need to know."

Gil had come out of the control room. He stepped up onto the set. "Jenny's at home, but you are right. You will fall in love with Hastings."

"I knew it. I knew it. I could feel it. I wasn't thinking about it, but I was totally in character, and I saw his face." She was shaking her head, still disbelieving. "Oh, God, I ruined the take, didn't I? I'm so sorry."

"That's all right," the director assured her. And it was. Karen was the most professional of actresses, always prepared, always punctual. She never held things up.

She went off to have her hair attended to, and people began moving off, going about their business again. Brian lingered on the other side of the set, laughing, talking. People were congratulating him. He finally had a story.

They finished the scene, and Alec returned to his dressing room. Ray wasn't in today's cast so he was alone. Back in his own clothes, he dropped into one of the chairs and propped his feet up on the coffee table.

Jenny had given Brian a story. She wanted to keep him on the show, keep him happy.

Alec had been taking a grim comfort in the fact that Jenny had based Lydgate's character on Brian. Whether she knew it or not, she saw all Brian's failings.

But Brian must have some strengths too. After all she had loved him for fourteen years. Maybe she was putting all the bad things about him in Lydgate and all the good things about him in Hastings. Lydgate was Brian at his worst; Hastings was Brian at his best.

Hastings was a fine fellow. There would be

nothing wrong with a woman pledging herself to him. Maybe Jenny still did love Brian. Or at least she wished that she still did. Maybe she was trying to persuade herself, remind herself, of the time when he had been worth it.

Well, shit. This hurt. Alec was surprised at how much. He had watched a sister die. He had had a wife refuse to carry his child. Why should this feel so bad?

But it did.

Karen and Brian began right away to build the attraction into their performances, and within a week they were getting the scripts that made the story clear. The bond between them was subtle, unspoken. A decision would need to be made and they would exchange a quick glance. One would nod, and the other would act. Amelia grew a little shy, averting her eyes when Hastings entered the room, and he, not the footman, would step forward to take her wrap.

It was a great story line. The barrier between them was absolute. There was no way the two of them could ever speak of their love, much less be together. It was the sort of story that could, depending on the needs of the show, heat up into a fiery climax within weeks or simmer along for years and years. Both Brian and Karen were doing a terrific job.

The show built a new half-set. It was the upper hall of the Lydgate House, the duke's London residence, right outside the duchess's bedchamber. Interested viewers got to see Lydgate rapping on Amelia's door and moments later, Hastings outside the door, his face tight with anguish and pain.

Alec identified with Hastings completely. This was exactly how he felt every time he saw Jenny go home with Brian.

Ten

Brian was happy with the new story. He was doing good work and he knew it. There was an ease about him, a looseness. He was interested in the show again, willing to talk with Jenny about story ideas. It was almost like old times.

Was this what it took? Giving him a story? Was that the price of domestic peace? A good part?

Jenny felt like she was paying him to be nice to her. Didn't either one of them have any self-respect?

She again raised the idea of him signing a long-term contract so that she could give him the dual-character story. "I could do a lot with an upper-crust character who looked like Hastings. Amelia might try to transfer her love to him."

Brian shook his head. "No, no. Especially not now. This story will give me lots of exposure. It's something I can build on."

Jenny hated hearing that. Why couldn't he value the good work he was doing now instead of always dreaming of something better? She hadn't just based Lydgate on him. There was also a great deal of Brian in Sir Peregrine, the irresponsible dreamer, ever ready to blame others for his failures.

She had first put these characters on paper more than three years ago, and she had been thinking about them even longer than that. On some level she must have known all this about him for that long.

My Lady's Chamber
Breakdown, Episode #647

ACT THREE C: AMELIA'S BEDCHAMBER (AMELIA, MOLLY). It's after the dinner party. Molly is helping Amelia undress. They are chatting about the evening, what Molly has seen from helping the ladies with their wraps. "It's nice to see Miss Susan in a new dress." etc., etc. Molly says that Mr. Hastings reports that Amelia's dinner partner Lord Varley was sleepy and difficult. "But he says Your Grace handled it beautifully."

"He did?" Amelia is pleased. She wants to talk about Hastings.

Molly looks at her mistress curiously.

Amelia is oblivious, happily brushing her hair, thinking about Hastings. She hopes Hastings knows how much they appreciate him. Would Molly tell him, would she be sure that he knows?

This is strange. A lady's maid carrying a message like that to the butler? Why doesn't Amelia convey it herself? "Yes, Your Grace," is all Molly can say. She takes the brush from Amelia and begins brushing her hair. She is now curious indeed.

My Lady's Chamber
Breakdown, Episode #648

PROLOGUE C: Replay final beats of #647
THREE C—Molly curious about Amelia and Hastings.
ACT ONE A: SERVANTS' HALL (HASTINGS, MOLLY). Hastings counting empty wine bottles, entering the count in ledger. Molly moves in. He is surprised. Why isn't she in bed? Does Her Grace need something?

His concern for Amelia is obvious. Molly gasps. She realizes the truth. These two people love each other. Only they aren't two people. One is a duchess; the other is in service. She can hardly believe it. To her, Amelia is simultaneously a goddess and a needy younger sister. How can a duchess care about a servant? It makes her look at Hastings in a new light.

"Oh, Jenny. Thank you. Thank you. Thank you."

Trina popped out of her greenroom chair and hugged Jenny. Jenny hugged her back. It wasn't hard to figure out why Trina was so happy. The cast would have picked up the script for episode 648 today, the one with the first suggestion that Molly—Trina's character—was also falling in love with Hastings. It would be Trina's first important story.

"Is it true? What's going to happen?" Trina demanded. "Is he going to get so wildly frustrated at being denied Amelia that he's going to rape me? Am I going to get so wildly frustrated at being denied him that I'm going to rape somebody? Tell me."

"I don't honestly know."

This whole story kept coming to Jenny in big, blinding flashes. It had nothing whatsoever to do with the outline for the autumn scripts that had been approved at the beginning of the summer. Truly she didn't know where it was all leading. But she knew it would work. Everything felt right.

She wondered what Alec thought of the story. She was probably being paranoid, but it did seem like he was avoiding her. She felt like it had been weeks since they had exchanged more than a few sentences. They had not been alone in that time. He never came up to her office. He never stopped her in the hall. She minded that, she missed him.

I am a woman of contrasts. Aren't you supposed to be drawn to me?

Probably not. He had, after all, been married to Chloe Spencer. But Jenny had thought that they were at least friends.

That afternoon she saw him leaving the building. She called out and hurried to catch up. He waited, holding the door for her. This was, she suddenly remembered, exactly how their last conversation had started.

"I feel like I should schedule a meeting with you." She started talking as soon as she thought he'd been able to hear. "It seems like it's been ages since we've talked. Is everything okay with you and Lydgate? I hope you'd tell me if it wasn't. I know he isn't the nicest guy, but we could talk about it if you were having a problem. You know, throw some ideas around, brainstorm."

She was talking too much.

"You don't have to schedule a meeting with me." He was smiling. "I'll talk to you anytime, anywhere. You know that."

His voice was warm, and there was something about the way he was looking at her, something . . . well, something warm.

What was with her these days? She was over-interpreting everything. Of course he was looking at her. He was talking to her, wasn't he?

She preceded him across the ramp to the loading dock where they had talked the last time they had been alone. She hoisted herself up. "I don't know why we put a conference room on the third floor, not when we have this great loading dock. I'd love to meet the network boys down here." She was rambling. She took a breath and started over. "I suppose you want to know how Lydgate's going to react when he finds out about Amelia and Hastings, but I don't know."

"I think he's going to be pretty harsh."

Harsh? Jenny didn't know about that. "He'll probably ignore it as long as he can."

"Maybe. But sooner or later you'll have to do something with it."

"I suppose."

There was an obvious way to figure this out. How would Brian react if he found out that she was in love with someone else? Yes, he'd avoid it as long as he could, but what if she confronted him, what would he do or say?

She couldn't answer that. It wasn't going to happen.

"It seems pretty clear to me," Alec said, "that he would want to make Amelia suffer."

"He would?"

"Yes. He's a punitive guy. He punishes people."

Jenny folded her arms across her waist. She felt a little sick. She supposed that Alec was right about Lydgate. But what about Brian? Was he punitive? Would he want her to suffer?

The days were getting shorter now. A long slanting shadow fell across the loading dock, just missing Alec. In a few more minutes it would touch his hand. Maybe they could just sit here quietly waiting for the shadows to move.

"We both know you've based Lydgate's character on Brian."

Jenny felt her mouth drop open. Her eyes jerked up, then dropped. She couldn't look at him. *Lydgate . . . on Brian . . .* She must have imagined that. Surely he hadn't actually said it.

"You have to have admitted this to yourself, I know you have."

What on earth? She jerked at the collar of her shirt. She wasn't going to talk about this. "Yes, but that doesn't mean I have to admit it to *you.*"

"Why not? We both know it is true. Why not be honest about it?"

Why not? Why *not*? It was a good thing that he didn't write soaps for a living. Behind nearly every daytime plot was a secret. Any soap he wrote would get through six months' worth of story in a week. All the characters would be honest with each other, and then where would they be?

There were skid treads at the edge of the loading dock. Jenny felt the ridges cutting into her own palms. She couldn't talk about this. Maybe she should be honest right back. *I'm sorry,* she could say. *But I can't deal with this. It is too threatening. Maybe I should be able to talk about it, but I can't.*

Alec would respect that. Of course he would. He liked honesty.

"So you think Lydgate is punitive?" she heard herself say. So much for honesty.

"I do. But I don't care about him. I care about you."

It was like he had turned over her Girl Scout sash and seen the big, staggering stitches or looked in her lunch box and seen the clumsy sandwiches. No, it was worse than that, much worse. Why wouldn't he stop? "There's no reason for anyone to worry about me." Her voice was stiff.

"You are sure you are not in any peril?"

Peril? What was he talking about?

He went on. "I know Brian seems very supportive of women. He helped you get the show started, and God knows he's the only one in the cast who's giving Rita half a chance. But it feels like a power thing to me, a way of keeping strong women feeling like they need him. Lydgate hates women, Jenny." His voice was gentle. "And that makes me ask if Brian does too."

"His mother," she had to concede that. "He probably does hate his mother. But me? He can't hate me. Why would he hate me?"

"You're more talented than he is. You're happier. You're more successful. You could make it without him. You don't need him anymore, and someday he'll make you pay for that. Lydgate is a very angry man."

"Brian's not angry," she protested. But as she said it, she had to wonder how true it really was. "I suppose he's not as calm as he seems. It's the ACOA thing, the adult child of an alcoholic. He needs to have everyone think he's perfect. But he would never hurt me."

"I know he wouldn't hit you. Lydgate doesn't express himself physically. He doesn't react through his body. But there are other forms of cruelty. He can still hurt you, I know that . . . and there's nothing I can do to stop him."

His voice had gone flat. *There's nothing I can do . . .* That was exactly what Hastings hated about loving Amelia. There was so little he could do for her.

Jenny shook herself. Why on earth had she thought about that? What did Hastings have to do with anything? What did loving Amelia have to do with anything?

No, surely not. It wasn't possible. Her hand came up to her eyes. She jerked it away and looked at him. And there it was, that look.

He spoke again. "I wish there were someone else to warn you about this. My motives must seem suspect."

"Your motives?" Her voice came out in a thin squawk.

"Of course. Surely you've realized—"

Realized what? She hadn't realized anything. Jenny felt frantic. He was about to say something, something that she couldn't let him say. It would be bad enough if it were true, but how much worse if he actually said it, how much more complicating, entangling.

She had to stop him. He couldn't say this. If he would just remain silent, then everything would be all right. She could handle secrets, she was used to secrets. You were safe when you had secrets.

"Alec, don't go on. Please don't go on."

"Why not? We both know that I—"

"I don't know anything. Really I don't." She dropped down from the dock. "Honest."

She was lying and he knew it. But what could he do? He was a gentleman, and she was the closest thing this scene had to a lady. He was going to have to respect her wishes.

He bent his head, a Regency's gentleman's slightest bow. He didn't like it, but she was giving him no choice. This was something they were not going to talk about, not ever.

Eleven

Alec was in love with her.

It was absurd. It was unbelievable. It was urgently, achingly gratifying. It made her heart lift, it made her stomach drop. Alec Cameron loved her.

She didn't know what to do. She felt awkward. She didn't know what to say to him, where to look when she was with him. The sound of his voice left her stumbling and flushing. But she couldn't keep away from him. He loved her. She was mesmerized by the thought. She was dying to know more. When had it happened? Why had it happened? What did it mean? She felt like she was fourteen, dizzy and confused, lost in the middle of the girl stuff.

But she wasn't fourteen, and neither was he. This wasn't an adolescent's daydream. Alec was an adult. He had a man's reflections and sensations. The stakes were high for him. And he loved her.

Alec's old network was finally giving up. The double exclamation points were not working. *Aspen!!* was being cancelled, to be replaced by a new talk show. *Soap Times* made it quite clear that Alec should feel vindicated; clearly he and his character had not been the show's problem at all. "Paul Tomlin simply didn't understand the daytime format, and he had no respect for the daytime audience," the article read.

Jenny went to post the article on the rehearsal hall bulletin board. Four copies were already up. She added hers anyway.

The cancelling of the show meant that a lot of good people would be available soon—not just actors and actresses, but directors and scriptwriters, cameramen and lighting people.

"Now's the perfect time for us to go to an hour," George, the executive producer of *My Lady's Chamber,* pointed out. "The network's ready to cancel one of the game shows if we'll do it."

A game show being cancelled for a soap? Jenny liked the sound of that. Paul Tomlin had just lost the soap community two network slots while Jenny Cotton would be picking up one. It would be another coup, even bigger than signing Edgar Delaney.

But an hour show meant five directors instead of two, a twelve-hour day, a cast that only knew the people in their own stories. She didn't like the sound of that.

All her original objections to the hour format were disappearing. She had said that soap veterans would not work well on a historical drama; Alec had proven that wrong. She had said that the visual style was too unique; the show could not have more than two directors.

But Terence and Gil had defined the style clearly enough that other directors could easily imitate it. She also had more than enough established characters for a sixty-minute show. She had gotten Tricia Steckler to postpone her return until the middle of November, but she would definitely be back then. Jenny had ideas for Georgeanna's character, but she didn't know when she would have time to do them. She had a great plan to have Robin not be the old duke's son . . . her ideas were endless.

The network was willing to promise her anything—more sets, more extras, even some location work—if she would agree to go to an hour. She wanted the sets, she wanted the locations, but she hated what going to an hour would do to everything. How could they feel like a family with so many new people?

Was she wrong? She needed to talk to someone who understood both her and the show. But Brian no longer seemed to care about either one. Alec would have been perfect. She longed to confide in him. He was so levelheaded, he had seen so much. He was exactly the right person to advise her. And two weeks ago she could have gone to him. But now she couldn't. It might seem like she was encouraging him.

On other hand, if she never talked to him, it might seem like she was punishing him. She didn't want him thinking that she resented him or anything like that.

This was too much for her to handle.

My Lady's Chamber
Script, Episode #659

	(ACT ONE A. AMELIA'S BEDCHAMBER. WE SEE AMELIA LYING AGAINST PILLOWS, AWAKE, NOT FEELING WELL. MOLLY MOVES IN.)
MOLLY:	Good morning, Your Grace. (SHE SETS THE CHOCOLATE TRAY DOWN ON BED AND MOVES TO OPEN CURTAINS.) It's a lovely day, very bright. (SHE TURNS BACK TO SEE AMELIA PUSHING TRAY ASIDE, GRIMACING.) Oh, Your Grace . . . I've been wondering. (SHE STRUGGLES TO STAY RESPECTFUL, BUT HER JOY IS BUILDING.) Is it possible? It has been two weeks since we would have expected . . .
AMELIA:	(NODS) I think so. Oh, Molly. I think so.

The Duchess of Lydgate was pregnant.

From the way everyone was acting, it could have been Karen herself who was pregnant. People were congratulating her, wondering when the baby would be born, speculating about the sex, as if it were an actual baby. As absurd as he knew it to be, Alec couldn't help joining in. "Is there something you can eat," he begged Karen during lunch, "to make sure that it's a boy? I don't want to go through this again."

"A heir and a spare," Ray jeered good-naturedly. "You've got to have two, Alec. Two."

"No, I don't. If the Prince of Wales quit after one girl"—and Alec was, of course, speaking about the Prince Regent, not the gentleman who currently held that title—"so can I."

"But I'm so much better looking than Princess Caroline," Karen argued. Caroline of Brunswick had been the Prince Regent's wife; they had loathed each other. These facts about Regency life were as familiar to the cast as anything in the current contemporary political scene, and in an instant they were all talking about the tragedy of dear Princess Charlotte—the Regent's daughter—dying in childbirth as if it had happened last week instead of in 1817.

"I don't think I want to talk about people dying in childbirth," Karen said.

My Lady's Chamber
Script, Episode #664

HASTINGS: Be careful of what you say. She has not yet told His Grace.

FOOTMAN: She hasn't? Why not? Won't he be pleased? I can remember when—

HASTINGS: (OVER) I'm sure he will be very gratified. But it is not our place to question what Her Grace chooses to tell.

FOOTMAN: (STILL QUESTIONING) But we all know.

HASTINGS: It is not the same. (FOOTMAN SHAKES HIS HEAD AND MOVES OFF.)

MOLLY: (IN LOW TONES, ONLY FOR HIS EARS.) If she asks you to, would you tell him for her?

HASTINGS: (LOOKS AT HER ODDLY. IT IS A STRANGE QUESTION.) I would do anything Her Grace asked me to. (PAUSE) But why would she . . . is she . . . why do you ask something like that?

MOLLY: She dreads telling him. She's pleased, she's relieved, but she wishes it had nothing to do with him.

HASTINGS: Ah. (HE UNDERSTANDS.)

My Lady's Chamber
Script, Episode #665

ACT THREE B. (LYDGATE FRONT HALL. CLOSE-UP ON HASTINGS. HE OPENS FRONT DOOR. LYDGATE MOVES IN.

LYDGATE: I have bought a new horse. (TURNS HIS BACK SO HASTINGS CAN TAKE HIS CAPE.) I'm pleased. He will do well in town. (HE'S QUITE CHEERFUL . . . FOR HIM) Is Her Grace within?

HASTINGS: Her Grace is unwell, sir.

LYDGATE: Again? (SLIGHTLY IMPATIENT) Has the doctor been sent for?

HASTINGS: He visited her this morning. I do not believe it is a serious disorder.

LYDGATE: Good. Good. (NOT PAYING MUCH ATTENTION) Has that

small parcel from Bond Street arrived?

HASTINGS: (DECIDES TO DO THIS) I believe Her Grace's condition is a matter for congratulation.

LYDGATE: (LOOKS PUZZLED, DOESN'T UNDERSTAND IMMEDIATELY, THEN) Oh. (MORE FEELING) Oh. This is gratifying news. (HE IS PLEASED. A NEW HORSE, A PARCEL FROM BOND STREET, NOW THIS) Yes, yes, it is.

Alec read through the script. This was going to be an interesting set of scenes to play. Of course Brian had the better part, struggling between Hastings's relief that Amelia's ordeal was over and his resentment and regret that she was carrying someone else's child. Lydgate's reaction was more limited, but all Lydgate's reactions were limited. Alec read the scene again, envying Brian his more challenging part.

Of course that wasn't all he envied Brian for. How complicated this was. On the show Brian loved Alec's lady. In life Alec loved Brian's. In life Alec had had to call Brian and tell him Jenny was having a miscarriage. On the show Brian had to tell Alec that Amelia was pregnant.

What are you up to, Jenny? What are you trying to say?

She was awkward and nervous around him. He hated that. He wished he could explain himself, tell her that he was asking nothing from her, he was expecting nothing from her. But she had made the rules—they were not to speak of this. It was like during the first year Meg was sick, everyone holding the truth inside, each moment of secret and concealment turning a family into a group of strangers living under the same roof. Hiding from the truth was wrong, it was folly. But it was Jenny's decision. He had to live with it.

He was in makeup. Brandi, his makeup artist, gestured for him to lean back. He let the script fall to his lap. The light brush of the makeup sponge was cool against his eyelids.

This would be easier to endure if he knew how it would end. If someone would just tell him that in so much time such-and-such would happen. Then he could get through whatever lay in between. But he couldn't imagine it ever ending. Jenny would never leave Brian, and Alec would never stop loving her.

That would be the best possible outcome, he supposed, for him to stop loving her, for him to wake up one morning and find that while he cared for her and respected her, he just didn't love her anymore.

But that wouldn't happen. He knew it down to his bones. He would love her until he died.

Brandi was done with the sponge, and now a brush was flicking across his face. The brush was soft, and her moves were light and expert. It was soothing.

Suddenly something clattered by the door. It was a rolling, metallic ringing sound. Alec sat up.

Karen was charging across the room. She had obviously burst through the door, knocking over the metal wastebasket. She swept over to Alec's chair and slammed him in the chest with a script. Brandi's hand slipped and a copper-bronze stripe appeared from the bridge of his nose down to his jaw.

"You bastard," Karen shrieked. "You son of a bitch, you rat. How could you?"

Alec picked up the script. It was 665. It followed the one he had been reading. Karen must have just gotten it. "What page?"

"The Prologue," Karen snapped. "You don't waste any time."

DUKE: So is this true?
DUCHESS: Yes, yes, I am sure.
DUKE: (CROSSING TO TABLE) Then I shall make arrangements to open Lydgate Abbey.
DUCHESS: (DISMAYED, SHOCKED) The Abbey? But, Lydgate . . . to go to the country now, with Parliament in session.
DUKE: (COLDLY) You shall spent your time at the Abbey.

Alec looked up. Karen was still standing there, glowering at him. "Gosh." He put on his best aw-shucks-I'm-just-a-Canadian-farm-boy voice. "Being stuck at Lydgate Abbey for nine months, that's not going to be much fun, is it?"

"It's going to be awful," she stormed. "I shall be all alone, nowhere to go, no one to talk to. There won't be any *newspapers.* Can you imagine, no newspapers? Parliament is in session. I shall know nothing."

It seemed as though Karen thought that she was going to have to endure this in real life.

"I suppose I can just do that?" he asked. "Ship you off without asking?"

Now even Brandi was frowning at him. "I don't think I like that. You ought to ask her, Alec."

Alec leaned back in the chair, hoping Brandi would attend to the stripe on his face. "I'm a duke. I can do anything I want."

He turned out to be wrong. Within days Hastings was spearheading a conspiracy to keep Amelia in London. Of course, the character had too much dignity to conspire openly with the servants under him so he had to lead by indirection. To the Lydgate coachman, he said, "Do take care of the traveling coach. It would be a shame if anything kept it from being safe enough for Her Grace to travel in."

And, lo and behold, the next day the coachman reported one of the coach's poles had snapped.

On the day the repair was to be completed, Molly swished into the servants' hall with a tray. Her hip brushed against a pine table. The dishes rattled and she quickly leveled the tray. It was nothing, but Hastings looked at her intently. "How fortunate that you did not break your arm. Surely Her Grace couldn't travel to the country without you."

Molly was smart. She instantly let go of the heavy tray. Crockery smashed at her feet. "Oh, my arm . . . my arm . . . I swear I've broken my arm."

The housekeeper came rushing in, full of fluster and concern. A doctor must be summoned.

"Oh, no," Hastings said artlessly. "We needn't be bothering a doctor for the likes of her." With a straight face he put Molly's arm in a sling. Molly, of course, liked him touching her.

The story was popular. It had a light, rompish quality, all the little guys, the mice, ganging up on the big cat. Alec could imagine that Lydgate had had a rigid, authoritarian nanny—Brian had apparently had such a mother—and he had spent his childhood silently raging at being overcontrolled. Not getting his way as an adult brought all this back, and the duke's cold fury grew with each episode.

Brian was relishing the story. "We're going to win, you know," he announced to Alec one day in the greenroom. "She'll never leave London."

Alec did not take well to such glee. "Any day His Grace could put his foot down and she'd be gone."

"But Karen hasn't asked for a write-out," Brian returned, "and there's no Lydgate Abbey set."

Brian had him there. If Amelia went to the country, either her actress had to be written out or some temporary sets had to be built, and this cheap show was not about to do that.

Brian was winning. There was no doubt about it. In life he was winning. Jenny might be blushing when she saw Alec, but she was not wavering in her commitment to Brian. And on the show

Brian's character was winning. The duchess was not leaving London.

Alec never expected things to be fair. But this was ridiculous. Brian got to play all the good parts of himself, and he got the girl. Alec got to play all the bad parts of Brian, and he didn't get the girl.

My Lady's Chamber

MEMO

DATE: October 30
TO: A much beloved cast
FROM: The incredibly thoughtful Jenny Cotton

Don't be alarmed when you read this script, folks. In the final scene Amelia acts like she's having a miscarriage. She thinks she's having a miscarriage. But she's not.

Ray laughed as he showed Alec the note attached to the latest script. "Jenny knows us, doesn't she? Karen would be suicidal if she thought she was miscarrying."

"I wouldn't be too thrilled myself," Alec responded. "If she loses this baby, I'll have to put my nose back to the grindstone until she gets another."

"Your nose?"

"Whatever." Alec flipped open the script, looking for the scene in question. He didn't miss the sex scenes, but he missed how challenging they had been. Lydgate was getting to be more and more of a one-note character, reacting in the same way episode after episode. Alec had to wonder if his forcing Jenny to openly acknowledge that she had been basing the character on Brian was the cause. Perhaps she was now less willing to explore the character's nuances.

He found the script's final scene. It was set in the Chinese room of Lydgate House, a set so gorgeous and difficult to dress that once it was up, it was used and used until the viewers were gagging. Amelia was writing at the table, Hastings entered with a message. She rose, she swayed and started to faint. He caught her up in his arms and carried her to the sofa.

Starting to faint . . . catching her in his arms . . . carrying her . . . Alec couldn't breathe.

This was exactly what had happened when Jenny had been pregnant—she had swayed and grown faint, Alec had lifted her and carried her into the hospital.

I did that for her.

So? Writers used their own experiences. That's what they did. It didn't mean anything.

No, it meant something. Jenny might use her own life to develop the show, but she also used the show to understand her own life.

What was Hastings like? He was calm, he was determined, he was orderly. He was a leader, the kind who didn't care about titles, medals, or other recognition just as long as people followed his leadership. He was a man who could pick and choose his battles. That was Hastings.

And it wasn't Brian. Not by a long shot. Brian

needed praise, he needed public acknowledgement, he needed approval.

Alec was not arrogant. But he knew his strengths. How had Hastings settled the Rose Hill Farm matter? A quiet word here, a firm look there, even though it had not been his responsibility. That was exactly how Alec would have handled it, how he did handle things around here.

Hastings is me. He was sure of it.

He was playing a character based on Brian, and Brian was playing a character based on him.

And the duchess loved the character based on him.

Jenny . . . Jenny.

She didn't love him. He knew that. But she was dreaming about it, she was fantasizing, she was imagining. And Jenny's imagination was powerful.

He didn't remember leaving the dressing room—if he said anything to Ray or if he just left. He didn't remember climbing the stairs, but suddenly there he was in her office. She was pushing back from her computer, looking up, smiling.

How he loved her. He loved everything about her. The callus on her finger which she had gotten from holding a pen; the little holes in her ears, always visible because she never remembered to put in earrings; the clutter on her desk; and the stack of books holding her office door open—he loved it all.

Why didn't she love him back? He felt a sudden spurt of anger. She wasn't stupid—she had to know. Brian was cold, selfish, irresponsible. *Why do you stay with him? Why aren't you with me? Why don't you love me?*

She saw his good qualities. Day after day she was writing about them. Why wasn't that enough?

He wanted to do something. That was the only thing that had made Meg's illness bearable—the feeling that the family was participating in her treatments, learning about her disease, doing something.

But what could he do now? Jenny had made the rules. He couldn't speak, he couldn't woo her. And Alec had a rule of his own. Brian might be a jerk, but he was Alec's castmate, his colleague, another guy. Alec wasn't going to do anything behind his back.

But he couldn't walk away. He couldn't do nothing.

"I just heard of a great new restaurant," he heard himself say. That wasn't true, at least it wasn't yet. "Can I take you and Brian out to dinner?"

Twelve

Brian wanted no part of Alec's dinner invitation. "He shouldn't be taking us out to dinner. You're the head writer. You're the one with the expense account. We should be entertaining him."

"But he asked us," Jenny argued. "We can't turn him down just because we should have asked first."

"Let's have him over to the house. He'll probably be glad of a decent home-cooked meal."

Alec wasn't exactly your basic starving actor. Why was Brian being like this? *You can't accept another man's hospitality, can you?*

Or was it just Alec's?

Surely he had some notion of what she was going through, how she could not get Alec Cameron out of her mind. How she was obsessing about him, fantasizing about him, dreaming about him. She had always been able to control her daydreams. She could stand back from them, see what the essential elements were and how she could use them in the show. She couldn't now. These dreams had a dizzying, frightening power.

I am in knots, Brian. I am scared. I am miserable. I don't want to think about anyone else. I want our lives to be as we had always planned. But I go in there every day, knowing that he loves me. What I am supposed to do? Help me.

Or Alec would.

My Lady's Chamber
Script, Episode #680

GEORGEANNA: Phillip is trying to forbid me from seeing Peregrine again. He says that when Peregrine returns from the Continent that I am not to receive him.

AMELIA: Mr. Courtland is your husband. He has that right.

GEORGEANNA: Everyone thought that I would stop loving him, that the baby, the time in the country, would make me stop. But I haven't. He is all I think about. I dream of him. The air I breathe, it smells of him. The food that I eat tastes of him. When I feel my clothes against my body, I feel his touch.

Jenny felt caught between the two men. She didn't think it was right to reverse Alec's invitation, but Brian was being impossible. Resisting him just wasn't worth it.

She felt spineless. But she was honoring her commitment to Brian. Wasn't that supposed to be noble and admirable? Why did she feel like she was pandering to him? Wasn't there any way to keep him happy without losing her self-respect?

She went down to Alec's dressing room reluctantly. But he made it all easy. Dinner at their house? Fine. Fine. He was completely gracious. "I'd like to see where you two live."

Then the next day she had to go back to his dressing room. "I'm sorry. Brian just remembered." She hated this. "He will be out of town Saturday. Can we do it Sunday night instead?"

She couldn't help being suspicious. Had Brian "just" remembered this? Or had he known and waited to tell her, because she then would have to change plans with Alec twice?

It was an awful thought. But she couldn't talk herself out of it.

"Sunday's fine," Alec said.

"I know that we'll have to break up early." She wanted to explain. "But Brian's doing some kind of personal appearance out west somewhere, Nevada—Reno, I guess—on Saturday. He gets back on Sunday."

"What's he doing? What's it for?"

Jenny ran a hand through her hair. She didn't want to answer that. Alec, like a number of well-established daytime actors, limited his personal appearances to charity work. They didn't ask to be compensated for their time, and they didn't expect any entrepreneurs to profit.

Brian didn't feel that way. "Oh, it's a thing for some new shopping mall. Actually"—she started to speak more quickly, trying to defend Brian—"he's really going to help Rita. This is her first appearance, and she said she would really appreciate it if he would accept the invitation too, show her the ropes and all."

"That's good of him."

My Lady's Chamber
Script, Episode #682

LADY VARLEY: Georgeanna questioned her life. That was her mistake. You cannot do that. You cannot wonder if the decisions you made—or the ones made for you—were right. You must live with them. Trust me, Amelia. If you dream . . . if you speculate about what might have been, your life will be intolerable.

AMELIA: Yes, aunt. (BUT THIS ADVICE HAS COME TOO LATE FOR HER)

LADY VARLEY: Dreams can make you miserable, my love. You must never let yourself question that your place is with your husband. Nothing else is possible. Nothing else is imaginable.

Jenny worked all weekend. She was dreading Sunday evening, having Alec at the house. What on earth were they going to talk about, the three of them? She knew what Brian would be like. He would show Alec around the house. He was proud of all the alterations and improvements. He would talk endlessly about why he had chosen blue granite over green marble. He would sound exactly like Lydgate. And Alec would know that he sounded like Lydgate, and she would know that he knew, and he would know that she knew that he knew and so on from there.

This would be easy if it were a scene on the show. The three characters would be in the room together. Tension and awkwardness would start to build. Then they would be interrupted, and the viewers would be left aching for the post-poned confrontation.

But this wasn't the show. They wouldn't be interrupted. The three of them would be stuck together all evening, trying to think of something to say.

Jenny expected Brian to be home by two on Sunday afternoon. He didn't come. She went on working. He had told her that if his plane was late, she should be sure and put the fish in the marinade by three. She forgot.

She was still working at four. Alec was sup-posed to come at five. She didn't let herself get up. She wasn't going to change clothes. If she changed clothes, if she tried to get herself all gussied up, she'd get nervous. Alec saw her every day. He already knew she was no good at the clothes thing. She went on working.

At five the doorbell rang. Jenny had been pac-ing down the hall and through the kitchen, wip-ing her palms against the legs of her khaki pants. She hurried into the vestibule. The doorknob felt damp in her hand. Even after the door was open, even after she had let go of the knob, she could still feel its shape against her palm.

It was Alec. Of course it was. He too was in

khakis with a red-and-white striped rugby shirt. It was warm for November.

"So you found us all right," she sang out brightly. Loudly.

"Of course."

Why had she said "us?" You found *us*? Was she trying to sound married? AS GOOD AS MARRIED: DO NOT DISTURB?

"Come in. Come in." That was pointless, stupid. He was already in.

He had a bottle of wine with him. "I know that Brian doesn't drink," he said. "I hope it's not a problem if other people do."

"No, no. It's fine." She took the bottle from him. "What am I supposed to do with this? Put it in the icebox?"

He followed her back into the kitchen and as she was crossing the blue granite floor to the subzero, pine-fronted refrigerator, she heard him whistle. "This is some kitchen."

"Isn't it though? But I can't take any credit for it. Brian picked out everything."

"He did?"

"Yes, he's worked very hard . . . even though legally it's my house, not his."

Why had she said that? She didn't go around telling people that. It wasn't anyone else's business. But Alec Cameron had been in the house for two seconds, and she had crammed the information down his throat. Why did she need to have him know?

"I can't imagine where Brian is." Again she spoke quickly. She didn't want Alec to ask any questions about the house. "His plane was supposed to be in by one, and here it is five already." *Stop talking so much. Calm down. Slow down.* "Maybe there's bad weather in Chicago. That always messes the whole country up. Or over the Rockies. Reno's on the other side of the Rockies, isn't it?"

She knew where Reno was. He knew where Reno was. Why couldn't she make herself shut up? Why was she so uncomfortable?

"Have you called the airline?" he asked.

"No, I guess I should, shouldn't I?" She turned back to the refrigerator to get the flight information. It wasn't there. "I can't get used to this. Have you ever had a refrigerator with a wood front? You can't magnet anything to it. How are you supposed to run a household with a refrigerator you can't put papers on?"

Shut up. You're a grown woman. Shut up.

"I can drive a couple of ten-penny nails in it if you like," Alec volunteered.

There was a soft laugh in his eye. He probably knew how unspeakably expensive this custom-made wood panel had been. Jenny relaxed a little. "What a perfect idea." And then she managed to keep her mouth closed long enough to get Brian's itinerary out of the drawer and dial the airline. A recording put her on hold; then a human voice came on and eventually told her that Brian and Rita had missed their flight but had made a later connection. That flight had already landed. Jenny looked at her watch. Brian should be home in thirty minutes or so.

She relayed this information to Alec. "I'm surprised. I don't know that Brian's ever missed a plane before."

"He probably didn't make allowances for how long it was going to take Rita to get ready. He's spoiled. He's used to you."

"Oh, well . . ." *He's spoiled. He's used to you.* "You." Nobody said that word like Alec. He was paying attention to her, thinking about her. Jenny put the itinerary back in the drawer. Brian would like that. He liked things neat.

"You're uncomfortable having me here, aren't you?" Alec spoke easily.

Jenny slammed the drawer shut. What was with this man? Why was he always so blunt? Didn't he know the value of secrets? She made really great money out of creating a world of secrets. Why did he have to go around speaking the truth all the time? Why couldn't he lie like everyone else?

"It's the 'here' part," she acknowledged. "I would have been okay at a restaurant . . . and I know, you don't have to say it, you suggested that we go to a restaurant."

"It really doesn't make any difference to me. I like seeing where you live."

"The house probably says more about Brian than it does me. I work up on the third floor, and it's totally me—a complete mess. He has made me promise never to show it to anyone."

"I wouldn't care about that."

No, he wouldn't. "You don't care about how things look, do you?"

"Are you asking if I care how *you* look?"

She blinked, surprised. But yes, that probably was what she was saying. "It just seems so amazing, a man who doesn't care what women look like."

"That's not me. I can't take my eyes off you. I love the way you look."

Oh. Jenny felt a prickling along her arms. She had never expected him to say that. "I guess I mean that you don't care what I'm wearing."

"Again you're wrong. I hate the fact that summer's over, and you've started to wear sleeves."

Jenny looked down at herself. Her shirt was a cotton knit in a soft buttery color. It was a Henley, with little buttons running partway down the front, and of course, it had sleeves. It might be warm for November, but it was November.

"Trina says that I'm short-waisted so I should either wear sleeveless turtlenecks or three-quarter length V-necks. Necklines like this are okay if you keep them flipped open." But she was supposed to push up the sleeves on this shirt. She had forgotten. She shoved the ribbed cuffs up over her forearms. "It has to do with lengthening the line of the torso or some thing like that."

You're talking again. You're babbling. You're acting like an idiot.

People were always judging each other on their appearances, drawing conclusions about your character because of how you looked. Did you have the self-discipline to diet? Were you organized enough to wear the right accessories?

But Alec's interest in her appearance had

nothing to do with judging her character. His response was strictly physical. His eyes—his physical self—liked the way her arms—her physical self—looked.

"I'm not used to anyone paying me this much attention," she said. "That's why I'm talking too much."

How about that? That was honest. She was learning.

"Do you want me to leave?"

"No . . . I mean, Brian would wonder. What would I tell him?"

"The truth. Say that you found it awkward entertaining me in your home without him here."

Oh, sure. She could see herself saying that. What if Brian asked her why she found it awkward? What would she say then? It would be easier to start off with a lie. *Alec had a headache.* That's what she would say, something like that.

The red and white stripes on his shirt were wide. The one along the shoulder seam was red. A white stripe followed the line of his collarbone. A red one spanned his chest. A little red maple leaf was stitched onto that red stripe. She hadn't noticed it before.

"I keep forgetting that you're Canadian," she blurted out.

"That's probably because you're from the Midwest," he answered easily. "When I like people right away, whenever I'm immediately comfortable with someone, they're usually from the Midwest. Canadians seem to have the most in common with Midwesterners. I felt it with you right away."

You. With you. He was doing it again. "Chloe, your ex-wife . . . was she Midwestern?"

He shook his head. "She grew up in Connecticut." Then he smiled. "But I never said I was comfortable with her, did I?"

No, but you did say you were comfortable with me. "Brian's from the Midwest too."

Alec shook his head. "But he's running away from it. You're not. That's the difference. A lot of Canadians run away from being Canadian."

"But not you?"

"I hope not."

Of course he wasn't. He wouldn't be running from his past. She couldn't think of anything wrong with him, anything she didn't like about him.

She heard the door opening, then a voice, someone calling her name. It was Brian. He was back. Quickly she turned, moving toward the kitchen door. "We're back here, in the kitchen."

A moment later Brian appeared. He was wearing a black T-shirt and a sage-green blazer. He had remembered to push the sleeves up. He would have done it in front of a mirror. He would have gotten it right.

At the doorway he turned, his arm extended back, his hand open, as if he were guiding someone's steps. He must have someone with him.

It was Rita.

She had on the strangest outfit Jenny had seen in her life. It was more or less a black leather mini-dress, but mostly less. It seemed to be made entirely of straps. Loose drippy ribbons of black leather looped down around her shoulders and dangled in a crisscross over her back and breasts. Surely it couldn't be covering everything that a garment was supposed to cover, but Jenny looked at all the key places, and there wasn't a nipple or a pubic hair in sight.

"We missed our flight and had a terrible lunch," Brian explained. "So I brought Rita home. She wants to see the house and there's plenty of the swordfish."

"Oh, shoot." Jenny slapped her forehead. "I forgot to put the fish in the marinade. Oh, Brian, I'm sorry."

He was at the refrigerator, taking the fish out. He hadn't taken his jacket off or washed his hands. "That's okay."

A prickling started to crawl up Jenny's arms. Something was going on. Brian hadn't looked at her once. And since when was it okay that she had forgotten to marinate the fish? Things like that always irritated him.

She moved close. "Brian?" Maybe things weren't so great right now, but they were a couple. This was their home.

He laid the fish on the counter. It was still wrapped in the fishmonger's white paper.

"I see there's some wine," he said. "Is that for now? Do you want to serve it or shall I?"

He still wasn't looking at her. "I can." She took the bottle from him, got the corkscrew from the drawer. She looked at the corkscrew for a second, trying to remember how it worked. Silently Alec took it from her. In a few quick moves he had the bottle open. She slid three wine glasses in front of him. He poured.

It was as if she and Alec were the couple, not she and Brian.

She offered a glass to Rita. Rita shook her head, she didn't want one, something, Jenny thought, she could have said before Alec had poured three glasses. "So how was the convention?" Jenny asked her politely. "Did it go well? Did you enjoy it?"

"Very much so. I'd never realized how interested people are in my character."

That was delivered with an aggressive air. "How nice," Jenny started to say, but she was speaking to the dripping straps across Rita's back. Rita had turned and was speaking to Brian.

"This kitchen is every bit as wonderful as you said," she said. "What about the rest of the house? You said you'd show it to me."

Brian had started to wash the four different kinds of lettuce he thought were necessary for a salad. He said something, but Jenny couldn't hear it over the sound of the running water.

"I can give you the tour," she offered.

"Oh . . . okay." Clearly Rita preferred to go with Brian.

But it's my house. Jenny felt a sudden spurt of bitchiness. *It's not his.*

Trina and Karen had always said that Rita brought out the worst in them. Jenny was starting to see why. She turned to Alec. "Would you like to come along?"

He had been leaning back against the kitchen counter. He straightened and spoke to Brian. "Do you need some help in here?"

"No, no. You go on."

Jenny's notion of a house tour involved opening doors and saying the obvious, "This is the dining room . . . this is a bathroom." But Rita was surprisingly interested. She wanted to see the closets and the built-in storage at the top of the stairs.

She was also critical. She didn't understand why Jenny hadn't put more closet space in her bedroom.

Because Jenny didn't have that many clothes.

Or why Jenny hadn't run the bathroom counter top all the way to the wall. It would make for a bigger vanity.

Because Jenny didn't need a bigger vanity.

But it was never too late to install a magnifying mirror.

Yes, it was. Jenny did not want to see her skin magnified. Maybe ten years ago, but not now.

"I hope I don't feel that way when I'm your age."

Jenny wanted to shoot her.

Alec said little during the tour. Clearly he had the sense to keep out of catfights—if that's what this was. But as they filed down the narrow hall toward the kitchen again, Jenny felt a light touch on her arm stopping her.

"Something's going on, isn't it?" He spoke in a low voice. "Do you know what it is?"

"No . . . unless she wants a job as an interior designer."

"She wants to score points off you. She's trying to make you feel bad."

"She did on the magnifying mirror. She scored big time on that one."

He smiled. "That she did." But from the way he was looking down at her, Jenny knew that he didn't care how cosmetical-commercial smooth her skin was. "This just may be the way she handles new situations, the best defense is a good offense and all that. But Brian, is he usually like this?"

"No, not at all." That's why Jenny's house-tour manner was so inexpert. Brian had always been the one to show people around. "But I don't suppose I can ask him anything until she leaves."

"Unless she's a part of it."

"A part of what?" Jenny didn't get it. Then she did. "No, that's not possible."

The hall was narrow, sandwiched between the stairs and the living room. Brian had thought long and hard about taking down the living room wall so that that room would be wider. But he had decided against it. The original arrangement, with the stairs separate from the room, was more formal.

But if the wall had come down, she would not be standing so close to Alec when they had this conversation.

Or maybe they wouldn't be having this conversation.

"Why not?" he asked. "You wouldn't be unfaithful to him, but that doesn't mean he wouldn't be unfaithful to you."

Why did he have to spell it out so clearly? "He just wouldn't." *Brian doesn't care that much about sex. You're the one who said that.*

Back in the kitchen Rita was standing at the counter near the chopping block where Brian was working. She had one hand on the counter and her body, with all its ribbony bits of leather, was turned toward him. She was saying something low and urgent.

So it was true. Jenny could feel it up her arms, at the back of her neck, along her spine. It was true. Brian had gone to bed with Rita. He had been unfaithful to her. After fourteen years of being together, after more than six months of not touching her, he had touched someone else.

Why had he brought Rita home? Did he honestly believe that the four of them were going to sit here and eat dinner? Of course he did. That was his style. Procrastinate, delay confrontation. Pray that it will all go away.

Jenny opened the silverware drawer. "Shall we eat in here or the dining room?"

"The dining room, I guess," Brian said.

Alec had his hand out, waiting to take the silverware from her. The ribbed cuff of his knit shirt was red, the same color as the stripes, as the little maple leaf.

If he hadn't been here, she would have let the evening play out Brian's way. It felt normal to her, this kind of avoidance. It was what she and Brian had always done. He had spent the first three years of their relationship never mentioning his father. Now he was going to try not to mention Rita.

But she wasn't going to put up with that, not with Alec here. She was learning something new from him. He was direct, he was honest, he faced up to things. She opened her hand and let the silverware fall back into the drawer. The utensils landed every which way, the forks slanted across the dividers, the spoons mixed in with the knives.

"Something happened in Reno." She was saying it as Alec would have, without any anger or any question, just saying it because it was true. "Tell me."

Brian had been lining up the spices for the salad dressing. "Why don't we eat dinner first?"

Oh, he'd love that, wouldn't he? He would be in control, he would know what the issues were, he would know what the secret was, while she would just be sitting there, helpless. Forget that. "No, now. Tell me."

He faced her, shrugging, his hands turned over, a gesture that somehow denied responsibility. "We didn't mean to hurt you."

So it was true. Of course it was. She had known it the moment she had walked into the kitchen. She wasn't going to react yet. She wasn't going to decide how she felt. Not yet. "Go on."

"It's hard to explain," he said. "It's not that simple."

"Go ahead and tell her." Rita's voice was keyed up and hard, a faint trill in it. "Tell her."

"It's not that simple," Brian said.

He had already said that. This wasn't like him. He always knew what to say. He was never at a loss. Except with his mother. He used to get like this with his mother. Jenny had always hated seeing it.

Alec stepped forward. "Come, my girl," he said to Rita. His voice was clear and firm. He took her arm. "These two have something to talk about. I'll see you home."

Rita shook herself free. "I'm not going anywhere. I have as much right to be here as *she* does."

Her voice was hostile.

She hates me, Jenny thought. *She hates me. Why on earth does she hate me?*

"No, you don't," Alec said. "You might have had a fun weekend, but now—"

"It wasn't a *weekend,*" Rita snapped. "Brian and I were married last night."

Married? Jenny felt her arms drop to her sides, her shoulders slump forward. Married? Last night. Brian and Rita. It could not be true.

No. It was only sex, a weekend quickie. She could handle that. She and Brian, they could figure something out, some way to go on.

He had never wanted to get married. He had wanted to be free.

"I don't know what you've done." Alec was speaking again. This time his grip on Rita's arm was firm. "But right now you and I are out of here."

He said nothing else. Jenny saw nothing else.

She heard a few protests from Rita and the door closing. And she was alone with Brian.

She was numb, blank, disbelieving. He didn't say anything. He wouldn't. That was his style. He wanted her to go first. Then he could react.

We were in this together. That's what we always said. It was you and me. We weren't like other people, that's why we didn't get married. It was just us, the two of us, together.

"Say something, Jen-o." He was pleading.

Why? Why should she have to speak? She hadn't done anything.

"We didn't mean to hurt you."

"You've said that. You've already said that. You can't say it again." What was she doing, scripting this? And why couldn't he say it again? In soaps people always said things over, endlessly, again and again. She wanted to laugh. She wanted to shriek, rip at her hair, she wanted to not be here. "This isn't some kind of joke, is it?"

"It's not a joke." He reached out as if to touch her. She jerked back. "You have to understand—"

"Understand?" Suddenly Jenny was furious. She didn't want to laugh or cry. She wanted to kill him. "No, I *don't* have to understand. Why do I have to understand? That's not my job here, understanding what you've done. I don't even *know* what you've done."

"She and I were at this fan convention together—"

"I know that," Jenny snapped.

"Do you want to hear this or not?"

No. I want all this to go away. I want it not to

have happened. She folded her arms, tight, sullen.

"Ever since she joined the show, the rest of the cast has been really hard on her. It isn't fair. Yes, she's young and ambitious—"

And she married a man who was living with another woman.

"And she's so attractive. Other women have never been very nice to her because she has such a great figure. She said that, that it's always been so unfair, the way other women won't forgive her for the way she looks."

That was crap. Women didn't hate other women for being beautiful. They hated them for being bitches. If other women hated Rita, it was because she was a Grade-A scheming bitch.

"I know she's made a couple of mistakes." It was as if Brian was pleading Rita's cause. "But that's only because she's so determined. She reminds me a lot of you."

Reminded him of her? "That's great, Brian. Why did you have to go after someone who reminded you of me when you already had me?"

He made a little gesture with his hands, an exasperated, giving-up gesture. "I knew you weren't going to understand."

"No. You're just saying that because you don't want to have this conversation. If you can convince yourself that there's no point in talking to me because I'll never understand, you can weasel out of here without having to face me, and that's what you want. You're a coward."

"I'm sorry if I hurt you."

"*If?* Brian, we have been together for fourteen

years, and without a word you up and marry someone else and you wonder *if* you've hurt me . . ."

"Jenny, we're never going to get anywhere if you're going to be like this."

"Okay, I'll be quiet." Jenny folded her arms again and glared at him. "All right I'm quiet."

He looked hesitant. "Well . . . I feel like no one has ever known me the way she does. She—"

"Knows you?" Jenny erupted. "Knows you? Brian, we've known each other since we were fourteen. Who could possibly know you better than I do?"

"That's in the past, Jenny. . . . The past doesn't mean anything."

Not mean anything? Hadn't she just spent the last couple years clinging to the idea that the past meant everything?

"She knows what I'm like now," he was saying. "That's what counts, now. She shares my ambitions. You're content to stay in daytime. I want more, and so does she."

"And I'm holding you back?"

Was that his image of her? That she was some kind of little mediocre drudge who was holding him back from fame and fortune? That was absurd, that was insane.

But he believed it. He goddamn believed it.

"But why *marry* her? Fine, leave me, have a fling with her, but *marriage*? You're the one who always wanted to be free. What happened?"

"This you will never understand. I had no choice."

"What do you mean by that? She's not pregnant, is she?"

"No, of course not. I would not have had any kind of intimate relationship with her behind your back."

What did he call marriage, if not an intimate relationship? "Then you're right. I don't understand."

"I knew you wouldn't. And you won't, not until you're really in love—"

"Really in love? What do you call—"

He held up his hand. "I know, I know. We said we were in love. We thought we were in love, but we weren't. Not really. Not like this. That's why you can't understand."

How dare he? How *dare* he? Deny their history like this? They had loved each other. Maybe not recently, but at first. Yes, yes, they had. How could he pretend that that hadn't happened? That the fourteen years had been a simple misunderstanding? *Oh, pardon me. I stepped on your foot.*

"Maybe I do understand." She was furious again. "She makes you feel important. She makes you feel big and strong. Yes, I understand. And it isn't understanding you want. You don't care if I understand. You want me to forgive you, to tell you that it's okay. Well, I don't. I understand, but that doesn't mean I forgive you."

"Understand . . . forgive . . . whatever." He obviously didn't get it. "You'll have to accept that this is an experience you—"

"Get out of here. Just go away."

Jenny dropped to the steps that led up out of the kitchen to the deck. She pressed the heels of her hands into her eyelids, then dragged her hand up over her eyebrows to her forehead, then her hair. Her forearms blocked her vision. All she could see was herself—the skin of her arms, the pale yellow buttons of her shirt, the khaki of her slacks. She wasn't wearing socks, and she could see her ankles.

She hadn't shaved her legs. She had been planning to when she changed for dinner, but then she hadn't changed for dinner. She pulled up one pant leg. Little stubble hairs dotted her calves. They looked awful, like stumps after a forest fire.

Rita probably shaved her legs every day. Or she got them waxed. She probably had her whole body waxed. Maybe she had her pubic hair waxed into the shape of a heart or something.

Is that it, Brian? That she's such a hot number and I'm not? With her little cut-out bras and her chains. Is it all about sex?

She had written about this, being jilted. It happened all the time on soaps. Just like miscarriages. Once again this was something she wrote about; it wasn't supposed to be happening to her.

She was sitting at the table now. She didn't know how she had gotten there, but in front of her was the antique Swedish pine table that Brian had so carefully chosen. Last week he had been thinking about the second floor. He had been full of ideas—knocking an arched opening between the two big rooms, enlarging the bath, moving the laundry up there. Just last week he had been talking about that. Seven days ago. He couldn't have been planning on leaving her. It made no sense.

She heard footsteps. Had he changed his mind? Was he coming back?

It was Alec.

"Oh," she said. "You waited."

He laid something on the table. It was a key, dull, scratched, well-used.

She didn't understand.

"It's Brian's key to your house."

"He left his key?"

Then this was real. It was happening. Brian loved this house. He might not have wanted it at first—a mortgage would keep him from feeling *free*—but it had become his creation, proof that he had left Oklahoma. Midwesterners didn't live in tall, narrow brownstones. That was a difference between them. Alec had already said that. Jenny liked being from the Midwest; she was proud of it. Brian hated it.

He had left his key. He had given up the house for Rita. *Was I the last piece of Oklahoma? Now that you're rid of me, do you finally feel like you've left?*

Alec spoke. "How much did you still love him?"

She couldn't answer. She had spent two years trying not to ask that question. How could she suddenly answer it now? She covered her face with her hands. "I feel like such a dope. I thought it meant something that we had been together so long. I thought that that mattered, but obviously it didn't mean a thing."

"Sometimes it's easier to go on being loyal than it is to know when to stop."

"So you think I'm a dope?"

"You have not lost your dignity."

Her dignity? What did he mean by that? Was she a dope, or wasn't she a dope? Why couldn't he just answer that? She was too tired, too confused to figure anything out. She had been dumped, jilted, discarded, unloaded. People were going to have to talk plain English. "He said we never loved each other. That's what hurts the most, the idea that we *never* . . . He says I can't understand because I don't know what love is. That's not true. We did love each other. He can't rewrite our past like that. He can't pretend it away."

"He shouldn't, but he will."

It wasn't fair. He was going to get away with this. He was going to get away with believing that he had never loved her. That was so unjust, so unfair.

"People shouldn't have the right to stop loving each other." Alec's voice was calm. "But they do it." She felt his hand on her arm. "They do it all the time."

His hand was warm, and it began to move, stroking her arm from elbow to shoulder. His hand caught on the fabric, pulling it tight against her arm. So the motion became circular, a light massaging of her arm, a few inches above her elbow. It was nice, comforting.

"You have always made me think of Tinker Bell."

Tinker Bell? What was he talking about?

"Not the pretty Disney version, but the one in the original play. She's a wonderful character. She's tough and courageous, she's loyal, she's feisty."

"But Peter and the Lost Boys . . ." Jenny knew the play too. "They want Wendy."

Wendy, the soft one in the white nightdress. Wendy the one who could sew pockets, Wendy the mother. Jenny had tried that for eight weeks last spring. But it turned out that her body had been playing one big practical joke on her.

"They were boys, Jenny." Alec's voice sounded far away. "That's why they wanted Wendy because they were boys. But men want something different."

Brian's still a boy. He doesn't want to grow up.

"Tinker Bell drinks poison for Peter, Jenny. He's too stubborn, too pigheaded to believe that there's poison in that glass so she drinks it herself. That's what you've been doing, Jenny. You've been drinking poison for the wrong guy."

Drinking poison? Was that what she had been doing?

She spoke. "At least he didn't leave me for a Wendy." She hated how bitter she sounded.

"She's not that," Alec agreed.

"But I'll bet she sure is good at the 'girl stuff.' "

"If you're talking about sex, I don't agree."

"Oh, come on. You've seen her. You've seen *lots* of her."

"She does dress like a hooker, no question about that. But it feels all about wanting power and attention, not any real joy in sensuality."

He was getting too complicated. "She had me fooled. And she must have had Brian fooled too. If you're right, then he's one unlucky son of a bitch, isn't he? First me, then her. He can't seem to find anyone who's good in bed."

"Why do you keep blaming yourself?" His hand was still on her arm. She could feel the warmth through her sleeve. "Why have you let him make you feel like some kind of sexual dwarf? You're not. You have to believe that."

She jerked her arm away. "A whole lot you know about it." He had never been with her. He had never seen how awkward she was. He didn't know how hard it was, how much trouble she had focusing, concentrating. Her mind would race, she would get distracted, and it wouldn't work.

"I know a lot," he answered. "I've paid attention. I've seen you move. I've seen the way you curl your hands around a cup of hot coffee, because you love to feel the heat of the cup. I've seen the way you pull your turtlenecks over your chin when you're thinking, how you rub the fabric against your cheek."

Yes, she did do that. She did like warmth against her hands and softness against her cheek. He had been watching her more closely than she had been watching herself. But liking warmth and softness was a long way from being any good in bed.

"And," he continued, "I've read your scripts."

"Oh." She brushed that aside. "Those are just fantasies." This always embarrassed her, people trying to conclude things about her from the scripts.

"Maybe they are. But someday someone is going to show you how close they are to reality. You have to believe me, Jenny. Brian's been telling you a lie. I don't know if he knows any better, maybe not. But it's a lie nonetheless. And someday you'll see that. Someone will help you see that."

Someday, someone . . . Did she believe that? No, she didn't. Brian was the only man who had ever loved her, and now even he had convinced himself that he never had.

Of course this man here, Alec, he'd been trying to tell her that he loved her. He couldn't mean it. Well, no, he did mean it, he did believe it, but he was probably wrong. Once he sat down and thought about it, he'd manage to talk himself out of it too.

"I don't hear you volunteering to be that someday someone," she said, and it sounded like a complaint, a thin, grousing complaint.

It took him a moment to understand her. "I'm not propositioning you, if that's what you're asking."

"Well, why not? You think you love me." She had been terrified of him saying that, but what difference did it make now? Everything was already ruined.

"I don't *think* it. I do. But, Jenny"—he was starting to sound exasperated—"for God's sake, look what just happened." He flung out his arm, gesturing to the door through which Brian had gone. "Don't you think it would be a little inappropriate? I'm not going to take advantage of this."

"Why not?" she demanded again. She pushed her chair out from the table, getting up so quickly that the chair clattered to the floor. "What's so wrong with me? This morning I thought that there were two people who were in love with me, you and him. Now twelve hours later he's married some bimbo, and you don't want to be near me."

"Jenny, I—"

She burst into tears.

Arms came around her, pulling her close. Hands were in her hair, running over her back, soothing, comforting. There was breathing against her cheek, the rising and falling of a chest, and in her ear was a heartbeat.

"I'm sorry," she sniffed. And she stepped back, pressing her hands across her eyes, trying to push back the tears. "I don't usually cry like that."

"Or go around demanding that people sleep with you."

"No"—her laugh was thin, a little watery, but at least it was a laugh—"I don't do that either. God, this has been one lousy day."

She ran a hand through her hair. She felt the hair lift, then drop back into place. She wished she hadn't stepped away so quickly. It had been nice, having him hold her.

He was trying to comfort you. Why can't you let him comfort you?

Because she never needed to be comforted. She was always the strong one, the cheery one.

God, but she hated this, feeling so pathetic, so powerless.

Why hadn't his breathing changed when he had been holding her? Why hadn't it quickened and gone shallow? Why hadn't the cords in his neck stiffened? Surely if he loved her, he wouldn't have been this restrained.

Surely if she had been worth loving, he couldn't have been this restrained. But, no. She was short-waisted, badly dressed, stubbly legged Jenny Cotton.

"You don't exactly find me irresistible, do you?" Brian had found Rita irresistible.

"That's not fair."

Who cared about being fair? She wanted to be irresistible. "I suppose you found Chloe Spencer irresistible."

"I didn't have to resist Chloe."

"Are you saying you could have?"

"I would like to believe that about myself, yes."

Oh, that's right. He was perfect. She had forgotten that. She suddenly felt hostile.

How she would love to show him, show Brian, show all men. Show Brian that he hadn't hurt her, show Alec that he couldn't resist her, show herself that she was someone else altogether.

"What would you do if I threw myself on you?" she demanded. "If I came up and put my arms around you?"

"Jenny, this is stupid. What are you getting at?"

She didn't know. She didn't care. "Tell me what you would do."

"I suppose I'd hold you, but I would be careful."

"And if I kissed you?"

"I'm sure I'd kiss you back—I know I would—but again I would be careful. It would be completely wrong to take advantage of—"

"You're thinking of me as some pathetic little worm, aren't you?" She hated that.

"No, of course not. But you're reeling, you're in a lot of pain, you're—"

"Oh, shut up." Reeling, in pain . . . that sounded pretty worm-like to her.

Wouldn't it be great to have one of those bodies—

No point in thinking about it. She didn't have one of those bodies. She was short-waisted, badly dressed, etc., etc.

You don't hate yourself. You don't. You don't. Why are you letting yourself think like this?

What did she like about herself? She should think about that. What was the single thing she liked most about herself?

Her imagination. Of course.

Alec was standing by one of the chairs. She could imagine him, his back and arms glistening with sweat. She could imagine his breath in her ear, ragged and gasping. She could imagine an urgent genital pressure, a determined, undeniable entry.

Let him imagine it too. He could resist her body, but would he be able to resist her imagination?

He liked her arms. She would show him her arms.

She turned and crossed to the counter, pulling open the knife drawer. She took out one of the small paring knives. Her father had taught her how to use tools. She was good with tools. She lifted the knife up to her shoulder, and with a deft flick, she slit into the fabric of the sleeve and then grasped the shirt by the cut. She pulled sharply, quickly, tearing the fabric. The sleeve curled down her arm, and she shook her wrist, and it dropped to the floor, pale yellow against the blue granite.

"Jenny . . ."

Imagine this, Alec. The power of her mind stopped his words. *Imagine this.*

She took the knife in her other hand and slit the fabric of the other sleeve. The fabric was cotton, it ripped in a soft whisper. She moved close to him and ran her arms up his, not merely her hands, but the whole sweep of her arms, touching the length of his. His hand was at her waist, firm, prohibitive. He wasn't going to let her do this.

For the first time in days Jenny felt triumphant, completely in control.

Her arm was up to his face now. She had let her muscles be soft, but now against his face she flexed, tightening, then releasing. She could feel his breath against her.

"Jenny, please don't. This is such a bad idea, you'll regret it."

But imagine it, Alec. These arms around you, pulling you down to me, holding you to me.

His hands were on her forearms, her wrists, as if he were trying to unclasp her hands.

I'm strong, Alec. But you're stronger. You could break free if you wanted.

"Jenny, this is madness. Please stop."

No, you stop.

With her arms overhead, her breasts were high. She moved yet closer to him, and she curved her arm around his neck, pushing down his collar so he could feel the bend of her elbow against his flesh.

All her life she had longed for a moment like this. All the reading, all the fantasies were about this—being irresistible. A man, the very best of men, with ideals of honor and restraint, standards he had always lived by, been able to live by.

Until you.

Alec was struggling, she could feel that. *I know what you're thinking. You're thinking that you're Canadian, that you ought to be able to resist this, that Canadians are sensible, Canadians are reasonable.* She traced the little red maple leaf on his shirt. *Then fight for your flag, Alec. But you'll have to fight my imagination.* She bent down and kissed the little embroidered emblem.

That did it. His arms crashed around her, pulling her against him, tight, low, and hard. His chin pushed her forehead back, and his kiss was urgent, almost rough. His hand came down her shirt, searching for softness. She felt him back her up toward the counter. He let go of her and picked up the black-handled knife that she had dropped. He slipped a finger inside her torn shirt sleeve and hooked the strap of her bra, pulling it out. One quick, businesslike slice and the strap separated, each half dropping down her arm. The same motion on the other side and then his fingers brushing against her back, releasing the hook, and her breasts were free, soft against the knit of her shirt.

Suddenly Jenny felt as if she did have one of those bodies. She was beautiful. She was erotic. She was powerful.

He pulled her close again, but his hand was between their bodies now, cupping her breasts. He was kissing her again, and he tasted of fresh air. She could feel his arm supporting her head. But she still felt glorious, in control. She had imagined this. She had made it happen. A moment later he was lifting her off her feet, scooping her up, carrying her up the stairs.

She pointed to the door of the bedroom, but he shook his head. "Not there. The third floor is yours, isn't it?"

There were three rooms up there. One was supposedly a second guest room, but they had never had two guests at once, and Jenny's stuff had spilled over into it. Books were piled up in front of the bureau, there were stacks of scripts on the chair, piles of paper on the bed.

"Do you care about these?" He gestured with his head toward the papers on the bed.

"No." She didn't know what they were. She didn't care. She loved this. The cords in Alec's neck were stiff. His eyes were dark and narrow. Just as she had imagined.

He jerked the bedspread off the bed, scattering the papers everywhere. They skated across the floor, spilling all over each other. It was a mess, a worse mess. He couldn't wait. She loved the thought.

He sat on the bed and pulled her to stand between his legs. He unfastened her slacks, his fingers brushing against her, and eased them down over her hips. His hands were hot on her body, and her skin was smooth, smoother than she had ever known herself to be.

She was at his side, lying next to him. "What is it that you like?" His voice was low. "I will do anything for you."

She knew that. She had made herself irresistible.

His body was as she had imagined, golden-toned and hard. And she could feel heat pouring out of him, he was aroused, desirous, wanting her, desperately wanting her.

He opened his mouth over her and the warmth of his breath, the moistness of his tongue seared through the thin silky fabric of her panties. She raised her hips, eased her underwear off, and an instant later he was warm against her again.

This too was as she had always imagined. She couldn't believe it. In the past desire had been such an uncertain road for her, so difficult and twisted, the end rarely worth the trouble of the journey. But here was a silvery path, the bright slick soaring she had always imagined, and then the sudden, bright bursting.

She had never felt like this before. She was gasping, she was breathless and laughing.

Yes, she had been drinking poison for the

wrong guy. But the poison was out of her system. She was free, and she was with someone else. She was someone else. She wasn't the tomboy with the wrong sandwiches. She wasn't the kid from the wrong side of the river with the wrong kind of blouse.

Alec was propped up on his elbow, looking down at her. He had his shirt off, but his khakis were still on. She ran a hand up his arm. "I suppose you're going to say 'I told you so,' but I don't care. It meant the world to me."

"I'm sure it meant more to me."

"What are you talking about?" She was laughing. "We haven't gotten to you yet." She pushed him back onto the bed, swiveled and swung her leg so that she was sitting with him between her thighs. She could feel the soft fabric of his slacks. She still had her torn shirt on, the armhole jagged and fraying over her lightly muscled arms. There were two dark circles on her shirt over her nipples, moistness from his mouth. He covered them with the insides of his wrists, lightly rubbing his pulses across her nipples.

"I'm talking about the fact that I love you. Everything you do, everything you say, everything that happens to you, means the world to me because I love you."

She believed him. For the first time she believed him. He did love her. He wasn't blind, he wasn't fooling himself, he wasn't daydreaming. He loved her.

What a wondrous gift. What could she give him in return? She ran her hand down his chest and started to undo the buckle of his belt. He stopped her.

"What about you?" she asked. "Don't you want to go on?"

"No. Not until you love me."

Thirteen

Alec's eyes opened to dim morning light. He was in a room with blue-striped curtains. Then he remembered. He was at Jenny's. And this rich tension in his body, even half-asleep he could feel it, the unfulfilled suppleness along his thighs . . . he remembered.

But she wasn't in bed anymore. He knew immediately, instinctively. He sat up, looking for her, hoping that she hadn't left.

She was asleep in the white wicker chair, her body turned sideways, her knees pulled up like a child's. There was a box of tissues in her lap. She had gotten out of bed to cry.

She must have awakened, and in the bleak darkness last night's new confidence had deserted her.

What had it been like for her, waking up in the guest room of her own home? What had he seemed like to her in that moment? She would have sat up and looked down at his sleeping form. Had he seemed like a stranger? But she hadn't retreated, she hadn't gone to her bedroom, she hadn't gone to cry in familiar comfort. There would have been too many memories there. Strangeness was better than memories. Memories of Brian.

Books covered the floor in front of the chair, and he had to push them aside to kneel down in front of her. She still had her torn T-shirt on, and she was breathing softly in her sleep, the pale yellow fabric rising and falling. Her cheek was pressed against the chair's striped cushion. She would have a crinkled red mark there when she woke.

She stirred. He wanted to scoop her up and carry her back to bed and keep her safe. But there was still a crumpled tissue in her hand. Even in sleep she seemed solitary, beyond comfort, alone with her memories of another man.

He's not worth it. Gently, pointlessly, Alec drew the tissue from her hand. Why had she pledged herself to someone unworthy of her? *I'm here. If only you would love me . . .*

He reached to put the tissue in the small wicker wastebasket. Automatically he turned his wrist over, checking the time.

Good God, it was 7:25. Rehearsal had started ten minutes ago. How could it be that late? He never overslept. Quickly, silently, he slipped on his clothes, the khakis, the red-and-white rugby shirt. He could shower and shave at the studio.

He knelt down in front of Jenny again. He touched her arm. He wasn't going to leave without saying good-bye. He ran his hand along her arm and whispered her name.

Her lashes fluttered open. She looked blank

for a moment. She didn't know where she was. Then he could feel it, as surely as if it were happening to him. He could feel the dead weight descending on her, crushing her, and then, dropping further and further, threatening to obliterate her.

"It's almost seven-thirty. I have to go." There was no point to apologizing or explaining. If he didn't show up at work, she would be the one called. *Stop whatever you're doing. Alec isn't in today. You've got to write him out of today's episode. This instant.* The best thing he could do for her was to go to work. "They may have already started."

"They . . ."

And he could feel beneath the leaden mass of her grief a dread building up. She was thinking about having to face everyone, having to see their curiosity and their pity.

It would be awful. He was not going to lie to her about that. He had dragged himself into *Aspen* day after day, hearing the whispers, feeling the silent glee of those who rejoice in the pain of others.

"It's Monday." This was all the comfort he had. "You never come in on Monday. Stick to your routine. Don't come until tomorrow. I'll be back the minute things are done."

"I'll be okay."

"I know that," he said. She had to hear that. "But there's no reason to make things harder than they already are." He had to leave. Time was passing. "Can I let myself out?"

He remembered last night, Brian coming out

of the house and turning, key in hand, to lock the dead bolt.

"No, you can't." Jenny ran a hand over her face, shaking her rumpled hair, trying to rouse herself. "The dead bolt needs a key, and Brian says we should—" She stopped, remembering that there wasn't any "we" anymore. "Oh, just go on out. The latchbolt will catch, that will be enough for this time of day."

She wasn't going to care about Brian's little rules anymore.

Brian was out of her life. Alec felt a grim, bitter triumph. He had first felt it last night when he had gotten that key back from Brian.

Rita had refused to leave. She had wanted to go back inside the house; she wanted to be a part of Jenny and Brian's confrontation. She thought that it was her right. Alec didn't. As determined as she was, as set as her little jaw was, he was more determined, more set.

But he couldn't leave her on the little square of flagstones that paved the space between Jenny's house and the sidewalk. It was dark and she was dressed in a leather cobweb. So he sat sideways on the wide stoop, leaning against the wrought-iron railing. He tilted his head back, looking up at the pale night sky. There were no stars, just the blank reflection of the city lights against the clouds.

Rita tried to speak, she wanted to tell him what had happened, how this madcap romance had come about.

"Stow it, Rita," he said, not even interested

enough to look away from the sky. "I don't care."

"But—"

"No, don't say a word. I'm only here because I don't know how safe this neighborhood is at night." His words were harsh, his tone mild. "Don't confuse that with me wanting to hear from you."

"Well!" She wasn't used to people talking to her like that. She stormed over to the front gate, treating him to a rear view of her dripping leather straps. A minute later someone in a passing car yelled something at her, and she had to retreat into the shadows.

She glared at him. "You're on her side, aren't you?"

Alec didn't answer.

"I don't get it." She jerked a strap back over her shoulder. "Why does everyone think she's so great? They do, you know. They think she walks on water. Everyone thinks she's so perfect."

Alec still didn't answer. So the kid didn't like Jenny's popularity. So what did she go and do? Steal Jenny's boyfriend.

Brace yourself, sweetcakes. You may be trash, but he's worse. He's going to disappoint the hell out of you.

Rita tried twice more, but eventually she understood that here at last was someone who was not going to pay attention to her, who had so little interest in her that he wasn't even going to be polite. He was going to be gallant—he wasn't going to leave her half-naked on a city street—but his responsibility stopped there.

So they waited in silence, she pacing on the flagstones, he staring upward at the sky. At last he heard footsteps inside the house. The door opened. It was Brian. Before Alec could see his face, he had turned to lock the dead bolt.

Alec scrambled to his feet. He thrust his hand out. "Give me that."

"What?" Brian drew back, puzzled. He didn't understand.

"Her key," Alec ordered. "Jenny's key. Hand it over. I'll get it back to her."

"But—"

"But nothing. You married someone else. You can't keep the key to her house."

"I live here, all my stuff—"

"You can get your stuff later. You may have lived here once, but you don't now." Hadn't Brian thought about that? *Legally it's mine,* Jenny had said. "Give me the key."

"What are you talking about?" Rita had started up the stairs. "Why should he give back the key? Maybe she should be the one who moves, not us."

Alec paid no attention to her. He supposed he was being ridiculous. What difference did it make if Brian kept Jenny's key for another week?

None and he didn't care. He was getting that key back and giving it to Jenny.

"The key, O'Neill, the key."

What was he going to do if Brian wouldn't turn it over? What if he just jammed it into his pocket and sauntered off with his new young bride?

Alec would hit him.

This wasn't the Duke of Lydgate. And it wasn't the nice-guy Canadian farm kid either. This was the Scotch blood finally boiling, charging down out of the heather. Three generations in Canada didn't wipe out five hundred years of clannish loyalty. He was a Cameron, and this man had harmed a Cameron woman. They would start here with this demand for a key. They would start being two civilized men on a Brooklyn stoop. But if they ended up with bloodied dirks and red-stained linen, that was fine by Alec.

Alec didn't take his eyes from Brian's. *You are going to hand over that key. I'm not giving you a choice.*

A muscle twitched along the side of Brian's face, Alec could feel something stiffening in him—maybe he was going to resist—but a minute later he was fumbling with his key ring. He had surrendered.

"What are you doing?" Rita demanded. "Why are you giving him the key? Why shouldn't we live here, not her? There's two of us, there's only one of her."

Brian didn't answer her. He took her arm. "Come on. Let's go."

Alec watched them leave. His palm closed tightly around Jenny's key. A fierce stab of joy surged through him. He felt the key in his hand. *You're mine now. Mine.* And he had used it to let himself back inside.

But of course he had given the key back to her. It wasn't his. Even after what had happened in the blue-and-white guest room, it still wasn't his, and he couldn't use it to turn the dead bolt this morning. He would have done anything for her, but he couldn't even lock her door.

It wasn't possible to get a cab this far out in Brooklyn, but the studio was only a quick subway trip away. As he waited on the platform for a train, he could feel a fierce urgency build in him. It was more than the usual need to get to work. It was a need to get back into character, to be the duke, to try and understand how Brian could have done this.

So far Lydgate had humiliated his wife only in private. Would he do something this public to her? Yes, if he thought he wouldn't lose face. He wanted to punish her, he relished the idea. He hated strong women. They were the smothering, controlling mothers. Lydgate had to avenge his powerlessness, he had to mutilate, cause pain. That's how he would become a man.

Or at least that's how people like Brian and Lydgate thought they would become men.

You are not going to get away with this. This was Alec's pledge, not to Jenny, but to himself. *Brian, you will pay for what you've done to her.*

The security guard inside the studio started to speak, but Alec held up his hand. "I know. I know. I'm late." He walked quickly down the hall. A wardrobe rack full of costumes had been abandoned outside the elevator. The big door to the studio floor was open. A makeup kit was sitting on the second floor landing.

So the word was out. People had dropped everything when they had heard. It was going to be another day when no one did what they were supposed to. Why was this an excuse for people to stop doing their jobs? Hadn't it occurred to anyone that maybe times like this were when you were supposed to work harder?

On the third floor he could see a crowd of people gathered outside the rehearsal room. They were makeup and wardrobe people, and people from the prop department. None of them had any reason to be up here. Ray was standing in the midst of them, saying something, gesturing with his hands.

He caught sight of Alec and broke free, hurrying down the hall, looking relieved. "Am I ever glad to see you. Have you heard what happened?"

"Yes . . . where's your script?" For the life of him Alec couldn't remember what was in today's episode. "I need to take a look at it." He was going to work even if no one else was.

"It's on the table . . . but wait, don't go in. There's something you should know."

"About Brian and Rita? I know."

He strode in the rehearsal hall, Ray at his shoulder. The cast should have been at the long table, each with coffee and an open script. Gil or Terence should have been on his stool, the day should have begun.

But no one was seated. Neither Terence nor Gil were in the room. The cast and production staff were gathered around the edges of the room, standing in little clusters of twos and threes. Mixed in with them were crew members, someone from lighting, one of the camerawomen, people Alec had never seen up here before.

And over by the bulletin board was Brian, standing by himself, rocking back on his heels, drinking a cup of coffee. He was in yesterday's clothes, a black T-shirt, a sage-green blazer. He seemed to be patiently waiting for rehearsal to start.

Jenny had gotten out of bed to cry. All by herself in a chair, crying over this man.

Now Brian was stepping forward, ready to greet Alec.

Oh, no, we're not going to be nice. We're not going to pretend.

Wouldn't it feel good to hit him? To feel the muscles in his arm tightening, his fist knotting, then the speed and the gathering power, followed by sound, the pounding of bone on bone and the crash of a body, the clatter of a chair. That would feel good, the brutish simplicity of being a man in a man's body with a man's psyche and a man's power.

But this was not a place for steel-hot simplicity. The glitter in this world came from silver, cool and elegant. Victors found their weapons from the metals at hand, and there was nothing more cool, nothing more elegant than the manners of the Regency.

Alec waited until he was sure that Brian was looking straight at him. But that wasn't enough.

He wanted everyone in the room to see this. He knew how to do that, how to get them all to look at him. And when they were, he looked straight at Brian for one beat more. Then he spoke to Ray. He didn't turn, he was still looking at Brian, he just spoke. "There's too much crap on that bulletin board." *You do not exist.* "How's a person supposed to know if there's anything new?"

He heard a faint gasp behind him. Somebody got it. This was the cut direct.

Here is the rule, Alec announced by the set of his shoulders, the line of his jaw, *work with this person when you have to, but otherwise he does not exist.*

Alec went toward the coffee table. His mug was thick white china that someone in the prop department had painted with the Lydgate coat of arms.

"I liked that," Ray said softly. He was impressed.

"That bastard." Alec pressed the black plastic handle on the coffee urn. The dark liquid steamed into his mug. His victory was bitter; what had he achieved for Jenny? Nothing. "Where's the blushing bride?"

"She's not in today. But her publicist left messages all over town yesterday."

Wonderful. Rita had probably called her publicist before her mother. "What's going on? What are we all waiting for?"

"Karen. She's locked up in her dressing room. She says she won't do her scenes with Brian. She has the big faint again. He lifts her up and carries her to the sofa. She doesn't want him touching her. She says it's out of loyalty to Jenny."

"Loyalty to Jenny?" Alec felt a sharp surge of impatience. "Tell me, precisely how does this help Jenny? How does getting us all behind and having to pay the crew overtime, help Jenny?"

Ray shrugged. "Gil's down talking to her."

"Gil?" Camera-shot Gil? "That's going to do a lot of good."

"I think he knew that. He wanted someone to let him know the minute you came."

"Me?" Oh, lovely. He was supposed to go down and do Gil's job for him?

Yes, of course. Hadn't this been going on for months? He had sworn that after *Aspen* he wasn't going to be the leader, the fixer, the cast ambassador, the laird. But he had fallen right back into the part. It was his own fault.

"Get everyone out of here who doesn't belong," he ordered Ray. If he was taking charge, then Ray would be his lieutenant, his adjunct.

This was what Ray had been trying to do before Alec had arrived, why he had been talking to the people out in the hall. But he was still new to command. He was a young man, not fully comfortable exerting authority. But he was eager for the knowledge, and he knew from whom he wanted to learn.

Alec set down his coffee cup and marched off to the second floor, knocking on the door of Karen's dressing room. She looked up as he came in, her lovely face tearstained and pale. Gil hovered over her, looking desperate.

"Oh, Alec!" She jumped up and threw herself

on him. "Have you heard? I mean, how could they? It's the—"

"I know. I know." Alec freed himself from her clinging embrace.

"You have to call Jenny." Karen's voice was rushed and high. "She has got to rewrite the scene. I can't do it."

Alec wanted to slap her. Jenny was supposed to rewrite the scene? Jenny who had gotten out of bed to cry? Who had been injured here, Karen or Jenny?

Couldn't Karen see that this wasn't about her? It was about Jenny, Jenny's pain, Jenny's humiliation. No, Karen couldn't see that.

But this was not the time to teach Karen maturity. Only one thing mattered, getting the day back on schedule. He spoke to her sternly. "There's a bottom line to all this, Karen. And that is that you are an actor. You are a professional. You are a duchess. So, yes, you have to go up and play a love scene with a guy who's a worm. Yes, you have to let some slimeball put his hands all over you and maybe feel you up." Not for one instant did Alec think Brian would ever do that, but the worse he made Karen's lot sound, the better she would respond. "You think you haven't done that before? And you think you won't do it again? You're an actor, and this is what actors do. They don't pay us to have any dignity. That's where the dignity comes from."

"What?" Gil couldn't help himself. "Say that again."

Alec was not going to say it again. It hadn't

made any sense the first time. Repeating it would only make it sound worse. But this was the sort of romantic nonsense that would have appealed to Chloe, and she and Karen were cut out of the same overly ornamented cloth.

It was absurd, but Karen was falling for it. She squared her brave little shoulders and gallantly prepared to do her duty. She was Mary, Queen of Scots, off to face the axe. Alec crooked his arm, holding out his elbow for her.

Over his shoulder he saw Gil mouthing a "thank you."

Karen was trembling as they went into the blocking room. Lady Varley, Lady Courtland, and other women clustered around her. They weren't quite applying damp compresses to her brow, but that was the general idea.

Why were they being like this? *Nothing happened to any of you. You just like being upset.*

How was Jenny doing? Had she gone back to sleep? No, she wouldn't have. Alec was sure of that. *I'm not with you. Maybe I should be. I don't know. But I am facing the world for you, fighting your battles for you.*

Ray had cleared the room and had gotten everyone organized. Gil lifted a hand. "We're a little behind schedule. Let's just go straight to the blocking. Now, Karen, you're at the desk—"

People started to move to their places. Ray handed Alec a script, already open to Alec's first scene. They had filmed episode 673 Friday which had ended with the duchess's fainting and the butler lifting her up. The prologue to 674 began by repeating the faint and the lift. The scene continued from there. Lydgate entered a page later. Alec focused tight and hard, running through his lines. A sudden hush broke his concentration. He looked up.

It was Jenny.

She did what she always did. She went over to the coffee trolley, got a banana, pulled a chair away from the wall, and sat on it as she always did, perching on the back, her feet on the seat. She was pale, but, by God, she did it.

This was courage. Forget Karen and her cold-compresses hysterics. This was courage—Jenny sitting on the back of a chair, a banana in her hand, facing everyone.

She was running up the colors. *I've been dumped, jilted, rejected, publicly humiliated. I know that's what you're all talking about. So talk away.*

Alec ached to be at her side. It was a physical thing, the need to be there, his arm around her, protecting her. He wanted to do this for her, be the one in the chair, facing the staring eyes. He had done it so often on *Aspen* that he wouldn't feel it. This was a lash his back knew well, but it would whip across Jenny's skin, drawing blood.

He forced himself to stay still. Jenny would get herself through the day.

Karen always turned in a fine, consistent performance. But today was clearly Emmy material. If a person had ever looked on the edge of fainting, it was she. This was dry rehearsal, and her agitation sent shivers through everyone. She'd maintain it all day. She'd be able to repeat it again and again, holding back just enough to peak at the taping.

Hastings was to lay her on the couch. Maids were to rush in, calling for Lydgate. A break in the line of folding chairs marked the set's door. Alec moved into position for his entrance.

Gil spoke. "We're going to need a couple cuts today. Let's lose the maids and go straight to the duke's entrance. What do you say, Jenny?"

She lifted a hand. "Whatever you think."

It was the first time Alec had heard her speak.

So Trina and the other maid sat back down. Alec made his entrance just as Hastings was turning with Amelia in his arms. Alec stepped forward, his arms out. That wasn't in the script. But in the original she would have already been on the couch by the time the maids had found him. Now he was standing there, watching another man carrying her, a servant. Wouldn't even Lydgate step forward?

Hastings, Amelia still in his arms, drew back. His gesture was tense, defensive. *I'm not going to give her to you.*

Lydgate cleared his throat.

It was last night's scene all over again. Then they had been on a stoop, Alec insisting that Brian hand over the key. This time Amelia was the key. Once again Brian had something, and Alec was demanding it back.

But the roles were reversed. Alec was playing Lydgate, a character based on Brian. *So this time I back down. And you get her. Only it's really me.*

He let the duke's face harden into ugly suspicion. It would be the end of the first part of the Prologue.

"Interesting set of choices, Your Grace." Gil's voice was cool. Then again he deferred to Jenny. "Does it change things too much, or shall we let it ride?"

She had come into the room empty-handed, but now she had a script. She was reading through the scene, then flipped forward. She shook her head. "Sorry. You'll need to go with it as written."

"Fine," Alec answered. It was the first thing he had said to her in public. "No problem."

He didn't care what happened in the show. All he cared about was that she understood. *I am not afraid of him.*

He put out his hand for Karen who was lying across the three chairs that served as the couch. As soon as she was on her feet, he moved back toward the table. With the day already so far behind schedule, Gil wouldn't have them run through the scene again. He knew Alec would get it right.

"Can I change my mind?" It was Jenny speaking again.

"Of course," Gil said.

"Then play it as you did," she said to Alec, looking at him steadily and clearly. "You suddenly realize that this person, your butler, this *thing* is in love with your wife. And then you look down at her and you wonder how she feels."

"Fine," he agreed. And then he let his voice go mild. *Oh, gee wilikers, I'm just a Canadian farm boy and I'm a mite curious here.* "But if I really believed that, that a servant of mine has been hankering after my wife, gosh, wouldn't I fire him tomorrow?"

Over his shoulder he heard Brian gasp.

Fourteen

It made for one hell of an interesting day. The episode called for Hastings to be at his most-Alec, full of a take-charge self-confidence. Everyone else was distraught, and while Hastings also cared about Amelia's sudden distress, he alone clamped down all his reactions in order to get things done.

The actor playing the character, however, must have felt the ground crumbling beneath him. He knew he had lost the support of the cast; the incident in the greenroom had made that clear. Then he had been hit in the face with what professional muscle Jenny had. She could write him out of a job overnight if she chose to, and Alec was giving her a perfect excuse to do it.

Nonetheless Brian turned in a credible performance when all was said and done. The guy could act. Alec would grant him that.

But see if you can do it day after day for a year. That's what Alec had had to do on *Aspen*.

Ray and Alec stayed down on the floor until the last scene was taped. They simply stood there, the duke and his heir, arms folded, legs braced, side by side, letting their presence be felt. It dampened the chatter, it kept people from gossiping, and the day finished more or less on schedule.

"Thanks, guys." Gil flicked his finger against his forehead as if tipping a cap. He knew what the pair of them had done for him.

I didn't do it for you. I did it for Jenny. Every problem around here ended up on her lap. Alec had saved her from having to deal with this, but had he done anything to take her misery away? No. He and Ray were doing all that they could, and it wasn't enough.

They went up to their dressing room, and were standing at the mirror taking their makeup off when they heard a knock on the door.

It was Jenny, her face so pale that her freckles almost seemed like drops of blood. She had her hands jammed down in her pockets. It pulled her jeans down low on her hips. He would have done anything to chase the staring anguish from her eyes. That's what he understood—doing—solving, fixing, finishing, making everything right again. But there was nothing he could do now. He was helpless.

He hated that.

Ray was turning from the mirror to greet her. Alec stopped him with a look, and with a quick jerk of the head, told him to leave.

Ray didn't blink. He asked no questions. He turned back to the dressing table, dragged a towel across his face, leaving the white terrycloth streaked with lines of bronze makeup. "I must attend to a matter," he said and disappeared.

That had been a line in today's script.

Jenny spoke quickly. "Gil told me how you helped out today. He said we wouldn't have made it through the day without you."

She wasn't looking at him. "Forget the show. I thought you were going to stay home. Why did you come?"

"I wanted to get it over with. And I wanted to say something to you."

He'd been planning on going back to her house as soon as he was through with work.

Why were they standing so far apart? When Ray had left, she had moved over to stand by the mirror, and he was still by the door. Why wasn't he next to her? Why didn't he have his arms around her? Why wasn't he kissing her, moving her against him, letting go of her only to lock the dressing room door?

Because the tight line of her shoulders, the way she had her arms folded flat against her, was making it very clear: she did not want him to touch her.

"I'm very uncomfortable about the way things ended last night. It wasn't fair to you."

"I don't care about that." His answer was immediate.

"I was using you."

"That doesn't matter." *I love you.* But she didn't want to hear that. "What is it, Jenny?" Then he knew. "You think last night was a mistake, don't you?"

He had known that. The instant that he had unlocked the door to her house, he had felt a certain urgent territorialness. But he had known it would be folly to act on that desire.

Yet he had done it anyway. He deserved this.

"I'm not a character on a soap, Alec."

"Of course you aren't. What makes you say that?"

"I can't solve all my problems by falling in love with you."

That was how characters on the shows solved all their problems, they fell in love. Get bounced off the board of your family company, find out that your mother is really your sister, wake up with amnesia, what should you do? Fall in love, it cures everything.

But it didn't. Not in life. Alec knew that.

Except . . . except . . . in this case, Jenny and him. Surely they were an exception. If she did love him, surely he would be able to make everything right for her, surely he would be able to make her happy.

No, no, he knew that to be absurd. Last night she had been devastated. No one could go from that to being in love overnight. Life didn't work like that. She needed time to recover her strength, her self-esteem.

But I want you to fall in love with me. Right now. I want you to come away from the wall. I want you walking across the room, saying that you love me.

He spoke. "This doesn't have to be about love. It can be about friendship, support."

She shook her head. That wasn't possible. He could pretend, he could be careful of what he said, but neither one of them would ever forget that for him it was about love.

"I have to do this alone, Alec. There's no way for anyone else to help me."

"I'll do anything for you, Jenny."

But what she was asking—for him to do nothing—would be hardest of all.

"I need some time, Alec, to sort this out in my own way. I just need some time."

"Of course. That's fine. I understand." She could have all the time she needed.

After she left, he turned back to the mirror to be sure all his makeup was off.

When the hell had time ever solved anything for Alec Cameron? "Give it time," they had said about Chloe's unwillingness to have a baby. "These things take time." "Give it time," they had said about Derek's rape story. "You'll get comfortable with it over time." "Give it time," they had said about *Aspen*.

And in all three cases he had ended up like Sisyphus, that poor son-of-a-bitch in Greek mythology who had been condemned to spend the afterlife rolling a huge boulder up a hill, only to have it roll back down each night. Time hadn't helped Sisyphus, and it hadn't helped Alec Cameron.

The next day was Tuesday, and Alec came into work early, thinking of nothing but Jenny. How was she feeling? How had she slept? *Where* had she slept? In her own room, or had some impulse taken her up to the room on the third floor? Had she sat on the white wicker chair, looking out through blue-striped curtains? Had she touched the pillows? Smoothed her hand over the quilt? He would have. But he loved her. She didn't love him. She didn't have blue-and-white stripes imprinted on her heart.

Why couldn't she love him? Everything would be fine if only she would love him.

He was at wardrobe without having been aware of walking down the hall. Someone else was leaving the department as he was coming in. It was Rita. There was no avoiding her.

He stepped aside, nodding formally, silently, almost fully in character. He was a duke, she was the upstart daughter of a merchant. He did not have to speak to her.

She was having none of that. She was not going to be brushed off. She planted herself right in front of him. She was wearing a skimpy little red knit tube, so tight that the fabric puckered as it stretched between her breasts. This was not a "I've done wrong, please forgive me" kind of a dress. She too was running up the colors.

"You don't like me, do you?"

That was direct. The Duke of Lydgate couldn't respond to such directness. Alec went back to being himself. "I don't like what you did. But as for liking or disliking you . . . you're nineteen years old. It's too soon to tell. You're too young."

"Too what?" That rattled her. She stared at him, dumbfounded.

She used her youthfulness aggressively. She flaunted her taut skin, the smoothness of her hands, her unmarked legs. She was proud of being young. It made her impervious, invulnerable. She liked being the youngest person in the room; that proved that she had come the farthest the fastest, and she believed that that was a guarantee, that she would always be traveling at that speed. It never had occurred to her that anyone would think her youth a liability, that a man would find her less interesting for it.

"It simply wouldn't be fair to judge you yet." Alec let his voice go heavy, fatherly. He was trying to sound as patronizing as possible. "Ask me in ten years."

She glared at him. "I don't intend to be here in ten years." And she flounced off, the high heels of her strappy shoes clicking angrily. The red dress cupped and strained over her pert little butt. That was one very expressive piece of anatomy back there. She was going to need it.

My Lady's Chamber

MEMO

DATE: November 6
TO: All Cast Members
FROM: Cathleen Yates, publicist.

Thursday, November 8, a reporter and a photographer from *Soap Times* will be preparing a feature on Brian O'Neill and Rita Harber-O'Neill, as arranged by free-lance publicist Dennis Cointreaux. They will have access to the second floor only.

Your cooperation is appreciated.

A feature in *Soap Times*. The rest of the cast did not appreciate that. The angle of the piece was happy-young-honeymooners-at-work—shots of the bride and groom kissing in the stairwell, holding hands and playing cute at the security desk. To get a picture of the pair side-by-side in makeup, the photographer asked Francine to move from her usual chair. He was gracious to her, flattering, even obsequious, and Francine complied, but she didn't like it.

"The Lady Varley," she said in an undertone to Alec, "does not care to be inconvenienced."

Then Pam and BarbEllen were kept hanging around in their costumes while Rita pretended to move out of the dressing room the three of them shared. Of course, Karen and Trina offered the use of theirs, but Pam and BarbEllen preferred to stay in costume, feeling cross and taken advantage of.

"You should see her lift a box," Pam complained. "She wedges it in under those boobs of hers and then lifts. Push-up city."

It soon became clear that Rita's move into Brian's dressing room was no staged photo op. It was for real.

It made a certain amount of sense. Brian was alone in the show's largest room. She was crammed in with two others. Nonetheless the rest of the cast was outraged.

"*He* shouldn't be there," one complained. "He only had that room because he was Jenny's boyfriend."

"And this hall is for men," argued one of the

"confirmed bachelors." "We can't have women here."

But no one seemed to know how to stop her, and by the week's end she had established herself as queen at the head of the men's hall.

So the big happy family now had a new stepmother—a tarty little thing, younger than all the grown children. And the grown children did not like it one bit.

Then Rita cooperated on a story with *The National Enquirer.* ALL FOR LOVE: SOAP STARS RISK WRITER'S REVENGE read the headline. The story was full of quotes from "daytime's hottest star."

"Brian and I share the same dreams, the same goals. You can't begin to know how much we love each other."

Daytime actors hated the tabloids just as much as other celebrities did, perhaps more.

"Jenny has accomplished a lot. I'm not saying that she hasn't. But she has no confidence in herself as a woman. She doesn't enjoy being female. She feels awkward and clumsy about it. She still thinks of herself as a tomboy."

No one on *My Lady's Chamber* had ever said anything other than "No comment" to a reporter from the tabloids. Even on *Aspen* no one had.

"No, we aren't worried about revenge. What can she do? We're both much too important to the show. She'll always do what is right for the show."

Alec went straight up to Jenny's office.

"What do you want?" she snapped.

The *Enquirer* was lying on her desk. No wonder she was snapping. "I wanted to see how you are."

"How am I? I'm just great, thank you. My ex-boyfriend's new wife is telling the tabloids that I'm missing part of my X chromosome."

"She's a tart, Jenny. She's trash."

"No, she's not. She's a fully confident woman. Look." She seized the paper and slapped the story with her hand. "It says so right here. They wouldn't print it if it wasn't true, would they?"

Alec longed to put his arms around her and comfort her. But she would shake herself free, he knew that. "You've been in this business for ten years. You know you can't expect to like everything you read about yourself. The tabloids print lies. You know that."

"I would mind if they were lies. I can deal with lies. I like lies. The bitch about this is that it's the truth."

"No, it isn't." *Don't you remember yourself that night in your guest room? Hold on to that.* But she couldn't. She was dismissing it, writing it off as an aberration. "Not anymore it's not."

"You know where she getting this, don't you? From Brian. That's what I can't stand, the idea that the two of them are talking about me. He's telling her everything he knows about me."

Alec could see why that would bother her. "You've got to expect that. You're the common enemy. Trashing you is the glue that holds them together."

"Oh, wonderful. I'm so proud to have a purpose in life."

* * *

"Shit." Ray slammed the dressing room door.

Ray didn't swear much. "What's up?" Alec asked.

"I can't decide whether to be thrilled or royally pissed off. I just met with Jenny. I'm getting a new story. So is Colley Lightfield."

"That sounds like good news to me." Ray was a terrific actor, and his character had great potential.

"Rita's in it too."

Oh. "I see your point."

It was to be a triangle although not a *love* triangle because as far as Ray could tell, not one of the characters loved one another.

Apparently Robin—Ray's character—was going to find out that he and the duke were only half-brothers. He was the result of an affair their mother had had.

"I didn't know that," Alec said.

"I didn't either. But apparently it's our own fault. Remember back in May or June when we were talking to Jenny about our dads? We were saying we were such totally great guys because we had decent dads. She got the idea then. You're a jerk and I'm wonderful because I had a father who paid attention to me even though I didn't know he was my father."

"Who is he?" In his head Alec ran through a list of the senior male cast members.

"Beats me. I'm not sure Jenny knows either. You know how she makes stuff up as she goes along."

"So what does this have to do with Isabella?" That was Rita's character.

The dowager duchess—Lydgate and Robin's mother—would make Robin promise not to say anything, at least not until the ducal succession was safe. "Technically I am legitimate and all. So if you croak and the baby's a girl, I'm the big kahuna."

"I can die in peace."

But Robin was going to want to end his financial dependence on the Lydgate estate. To that end he would court Isabella.

"Jenny says that it would be more sympathetic than that makes it sound. I don't love the girl, but I like her, and I'm decent to her. It would be a good enough marriage by the standards of the time."

Isabella would feel much the same way, that Lord Robin was a man she would do all right with. Even if she was not from as lofty a social background, he would treat her honorably. "But she knows her father wants her to have a title."

"And that's where Colley Lightfield comes in?" Colley Lightfield was the poor baron with forty jillion sisters.

Ray nodded. "So she accepts a proposal from him. But then in some incident that Jenny hasn't figured out yet, I get a pretty good inkling that he is a practicing homosexual."

So Robin had an interesting set of choices. Should he warn Isabella's father? Encourage him to discreetly get his daughter out of the engagement? But James Marble was from a different class. Robin couldn't count on him to protect the

Lightfield name from scandal. What were Robin's responsibilities? Were they to his fellow aristocrat? Or to this middle-class girl for whom he had some affection?

"It's a good story," Alec acknowledged.

"If only it didn't involve Rita."

Unlike the writers on *Aspen,* Jenny never gave a story to a character until the viewers cared about him. In the weeks before a story was to begin, she always gave an actor plenty of screen time to reinforce the viewers' interest in his character.

So it was clear to everyone that Rita was about to get a story.

Exactly what Rita's story line would be, the cast did not know, but they were familiar enough with Jenny's old-fashioned storytelling techniques to know that one was coming. A new character was introduced, a valet for the merchant, Rita's character's father. His introduction was the excuse for a lot of recapping, and most of it was given to Rita—a sure sign that something big was about to happen for her character.

Rita got four such scripts, one right after the other. Then there was the weekend break and on Monday a fifth script showed up, with her doing just as much.

She was ecstatic, talking endlessly in the greenroom about all the publicity she was getting—she and Brian were repeating their vows at a fan convention and she was going to wear a full-scale bridal gown, cascades of satin and tulle that she was describing in unceasing detail. She was decorating Brian's dressing room; she was insisting that wardrobe lower the necklines on her character's new dresses.

"It's such a good thing I have a phone in my dressing room," she trilled. "I'm getting so many calls. We've had to get an answering machine."

Alec was waiting for someone to stab her with the lunch-table mayonnaise knife.

"I don't get it," cast member after cast member complained. "Why's Jenny giving her a story?"

"It's like she's rewarding her."

"If someone stole my man, she'd be pouring tea once a week for the rest of her career."

"Is that what you have to do to get a story around here? Hire your own publicist?"

Alec felt like he had been here before—in the middle of a nervous, dissatisfied cast. On *Aspen Starring Alec Cameron,* he had felt that he owed it to the cast to do as much as he could. On *My Lady's Chamber,* the cast deserved whatever hysteria they fretted themselves into. His obligation this time was to the writer.

It was time to pay a call upon the lady.

He had been careful not to seek her out. He was determined to give her the time she had asked for. He also discovered that seeing her was not an uncompromised pleasure.

When a fellow had learned to live without something, he should go on denying it to himself until he can be sure of a steady supply. Air-conditioning, coffee, tobacco, enough closet space, these were all things you could teach yourself to live without. Sex, too.

Alec had not been in a relationship in some

time, and that had been okay. There had been moments during the duke's efforts to impregnate the duchess when he had had to stare sharply at the ceiling for a moment or two, but he had always been able to get himself in order without much difficulty.

Then one night with Jenny, and he was having all kinds of difficulty. It was a very specific desire. Rita's twitching mounds of flesh or Karen's graceful throat did nothing for him. He wanted Jenny.

Miss Royall was at her desk outside Jenny's office. "Is she in?" Alec asked.

"She's not happy."

It wasn't like Miss Royall to worry about people's feelings. If people kept their scripts neat and their spines straight, then she was doing her job. Alec felt like he had been given a chore. *Erase the blackboard, sharpen the pencils, and when you are finished, make Jenny happy.*

He knocked lightly. Jenny looked up from her keyboard. She didn't smile, she didn't pop up out of her chair.

"Hello, Alec." She sounded wary.

I'm not going to jump you. You don't have to be scared of me. But she was.

"I'm here to talk about the show," he said.

"Oh." She was relieved.

What had he done to deserve this? Had he been dogging her footsteps? Had he gone to her house, climbed on her garbage cans, and chanted Romeo's half of the balcony scene? He could. He knew where she lived and he knew the part.

He had been conducting himself with dignity

and self-restraint, and she was inching away as if he were a piece of unexploded dynamite.

Which, of course, he was. But he would never explode in her face, and she goddamn well ought to know that.

"Rita's about to get a big story, isn't she?"

She shrugged, lifting her hands in an empty gesture. She didn't have to discuss future story plans with an actor.

That was crap. "Why are you being so goddamn noble?" he demanded. "You're bending over backwards for Rita. Why not be as petty as everyone else? You're entitled. Why not be vindictive?"

"She wanted her chance."

Oh, for God's sake. Every actor on earth wanted his or her chance. That didn't mean they got it. "Is George making you do it?"

"Actually George offered to fire both of them."

Alec blinked. That was a surprise.

An irritating surprise. He expected better of George. Firing Rita would have been vindictive and unprofessional. Firing Brian was just flat-out stupid. His character was much too important to the show. George was being as big a baby as everyone else.

"I suppose you were the one who told him not to."

She shrugged. "Did you notice how Terence and Gil had stopped giving either of them close-ups and how makeup was starting to harden her look?"

No, Alec hadn't noticed and he usually noticed

such things. "I suppose you stopped it all before I saw."

"Yes."

This was wonderful, perfectly wonderful. Everyone was angry at Brian and Rita, everyone wanted revenge. None of it would have been good for the show, and because she cared about the show, Jenny—the person with the greatest right to be angry—had to be the moderate one, the professional one.

Alec wanted her to be fighting, he wanted her to be raging and storming, but how could she? Everyone else was stealing all her lines.

She was trapped. She was stuck in some sort of long, dark tunnel. She didn't care if she were found.

She was sitting with her chin in her hand. She let her head tilt so that her cheek was bearing the weight.

The next Tuesday they taped the first of Rita's big scripts. She did a terrific job. She was funny and pert, suffusing the most routine recapping lines with Isabella's lively personality. Even Ray was impressed. "I've been doing this for two and a half years," he said, "and I'm just now getting the hang of scenes like that."

The next day she distinguished herself again. Was it possible that she really was going to be the next Chloe Spencer?

The third day she had trouble with a couple of her lines. It was nothing much, and if she had been playing the scene with an experienced actor, he would have been able to cover for her.

But David Kendall, the young actor playing the valet, was new to daytime and so it took a couple of takes to get the scene right.

By Friday she was clearly unprepared. Alec could guess what had been happening. To get these performances she—and quite possibly Brian—had had to spend every waking minute preparing. She had energy and stamina, there was no doubt about it, but you couldn't spend four days learning one script if you had five scripts in a row. That was one thing about day-time: the scripts kept coming. It was a never-ending conveyor belt, script after script, episode after episode—they never stopped.

The weekend break didn't help her. She had too many personal appearances to have much of a chance to prepare. So through the next week she was desperate, scrounging, just trying to get through the takes, writing her lines on props or the cuffs of her costume. She was alone out there; no one was going to help her. Edgar De-lany accidentally—Alec did believe that this was a genuine accident—held on to her hand at a moment when she needed to flip her wrist and read her line. Francine accidentally—and Alec wasn't so sure about this accident—filled a tea-cup so that the line written inside it disappeared.

"Oh, my dear, I do apologize," Francine drawled majestically after Gil called for a cut. "I simply forgot. No one has ever needed to do that on this show."

"Some of us already know our craft," Lord Varley said nastily.

Rita was flushed, furious, but she didn't reply.

She started relying on the teleprompter which gave her scenes a vague distracted quality as her eyes shifted toward the camera to read her lines off the rolling screen.

And the teleprompter could only do so much. One day in the middle of dress Terence's voice boomed out over the loudspeaker. "Okay, people. Take five. Rita, please go learn your lines."

Rita froze. This was total humiliation. A production assistant handed her a script and she took a step or two, moving toward a corner of the Bond Street set. Everyone else was standing around, whispering, waiting for her.

She couldn't concentrate. Alec saw that. Her eyes weren't moving across the page; her lips were drawn into a right fierce line. Controlling herself was all she could do. She couldn't possibly focus on the script.

She needed help. It was too bad that Brian wasn't there. He could have gone to her, he could have run her lines with her.

Brian was in today's cast. Alec had a scene with him. There he was, over by the Chinese room. He was idly stretching his neck and shoulder muscles, not looking toward Bond Street where his wife was. *This has nothing to do with me.* His body language was screaming the message. *It's not my fault, not my problem.*

What a rat. He ought to be over there helping her. But he wasn't. He saw that her ship was sinking and he wasn't going down with it.

Rita hadn't moved. The five-minute break was nearly over, and she had hardly looked at the script.

Brian's muscles were all nice and loose now. He began to examine his lapels.

Alec grabbed a script. An instant later he was at Rita's side. "You can do this, my girl," he said to her. "You know you can."

"I don't need your help," she hissed.

"You won't for long, but you do right now. What page are we on?"

She didn't answer. He looked over her shoulder at her script, found the right place in his, and fed her her line. After a moment she cooperated.

She was a quick study, and even though it wasn't much of a performance, they all got through the day.

"I was surprised you helped her," Ray said in their dressing room afterward.

"Someone had to, and that thing she married obviously wasn't going to."

"He sure made a bad bargain, didn't he?"

"Actually I think she did worse. What would you rather be married to, someone who needs help or someone who refuses to give it?"

Fifteen

Jenny saw it all on the monitor in the corner of her office—Rita struggling with the scene, Gil calling for a break, the other people in the cast pulling back from her.

You should be thrilled, Jenny told herself, *thrilled.* Brian was in today's cast, he would be seeing all this. *This is the person who understands your dreams better than I do. This is the person you left me for.*

But she wasn't thrilled. Rita looked so young and alone on the set, the script trembling between her clenched hands. She was stiff with panic and fury.

Then on the monitor Jenny saw Alec crossing the set, coming to help the girl. Rita jerked away from him. He was patient, looking for the place in the script.

Why did he always do the right thing? Jenny glared at the monitor. Where did he get off being so perfect all the time? Why couldn't he screw up once in a while like everyone else?

She wasn't used to perfect men. Her dad had done his best, but he had been nineteen—Rita's age—when she had been born. And Brian, no one could call him perfect, except maybe his mother. But Jenny had loved both of them. So what was a person supposed to do when Mr. Perfect showed up on her doorstep declaring himself in love with her? She didn't have a clue.

I'm supposed to fall in love with you, aren't I?

That's how the story should go. She knew. She had been telling stories all her life.

But I can't.

There was nothing inside her to love with. When she had fallen in love with Brian, she had had a young girl's warmth and spirit. She had been full of a rushing, tumbling, sparkling energy, and her love had glowed. Now she was weary, weighed with doubt.

An hour later George was at her door, coming in and sitting down.

"I suppose you heard what happened on the Bond Street set today," he said.

She nodded.

"It's time to recast Isabella."

Recast Isabella. Jenny shut her eyes. Here it was again. George wanted to fire Rita.

"I know, I know," he spoke quickly. He knew what she was thinking. "I said that right after the two of them got married, but this is different. She's clearly not up to the work."

"She's had a tough couple of days, but surely we can't get rid of her because of a couple of days."

"The timing's such that we have to. Her contract cycle is up next week, and the next chance we'll have to let her go isn't until after the February sweeps. That's when you wanted her story to start."

Jenny glanced at the big calendar on her wall. George was right. If they didn't let Rita go now, they'd have to use her through February, and it made no sense to recast a character right after using her through a sweeps month. Any recasting should be done before.

The weight of the story about Robin and Colley's courtship of Isabella would fall on Ray. But Isabella would have some difficult scenes. She wouldn't know that Colley was homosexual, but on some level she had to feel an uneasiness, a sexual disquiet. And there was no way Rita Haber . . . Rita Haber-*O'Neill* was going to be able to do that.

"I know you feel bad about it," George continued, "but we aren't being unfair. We aren't letting her go because she married your boyfriend, we're letting her go because she can't do the work. She's done this to herself. You aren't to blame. You gave her her chance."

Yes, Jenny had given Rita her chance. Her chance to ruin her career.

She hadn't been noble when she had given Rita this story. She hadn't been bending over backward to be fair. Alec had been completely wrong about that. She had indeed been out for revenge just as surely as George had. Only Jenny was craftier than George. She had gotten her revenge on Rita by giving the girl exactly what she had asked for.

Jenny had known that Rita would not be able to handle this much material. It was too soon in her daytime career; there was too much she hadn't mastered yet. The girl had talent, she had potential. If Jenny had allowed her to develop slowly, she might well have become an important force in daytime. At the very least she would have matured into a useful, productive actress. But she now felt under seige. She would never in this production learn how to be an ensemble player. The damage done to her career might well be irreversible.

Who said that revenge was sweet? Jenny felt sick, utterly disgusted with herself. Yes, Rita had asked for this. Yes, she had spied the bottle on the shelf and pointed to it, insisting that it be served to her. But Jenny had known there was poison in the bottle. She should not have let Rita drink it.

George was still sitting across from her desk, waiting for her to say something. "We don't have to decide anything today, do we?"

"No, no." George stood up. "We can talk tomorrow."

Tomorrow wasn't going to change anything. Jenny knew what was in that script. There was a range of emotion that Rita couldn't possibly pull off, especially since it wasn't anchored in the story or the character. Isabella was getting angry at things the character shouldn't care about. Rita would be worse than ever.

Jenny watched George leave. The churning sickness in her stomach spread. There was no excusing what she had done. She had hurt another woman. She had done something wrong, and someone else would have to pay.

She found herself on the second floor in front of Dressing Room Six. She was knocking. She heard Alec's voice.

Why had she come down here? Why did she keep turning to him?

Because she had no one else.

My Lady's Chamber
Script, Episode #684

LYDGATE:	Those are not the Lydgate pearls, are they?
AMELIA:	No. (TOUCHES HER NECKLACE) These were my mother's. I've always loved them for that. (SHYLY ENTHUSIASTIC, ENDEARING) I know they are small, but she was wearing them in the portrait she sat for just before she died.
LYDGATE:	(HE DOESN'T GET IT) Surely the Duchess of Lydgate should wear the Lydgate pearls. You must change them.
AMELIA:	(DEFEATED) If you wish. (BEGINS TO TAKE OFF NECKLACE)
CUT TO:	PORTRAIT OF AMELIA'S MOTHER, A LONG-DEAD WOMAN WHOSE DAUGHTER IS NOT ALLOWED TO WEAR HER PEARLS.

Alec opened his dressing room door. He was still half in costume. His coat was off and the duke's flowing white shirt was open over the slim black breeches. Cascades of ruffles spilled over his wrists and on either side of his chest.

"You know how you thought I was being so noble," Jenny blurted out. She knew she sounded belligerent, but wasn't this what he liked, honesty? "You were wrong. I did this on purpose. I knew this would happen."

He blinked. It was a moment before he understood. "I assume we're talking about Rita's material and her problems with it?"

"It made no sense." She charged on. "Why would the daughter of the house be talking to the new valet so much? One of the servants from the other houses should have been doing it. That's what I had always planned. Brian could have done this in his sleep. Or Trina, she deserves more work. I gave it to Rita because I knew that she couldn't handle it."

You thought I was wonderful, didn't you? Well, I'm not. So how do you like that?

He was quiet for a moment. "No one can blame you for wanting revenge."

"But that doesn't make it right." She didn't want him excusing this. She would cry if he were nice. "I was wrong and you know it."

"Perhaps you were." He was still calm. "But you might have assumed that the cast would have covered for her more. It wouldn't have been such a mess if she had had some support, but she didn't."

"That doesn't change what I did."

"No," he agreed. "But the system did fail. George should have seen this coming. I know you love it that you don't have to fight for all your good ideas, but that means that there is nothing to protect you from your bad ones."

Why was he talking about George? She wasn't going to blame this on anyone else. It was her fault.

He went on. "And I think you should ask yourself why you went after her when it's *him* you're mad at."

Jenny jerked. As a kid on the playground, she had once been hit in the stomach by a dodge ball. No one had meant to do it, it had been an accident, but it had still been a dull, sickening blow. She felt like that now, sick, unable to breath.

Alec was telling the truth. Of course, it was Brian she was angry with. Rita owed her nothing. It was Brian who had promised everything, it was Brian who had broken his vows.

But she had spent fourteen years trying not to get mad at Brian, fourteen years trying not to see his faults. How was she going to start now?

She was going to cry. In a minute she would be sobbing, and Alec would put his arms around her and murmur all sorts of comforting things into her hair. It would be the same thing all over again, just like during her miscarriage, and after Brian had left her. She would be the weak one, helpless, pathetic. She hated it.

She was not going to let that happen. She could face this with her chin up. "George wants to fire her. He's serious this time."

"You can't ease up on her? She may be very good someday."

"If she ever finds work again."

If *My Lady's Chamber* let her go, the word would be out in hours. Everyone in daytime would hear that Rita couldn't keep up the pace. Who would hire her, knowing that?

Alec was nodding. He understood. "Is there anyway you can monkey with the story to give her the year that she needs?"

Monkey with the story? Again? That's all she had been doing all fall, revising for Edgar Delaney, adding Hastings and Amelia's love story. There was so much to consider—contracts, deadlines, ratings. She felt she was stretched as thin as she could go.

"Did you have something in mind?" she asked.

"No, of course not. You're the one with the imagination, not me."

Jenny guessed that she appreciated that. The network executives never seemed to understand imagination. Half of them assumed that anyone could do her job, and they would come up with story ideas which were creaking retreads of things that had been done and done. At least Alec understood that this was something only she could do.

She moved toward the door. That was one thing she could almost feel good about. She had confessed, but her error hadn't become something he was going to solve for her. She hadn't become Chloe. She put her hand on the door knob, and just as she was moving across the threshold, she stopped and turned back.

"Have we ever said that Isabella is an only child?"

My Lady's Chamber

MEMO

TO: George
FROM: Jenny "When The Going Gets Tough, The Tough Enlarge the Cast" Cotton

Isabella has had it. Town life has gotten to be too much for her. That's why she's been so wooden and flat during the last few episodes. (And you thought this was unintended!!) So her *YOUNGER SISTER* arrives to comfort her. She has all the energy and spunk we saw briefly in Isabella, but she's tougher than Isabella. She'll be able to handle things. And she'll get the Robin-Colley story.

My Lady's Chamber

Audition Script for the Role of Sophie Marble

SOME BACKGROUND NOTES ON THE CHARACTER:

For all that she is a wealthy young heiress, Sophie is a tomboy. She's alert, intelligent, talkative. She has little interest in changing clothes three times a day. The elaborate, artificial manners of the upper crust make her laugh.

> Her beautiful older sister Isabella has always been an abstract ideal to her, someone who she was supposed to be like. But as she sees how town life has crushed her sister, she appreciates her own strength. Sophie likes herself.

Jenny watched the paper curl out of the printer. Sophie was going to be a good character. The audience would love her.

Ever since she had started creating this new character, Jenny had felt the darkness receding. She knew she wasn't over what had happened with Brian, but she now knew that she would get over it. She was starting to feel like herself again. It started with her body, the light, lilting, skipping feeling had returned. She felt eager to move again, she was back to her old ways of twisting herself up like a pretzel whenever she sat down. She was sure of her grasp, she was again interested in the way things felt, the warmth of a coffee cup, the soft knit of a shirt.

My Lady's Chamber
Script, Episode #692

AMELIA:	Pearls, I think, Molly. Wouldn't you agree? With this lace?
MOLLY:	They will look lovely. (SHE TAKES SMALL JEWEL CASE FROM LOCKED DRAWER OF DRESSING TABLE, OPENS IT, AND HANDS IT TO AMELIA. AMELIA DRAWS BACK AND STARTS TO PROTEST. THESE ARE NOT THE LYDGATE

	PEARLS. MOLLY SPEAKS QUICKLY) The other pearls, Your Grace . . . I know they are larger, but they have too much pink in them. The lace will look yellowish.
AMELIA:	Oh. (SHE TAKES HER MOTHER'S NECKLACE OUT OF THE CASE AND HOLDS IT UP TO HER THROAT. SHE LOVES IT. RELUCTANTLY SHE RETURNS IT TO THE CASE) I don't think—
MOLLY:	(OVER) Mr. Hastings says that His Grace sent word that he will not be in for dinner.
AMELIA:	He won't? (THE TWO EXCHANGE GLANCES. A DECISION IS MADE. AMELIA TURNS SO THAT MOLLY CAN FASTEN HER MOTHER'S PEARLS. AMELIA WATCHES IN THE MIRROR)
CUT TO:	PORTRAIT OF AMELIA'S MOTHER

The greenroom was empty when Jenny entered. Something must be delaying the cast. It was lunchtime. The deli platters had already been delivered. Jenny went over to the table and started peeling off the plastic wrap. How domestic she was becoming.

"Hello. Are you the new waitress?"

It was Alec. She knew that without even turning around. "Where is everyone?"

"Hung up on the Almack's set. You put too many people in that scene."

She knew that. But it was getting harder and harder to use everyone.

He had his mail tucked under his arm. "Look at the revised pages," she said. "Page seventeen."

He deposited his other mail on the end table and started to read the salmon-colored pages. There was only a brief mention of the new character. James Marble was flipping through his letters. He exclaimed in delight at seeing one from his younger daughter—this was the first mention of his having more than one child. "Perhaps we can bring her to town," he said to Isabella. That was all.

But Alec knew immediately what it meant. He raised his eyebrows. "So the sister gets the big story? And Rita stays with us?"

Jenny nodded.

"That seems a good solution." Clearly he approved.

She was glad.

The duke was to go out riding in today's episode. Alex had on tall riding boots with spurs. His trousers were buff, his riding dresscoat was a crisp dark green. There was no frill on his shirt today, just narrow vertical pleats. The collar was still open, and between edges of the starched white placket, his chest glowed bronze.

The night they had spent together . . . she had trouble believing that it had really happened. She had been so unlike herself, so full of confidence. Fulfillment had come so easily. She wondered if she could ever be that way again. As the weight of grief and humiliation eased, she thought more and more about it. She wanted it to happen again.

But she knew what Alec would say. *Not until you love me.*

People began to come into the room. Then suddenly it was full, all the cast members who had been in the Almack's scene were crowding in for lunch. There was no place for private conversation, but she remained at Alec's side, taking slices of meat and cheese off the same platter.

Murr and Frank—Lord Courtland and Jaspar—wanted to talk to her about something. They drew her aside. She listened to them while she ate, at least she was partly listening. She kept glancing at Alec.

Murr and Frank finished. Jenny moved back toward the table. Brian was there. He was looking at her, his expression puzzled, surprised.

So he had noticed what she was looking at. *I can look at whatever bodies I want to look at.* She smiled at him with a simpering sweetness. It was the first time she had exchanged any voluntary communication with him since the night he had left her house. *And believe me, there are far better bodies out there than yours.*

"A sister! What do you mean I have a sister?"

Rita's voice rang out across the greenroom. Jenny jerked around. The sandwich almost slid off her plate.

Rita was standing at the door to the greenroom, her face flushed, her gauzy white costume swirling at her ankles. She had the revised pages clutched in her hand. "Nobody said anything about a sister." She was furious.

The greenroom went silent. Everyone drew back, unsettled by Rita's anger, wanting to escape it. Jenny laid her plate down next to the cheese platter. "Yes," she answered mildly. "She's younger. Her name is Sophie, and—"

"I know *that.* I can read. Why do I need a sister? You're taking my story away from me, aren't you?"

Jenny didn't have to answer that. She had no obligation to tell actors about future stories.

"It's because of the other day, isn't it? Because I held things up for all of five minutes?" Rita was livid. "I'm not the only one who had made a mistake. What about the time Karen knocked over the dressing table? That took forever, but she didn't lose her story. I know what you're doing. You're trying to make me quit."

That was the exact opposite of what was happening. Jenny was trying to keep her from being fired.

"If I were trying to make you quit, Rita," Jenny answered, almost gently, "I would succeed."

Rita glared at her. "You're jealous of me." Then her eyes shifted, taking in everyone in the room. "You're all jealous of me. You've hated me since the very first day because I'm going somewhere. I have ambitions, not like the lot of you."

"Maybe what you perceive as the lack of ambition," Murrfield Thomas said, "is simply the knowledge of our craft."

This was the one thing that no one in the cast would ever forgive her for, saying that she was in daytime simply to learn her craft.

"I am not going to stand for this," she announced. "I'm going to go to George. He knows how much viewer support I have. He knows how important I am to the show." She slammed the new pages down on a table and stalked out.

Jenny started to follow her. She needed to stop her. Going to George was the worst possible thing the girl could do. George hated confrontation. Jenny knew what he would do if an actress burst into his office ranting. He would nod and smile, he would make her think that everything was fine, but as soon as the door closed behind her, he would be on the phone with her agent. The girl would be out of work.

But there was no point in Jenny going after Rita. The girl would never listen to her. She needed to act quickly. George was probably in his office. Rita could be there in two minutes.

Jenny moved around the table. She caught Brian's eye and nodded her head toward the corner, indicating that she needed to speak to him.

"You have got to go stop her," she whispered urgently. "You can't let her go talk to George. I can't tell you why, but you can't."

Brian looked at her for a minute, his face more cool and distant than she had ever seen it. "Why ask me? I just open doors around here."

Jenny stared at him. He wasn't going to protect his wife. *But you did so much for me, back when we were putting the show together. Why can't you do as much for her?*

Because he hadn't done all the work on *My Lady's Chamber* for Jenny. He had done it for himself. He wasn't going to do anything for anyone.

Jenny moved back to the table. She picked up her plate and looked down at her sandwich. Ten years in New York and she still liked white bread with mayonnaise. Everyone laughed at her for it, but she didn't care.

How could she have loved Brian? Had he always been so cold and selfish? Why hadn't she seen it?

She moved over to the trash can and dropped her plate in. She wasn't hungry anymore. She had done all that she could for Rita. She had failed.

A hand closed over her arm. It was Ray. "Can you hang around here for a couple more minutes? Alec went after Rita, and he asked me to keep you out of the way."

An hour later Jenny saw George in the third floor hall. It was clear from his easy greeting that he had not seen Rita.

She went into her office and switched on her computer, but she wasn't quite sure what to work on. She needed to find out a lot more about homosexuality in the Regency, what the upper class's attitude really was. That was going to take some fancy research. Maybe she should hire someone else to do it.

Everyone had always been telling her to do less herself. The show was making plenty of money. Jenny could get more help. An editor, a continuity person, a researcher—a couple of part-time people would make an enormous difference in the amount of work she had to do.

Now she understood why she had never wanted to hire those people. It had nothing to do with the budget. She had needed to be busy, desperately, overwhelmingly busy. That was the only way she had been able to hide from how empty her relationship with Brian was.

And suddenly there he was, crossing her office, coming up to her desk.

He hadn't knocked. Of course, he had never knocked before. *Things have changed, Brian. You changed them. You must knock on my door.*

He sat down. She hadn't spoken. "I know things are hard on you right now," he said.

Now that was interesting. After fourteen years he was at last admitting that something might be hard for her.

She still didn't speak.

"I want to help you in any way that I can."

Again very interesting. An hour ago he hadn't been willing to help his wife. Now he was all fired-up to help his ex-girlfriend. "What did you have in mind?" she asked politely.

"If you still want to do that look-alike story between Hastings and a nobleman, I'll sign a two-year contract."

Sign a contract? This was beyond interesting. For two and a half years he had been resisting committing himself to daytime. In fact, wasn't that the great appeal of Rita? That together the two of them would rise out of daytime? Well,

Rita had almost been out of daytime, but "rise" wasn't the right verb.

"Why do you want to do that?" she asked.

"To make things easier for you. I know you've put a lot of time thinking about the story. It must be like money in the bank, a lot of the work has been done. I just want to help you."

The hell he did. Jenny did not believe that for one second. "That's good of you," she said briskly. "But you're too late." This was the truth. "We're working that story up for David Kendall."

"David Kendall?" Brian stared at her blankly.

David Kendall was the young actor hired to play James Marble's valet; he had been on the receiving end of Isabella's recapping. If viewers took to him, this was going to be another one of the big stories for the February sweeps. Into town would come a young viscount, a cousin of the Varleys' impoverished niece Susan. He would look exactly like his bastard half-brother, a valet.

"You're giving the story to someone else?" Brian was stunned.

"When we planned the story for you, we didn't know as much history as we do now," Jenny explained. "A duke's not going to hire a butler that's crawled out of the woodwork. You grew up on the Lydgate estate. We've said that a couple of times. And if you were someone's bastard, people would have known about it, kept track of it, and never put you in such a visible place. But a rich merchant might hire someone whose history was spottier."

"This is beneath you, Jenny. I had thought better of you."

No. What she had done to Rita was beneath her. That had been wrong. This wasn't. This was routine. An actor refuses a story line, so the story goes to someone else.

"You said you didn't want it." *You've done this to yourself, Brian.* "You said that all along. So I gave it to David."

"Then ungive it." Brian's tone was sharp. "The audience cares a lot more about me than they do him. Change it."

There was a white streak running around his mouth. He was raging inside. This was how he used to look at his mother. *So I'm your mother now, am I? Keeping you from doing what you want.*

What was this about? Why did he want this so badly?

Ten minutes later she was back at the door of Dressing Room Six. Ray and Alec were both there. Ray started to leave. "No, no, stay," she told him. "I need some information. Where are Brian and Rita living?" She had never thought to ask that before, but she wanted to understand what had just happened. She needed to know more.

"In your old place in Manhattan," Alec answered. "The Storage Shed or whatever you called it."

"The Broom Closet. Why on earth are they there? It's really small. It would barely hold his clothes, much less hers."

"I imagine that they haven't been able to find anything else."

Housing in New York was expensive. "But they have two incomes."

"Don't overestimate that." Ray spoke up. "You both make too much money to have any feel for this. But the amount Rita has been spending on her clothes, her fan club, her publicist, that's got to be her whole income. I don't know it for a fact, but I'd bet a month's pay that until she married Brian, she was living with her folks, not paying for food or rent or anything."

Rita had not stopped buying new clothes since she had gotten married, she had not stopped using her publicist. She was undoubtedly expecting Brian to pay for room and board, just as her parents had always done.

But Brian had always spent all his salary, even though he had paid for none of the expenses associated with the Brooklyn house. Clothes, restaurants, theater tickets—a person could drop a lot of money living in New York. And Brian had.

He needed money. That was why he had at last been willing to sign a long contract. That was also why he had been so angry with Jenny, why he had felt entitled to the story. She had been paying his way for the last couple of years; in his heart he expected her to continue.

Did he feel he deserved "palimony?" No judge would ever award it to him, not after he had left her. Even if she were in the clear legally, maybe morally she did owe him something for the year he had supported her. If he asked directly, she would hire a lawyer and come to some kind of settlement. But she wasn't going to offer. He was going to have to ask. In fact, he was going to have to beg.

Sixteen

ZELDA OLIVER TO LEAVE *DAY BY DAY*

We can't confirm it, but the rumors won't stop. Zelda Oliver may leave *Day By Day* to join the cast of *My Lady's Chamber*. The highly popular twenty-year-old actress has become one of the mainstays of *Day By Day*.

"She's grown up in our living room," says Dot Ellsworth, president of Zelda's fan club. "She has been playing the part of Nicole for fourteen years. We love her. It's impossible to imagine *Day By Day* without her."

Zelda is reportedly fed up with the turnover in the *Day By Day* writing staff; there have been three different head writers in the last eighteen months. *My Lady's Chamber* does appear to have a part that would be perfect for her, Isabella Marble's younger sister.

No one from either show will say anything official, but we're going to be surprised if it doesn't happen.

—*Soap Times*,
December 15

Everyone in the greenroom was upset, but then everyone in this greenroom was always upset. They liked it. Alec listened patiently.

"Zelda Oliver's going to join the cast?" Murrfield Thomas slapped some mustard on his bread. "That's not possible."

Alec wondered why not.

"She's been Nicole for fifteen years." Francine speared a piece of low-salt turkey breast. "She *is* Nicole."

No. She was an extremely talented actress.

"The audience will never accept her as anyone else." Pam broke a cookie in half.

That's what people had said when Alec had left the part of Derek.

"What do you think, Alec?" Ray asked.

"I think we need someone who can hit the ground running." With the February sweeps approaching, Sophie Marble was going to be in the thick of things from her very first episode. "We don't have time to ease anyone else in. We can't afford to take a risk. Zelda Oliver is going to be able to do the work."

"But she's a star," Frank complained. "She'll be expected to be treated like a star. She'll change everything."

This was everyone's real concern, that Zelda would not fit in, that she wouldn't become a part of the big, happy family. And she probably wouldn't. She already had a well-established life within the daytime community. She had her own circle of friends, her own selected charities. She would not be the emotionally needy foster child, grateful for every smile.

There's a reason for that, folks, Alec thought. *What we have here isn't right. It's warm, it's satis-*

fying, but it isn't keeping the trains running on time.

Soap Times had hit the newsstands in the middle of the morning. When Jenny came into the greenroom to get some lunch, people pounced on her, full of questions about Zelda.

"I'm sorry," she said. "I can't discuss it." She looked pale and tense.

"Come on, Jenny," someone protested. "This is us. You can tell us. You can trust us."

Alec waved them off. Jenny didn't need this. The idea of the big, happy family was as important to her as it was to anyone, if not more so. Writing was so much more solitary than acting. That left her every bit as afraid of change as the cast was. And she also had to face that this particular change was her fault. If she hadn't pushed Rita too hard, there would have never been a need to cast this new character.

He watched her get a carton of yogurt. *Leave,* he willed her. *Eat upstairs today. Let everyone know that things must change. Show the big happy family that they are neither happy nor a family.*

But she had been alone too much as a kid. She wasn't going to seek solitude now. She sat down next to Trina and BarbEllen. From the way that the two of them drew close and started talking quickly, Alec knew that they were asking about Zelda, wanting to know more.

Jenny's face went tight and tense again. Clearly she hated being in this position, having information that she couldn't share. It made what she did seem like a job.

This is going to keep happening, my love. Again and again. Because the bottom-line truth is that, however much you love what you do, it is a job.

Alec felt a movement at his shoulder, a light warmth. It was Karen. Her hair hadn't been done yet, and it floated over her shoulders like a dark cloud outlining her long, graceful neck. She drew close to him. "Can we go out in the hall?" she whispered. He had to bend his head to hear her. "I need to talk to you about something."

"Of course."

They went down the hall past the doors to the studio floor. Karen stationed herself so that she could see both the fire door leading out of the stairwell and the guard desk near the front entrance. She glanced both ways. Clearly she considered herself to have a major secret.

Again she spoke softly, conspiratorially. "Have you talked to Jenny recently?"

Alec shook his head. "No."

"I think you need to. I really think that—"

"If this is about Zelda Oliver, I will not get involved." He made no effort to lower his voice. He didn't care who heard. "The cast has no part in this decision."

"No, no." Karen's mass of hair shimmered as she shook her head. "It's about you. You need to talk to her about you." She put her hand on his arm. "She can't write for you anymore."

"Can't write for me?" Alec drew back. "What are you talking about?" He had seen the schedule for the next two months. He was appearing as regularly as ever. Of course, Jenny was writing for him.

"I don't know for sure, but it's an instinct I have—"

Karen's instincts were the gloomiest creatures on the face of the earth. Alec was not going to get too upset by anything Karen's instincts had to say.

"When we were doing today's scenes, I could feel Amelia start to relax. She's starting to be able to predict what you're going to do. That's great for her. She's starting to feel safe again. But it's terrible for you, Alec. If she can predict everything Lydgate's going to do, he isn't dangerous anymore. Then he has no purpose. I think you're going to die."

"Oh, come on," he scoffed. "Jenny's not going to kill me."

She felt too guilty about not loving him to ever fire him.

"Well, maybe you won't *die,*" Karen answered. "But if Jenny can't write for you, your part will get so boring you'll go mad. I know you don't want to believe me, but I'm right about these things. You know I am."

She had him there. Hastings falling in love with Amelia, Rita being a danger to Jenny—Karen had sensed those long before anyone else, and she had been right.

She could tell that he was relenting. "It's like Jenny's imagination is no longer engaged with the character." She was speaking quickly, relieved that he was going to listen, that she wasn't Cassandra prophesying the future only to be disbelieved. "He's a placeholder, a stick figure that she has to use, but she's not interested in him. She doesn't want to write for him anymore."

Because she's not interested in Brian anymore. Maybe this had nothing to do with him at all. It was about Brian. Jenny had used Lydgate's character to hide from her doubts about Brian, but she had faced those doubts now. She didn't need the character. She had nothing left to say about him.

But she would never get rid of the character because she felt too guilty for not loving the actor.

Alec didn't want to keep his job because she felt guilty. Why did she keep living her life through the show? Why couldn't she deal with her feelings, her doubts, her anxieties directly? Why did she always have to route everything through the stories she was telling?

"So you'll go talk to her?" Karen was insistent. "You see the importance of it, don't you?"

Of course he saw the importance of it. After all, he was the one who would be stuck playing a stick figure for the remaining two and a half years of his contract. But what earthly good would there be in talking to Jenny? If she wasn't interested in Lydgate, she wasn't interested in Lydgate. It was infuriating, it was all so stupid, so unnecessary. If only Jenny wouldn't—

If only Jenny would love him.

That's why he was mad at Jenny. He wasn't mad at her because Lydgate was a stupid role. Stupid roles were part of the ebb and flow of an actor's life. He was mad at her because she didn't love him.

It was the show's fault, or rather her obsession with the show. He was suddenly convinced of that. Every time something seemed halfway wrong with her life, she closed her eyes and stuffed the cracks in her heart with padding from the show. It kept her from needing anything else. She wasn't going to fall in love with Alec or with anyone else as long as she was so obsessed with the show.

And you couldn't rescue someone from their obsessions. There wasn't anything you could do, not a blessed thing. As long as Jenny was writing the show, she would be obsessed by it.

What did he want to have happen? For the show to be cancelled? For her to be fired? Of course not. Either one would destroy her.

And the show wasn't going to be cancelled. She wasn't going to be fired. There was no way out of this. There was no happy ending. There was nothing Alec could do.

Wordlessly they joined hands. Everyone was there, except Meg. The memory came back, sharp and urgent. *His father's voice was heavy. "There is nothing more to be done. We must let her die in peace."*

Jenny got the first call at 7:30 the next morning. It was from Steve, one of the production assistants. "Alec's not here. He's late. Where is he?"

"How should I know?" Why did everyone assume she was going to know everything? "Did you call his house?" Of course, they had called his house, but his answering machine had picked up the call. "Sometimes he takes the subway. Maybe there's a problem on his train."

Miss Royall called the Transit Authority. His subway line was running as normally as it ever did. Jenny refused to get upset. People were late. It happened.

He still had not arrived by 8:00. By 8:15, they needed to do something. If he wasn't coming in, they needed to rewrite his scenes. Jenny went down to the rehearsal hall.

Things were a mess. Terence hadn't taken control; he wasn't keeping things on schedule. All anyone could talk about was Alec. "He must have been in some kind of accident."

"Maybe he's dead."

"He's not dead," Jenny snapped. She would know, wouldn't she, if he were dead. Wouldn't she feel it?

"This may be my fault." Karen looked as if she had been telling everyone that all morning. "I have some grave concerns about where Lydgate is going, and we talked about it yesterday."

Was Karen suggesting he had bolted because he was in a snit about his character? "Alec has been on daytime for ten years." Jenny's voice was tight. "He's not going to pout because his character isn't in a front-burner story every second."

There was no way to explain this. Jenny couldn't imagine what would keep Alec from coming to work.

She picked up the script. Lydgate was in three

scenes. She would need to rewrite them all. She glanced through them. He was mostly doing recapping. She hadn't realized that. Why wasn't he doing something more interesting? Oh, well, she hardly had time to think about that now. She should just be grateful. It would make it that much easier to write him out.

Whom could she give Lydgate's lines to? She glanced through the day's cast list on the first page of the script. Hastings was in the line-up. Brian was good at recapping. He had a quick memory and he could take a heavy dose of new material.

But she didn't want to give anything to Brian. Robin was also in today's cast. It was time to let Ray prove himself. She started slicing away at the script.

She had to completely rework the scenes, adding new entrances and exits. It felt like as much work as writing a new script. *Like I didn't have anything else to do today, Alec Cameron.*

At ten George called Alec's agent. "She tried to cover for him, but in truth she was as surprised as we were. She asked for a week's emergency leave of absence, but she's really in the dark."

By now Jenny was furious. She might have expected this from other people—Karen, Frank, Murr, or Francine. They were all capable of fits of artistic temperament. But Alec? He was the one they all counted on. He couldn't suddenly blow off like this. He didn't have the right.

She stormed up to her office and called him herself. The phone rang and rang. Now even his machine wasn't picking up. He was home. Why wouldn't he answer the phone? Why couldn't she make him answer the phone?

Here she was, in the middle of all this crap with Zelda Oliver, reworking the story outline once again to accommodate Zelda's agent's demand for a three-times-a-week guarantee, and now Alec didn't come into work. He was supposed to be on her side. Wasn't that what he had been claiming? That he was in love with her, that he would move the moon and the stars for her?

I don't need you to move the moon and the stars for me. I just need you to come into work.

She was going to go get him. She picked the phone back up to call the car service. She would plant herself on his doorstep. She wouldn't leave until he came out and talked to her.

Five minutes later she was in the car. She sat in the backseat, her arms folded angrily. He was the one person she had thought she could count on not to cause problems on the set. *You didn't do this to Paul Tomlin on* Aspen. *Why are you doing to me?*

She had gotten his home address from personnel. He lived on the Upper West Side, in a quiet, residential street of well-tended brownstones. It was such a perfect New York street, the kind that got used in movies that were romantic comedies, movies where the characters "met cute." Well, there was nothing romantic or cute about any of this, and it sure as hell wasn't a comedy either.

She marched up his front steps and knocked

on the door. She didn't hear anything inside. She knocked again. *You might as well answer, because I'm not leaving.* Just as she was about to knock yet again, she saw the peephole darken. He must be looking out. She had read a murder mystery where the killer shot through the peephole. That way you caught the victim right in the eyeball. Sounded good to her.

He opened the door. She didn't give him a chance to speak. "Where have you been? Why didn't you come to work? People are counting on you, people are relying on you. Don't you know that?"

"Why don't you come in?"

Why didn't she come in? What did he think this was, some kind of social call? "No, I don't want to come in. I just want to find out why you didn't come in to work."

"Jenny, it's December." He was speaking patiently. "It's below freezing. Please come inside."

"What's wrong with out here? Why can't you tell me what's going on out here?"

He popped the lock on the door and stepping out onto the stoop, pulled the door closed behind him. He had on a long-sleeved undershirt and a flannel shirt. That wasn't enough in this weather.

Well, great. She had at last pulled off a major girl-stuff move—getting a man to put up with total and complete irrationality.

"Oh, all right. We can go in." She could back down, but she couldn't be gracious.

He opened the door and stepped back. She went into a narrow, ivory-walled hall. The floor boards were sanded and stained. A recessed light shined on a small watercolor portrait. It was of a little auburn-haired girl. She had Alec's eyes. It must be his sister Meg.

Jenny felt him at her back, his hands at her shoulders. She tensed. What was he doing?

Helping her with her coat. She felt like an idiot. She pulled her arms free and watched as he laid it across the bannister.

Why on earth was she here? Why had she gotten so angry with him? If anyone else had missed a day of work, she would have rolled her eyes. *Oh, the things the children will do.* She could be the forgiving mother. Except with him. She had been the betrayed wife.

He directed her through an arched opening to the living room. The room had all the right furniture—a sofa, two side chairs, a few little tables, everything fresh and sleek—but it was clear that Alec never used it, except maybe as a closet. One basketball nestled in the seat of the wing chair, another one rested on top of a wastepaper basket. A hockey stick was propped up against the sofa, and a pair of unlaced skates were in front of the fireplace. Three different kinds of racquets were by the door. The table was piled with mail, magazines, loose change, and cans of tennis balls.

Jenny could imagine him coming home, dumping his mail on the table, aiming the basketball at the waste can. It would have to be a soft, perfectly aimed lob. Otherwise the ball would glance off the metal rim, roll to the floor, and ricochet off the skates.

She spoke. "I've never been ice skating."

He must think she was crazy. Walk out of work, sit in traffic for forty-five minutes, just to tell him she had never been ice skating? She thought she was crazy.

"I could have taught you." He motioned for her to sit down. "You would have been good at it. You have a strong sense of balance."

It was a nice thought, going ice skating with him. Thick sweaters and long mufflers, frosty air, hot chocolate, gloved hand in gloved hand.

Could have taught you. Why not can?

Jenny sat down. "Not showing up for work . . . that's not like you, Alec."

"No, it isn't. I have always been Mr. Responsible."

He had been more than responsible. He had been resourceful and insightful, patient when patience was called for, firmly decisive when the time for patience was over. What had happened?

"Karen said that the two of you had talked about how flat Lydgate might be getting. I know he doesn't have a lot of ambiguity, but that's something we can work on, something we can fix." Alec's expression hadn't altered. Jenny had no idea what he was thinking. "I mean, if that's the problem." She could hear herself falter.

"This isn't about Lydgate. This isn't about the show."

"It's not?" Jenny didn't understand. If it wasn't about the show, what could it be about?

"It's about you and me."

Oh, of course. Jenny waited for herself to say something. She was never speechless. Sometimes it was mindless babble stirring the air current, but there was always something coming out of her mouth.

Not now.

It's about you and me.

What could she say to that?

"Karen's right," Alec continued. "Lydgate's a selfish chowderhead. Another six months of playing him and I'll be out of my mind."

"But that's what I was talking about," she protested. "We can work on that. I don't know how yet, but—"

Alec held up his hand, stopping her. This wasn't about the show. She gripped the arms of the chair, forcing herself to stay quiet. How could this not be about the show? Everything was about the show, wasn't it?

"I can't make you love me, Jenny. I would do anything, anything at all, but there's nothing I can do."

Nothing. His voice was flat. There was a painting over the fireplace, an oil. It was a seascape, a narrow beach bounded by boulders and trees. She wondered if it was a painting of his home, Prince Edward Island. She wanted to ask. They could talk about that, about the terrain, the climate. His voice would not be so flat if they were talking about that.

He went on. "Every other time I've faced something hard, I've always felt like there was something more I could do, if I just tried harder, if I kept soldiering on, then there was a chance." His voice seemed to be coming from a long way off. "But there isn't now."

The world was swimming, the picture over the fireplace was a gilt-edged blur.

"I've never quit at anything." He was still speaking. "I'd still be married to Chloe if she hadn't asked me to leave. I wouldn't have quit *Aspen*; they had to fire me. I don't quit. But I think I have to now. There's nothing more I can do."

He seemed so faraway. "I don't understand. You're quitting the show?"

It was the wrong thing to say. She knew that, but that's how she always thought about everything—what it would mean to the show.

"I don't know," he answered. "I don't care. This is all about you. I can't quit loving you, but I can quit hoping that you will love me back. That's what I am doing. Quitting."

The ribbed collar and cuffs of his heavy, white undershirt showed beneath the dark plaid of his shirt. She used to know the names of a lot of plaids. The Camerons must have one. She couldn't remember what it was like.

"I'll keep your part open." That was all she could think of to say.

But he didn't care about his part. This wasn't about the show. *I'm no good at anything but the show. Unless we talk about the show, I have nothing to say.*

She stood up and let him walk her to the door.

"You write the best show on daytime, Jenny." His voice was steady. "But that's not enough for you. You have let it become your life. You get everything you need from it. I can't compete with that."

Things were whirling. She heard what he was saying, and yes, there was truth in it, but there was more, much more. Only she didn't know what it was. She felt his fingertips at her chin, lifting her face so that she was looking at him.

"When Chloe and I split up, I told her that I would always be there for her. That's still true. I would do anything she asked of me. It would be easy because I have stopped loving her. But I cannot say the same to you. I am not going to be here for you, Jenny. I cannot be your friend. I cannot help you solve your problems. I don't want you to ever come back here. It would hurt too much. I cannot help you, because I will never stop loving you."

He nodded farewell and eased the door closed, and she was left on the street, the street where they make romantic comedies, the street where people are supposed to "meet cute."

Seventeen

It took her two eighteen-hour days to write Alec out of the next three weeks. She didn't go into the studio, she didn't answer the phone, she didn't open her mail, she simply worked.

It was hard, nightmarishly hard, but it was her punishment, the penalty she owed for not loving Alec. And it was something she could do for him. She could protect his job . . . even though he didn't care about his job.

She went back to the studio, feeling weary and fragile. This was how she had felt after the miscarriage, filled with a strange, silvery grief for something that hadn't happened, that couldn't have happened.

And just like after the miscarriage, she went back to work and no one seemed to notice that anything was wrong with her. She wanted help, she wanted sympathy and support. All anyone could talk about was dressing rooms.

"I can't believe it." She couldn't even try to be patient. "We have two incomplete shows in the can." They had had to tape two episodes leaving out Lydgate's scenes until Jenny rewrote them. "That means we're almost down to a three-day delay, we've got two holidays coming up, and people are worried about dressing rooms?" She could hear her voice rising, shrewlike. "For God's sake, what's the problem?"

"It's nothing," George waved his hand. "Just actor-to-actor stuff. It will sort itself out."

Jenny left his office in disgust. Things around here never sorted themselves out. Someone had to do the sorting. George was simply making it clear that he wasn't going to be that someone. How on earth did you get to be executive producer on a soap when you were afraid of confrontation?

Brandi in makeup explained the problem to her. David Roxbury—Sir Peregrine—was finally rejoining the cast after New Year's. He had previously shared a dressing room with Ray, but Ray liked sharing with Alec. Edgar and Murrfield Thomas, the cast's two senior males, were comfortable together, as were the "confirmed bachelors" in their rooms at the far end of the hall.

"So David thinks that he should share with Brian."

"That makes sense." Brian did have the biggest dressing room.

"Rita's moved in there."

Oh. Jenny had forgotten that. She had known about it, but she hadn't wanted to deal with it so she had let herself forget about it. "Then why not get Rita out? That's the men's corridor. She needs to move back into wherever she was before."

"She says she can't. She needs the phone." Brandi's voice grew sarcastic. "In case her publicist calls."

"I don't get it. Does Brian have a phone?" She thought the dressing rooms didn't have phones.

Brandi nodded. "One was put in before you got your office."

And no one had taken it out. And no one had ever been assigned to share Brian's dressing room. He had been the head writer's boyfriend. Everyone must have assumed that she had wanted him to have special treatment. She hadn't. Even when he had been her boyfriend, she hadn't wanted it.

"Then let's rip his phone out. There's no reason why one actor should be treated better than the others."

An hour later she could see that that was not the best solution. If phones were such a big deal, why not put phones in everyone's dressing room? How much could it cost? The show made all these people schlep out to Brooklyn every day. At least they could have phones.

She drafted a memo to George, suggesting better lunches, new furniture in the greenroom, phones in the dressing rooms, cushioning and carpeting the stairs. She clicked on the final *Print* command reluctantly. The shoddy greenroom, the drab deli lunches, these deprivations gave the studio its character; complaining about them united everyone, made them comrades in arms, a family. She hated the idea of that changing.

You have let the show become your life. You

get everything you need from it. I can't compete with that. Alec had said that.

Jenny did not have a merry Christmas.

David Roxbury returned after New Year's, and Zelda Oliver joined the cast. Her performance was dazzling. Sophie was instantly heralded as one of the most delicious characters to hit daytime. But whenever Zelda was not rehearsing or taping, she was in her dressing room. She didn't hang out in the greenroom, she didn't want to make friends.

David too had changed. His run on off-Broadway had lasted nine months. He was glad to see everyone on *My Lady's Chamber,* but he had another set of friends now. He had developed relationships with the cast of the play he had been in. *My Lady's Chamber* wasn't his whole life anymore.

Nothing felt normal. Gil got sick, a prostate infection that wouldn't clear up, the doctor told him, unless he spent a week in bed. Terence couldn't bear the thought of bringing in a substitute director even though some very good ones from *Aspen!!* were still looking for work. So he did all five shows that week, and he was bleary-eyed, unable to keep the taping on schedule. Every single night that week people were working until eight and nine o'clock.

On the day Gil returned, the stairs were being carpeted, and everyone was having to use the freight elevator. It was very slow, and crowds of people developed on every floor. Jenny couldn't believe it. Why hadn't someone paid an extra ten percent to get job done on the weekend? The show was making a lot of money for the network.

After lunch she joined the group of actors who were waiting for the elevator to take them back up to their dressing rooms.

"We have been here late every single day since December twentieth," Francine complained. "We need Alec back."

"No, we don't need Alec," Jenny snapped.

He was an actor. They had done the show for two years without him; they could do the show for another twenty without him. It was George's job, Gil and Terrence's job, to get them all through each day, not Alec's.

Everyone was fractious, bewildered. They wanted to know where Alec was. They wanted to know why he wasn't coming in.

"Maybe I overreacted to his character," Barb-Ellen said. "Maybe I wasn't nice enough to him."

Maybe Lord Courtland had tried too hard to upstage him. "I do that, you know," the actor admitted.

Jenny couldn't stand it anymore, listening to all of them trying to put themselves in the center of this drama. She broke free from the crowd around the elevator. She didn't know where she was going. All her work was upstairs, but if she stayed another moment, she'd blurt out everything to everyone. *This has nothing to do with any of you. It's because of me. Alec isn't here because of me.*

But she couldn't say that.

She found herself in the greenroom. Some extras were playing cards. They looked up when she entered. Did she want them to move? Did she want their table? They would have done anything. She was a head writer; they were extras. No, no. She waved at them to keep in their seats.

Suddenly Ray was at her elbow. "Jenny, are you all right?" Trina and Karen were there too. They all looked worried, their faces anxious, their eyes drawn. They cared about her. They didn't like to see her distressed.

Why shouldn't she tell them what was going on? They were her friends, her family. How could they comfort her if she didn't tell them?

It was the most foolish thing she had ever done. Within twenty-four hours everyone knew. *Alec won't come back until Jenny falls in love with him.*

Every day she felt like she was being surrounded by twenty doctors, constantly taking her temperature. *Are you in love yet?* They wanted to speed the cure. They were constantly praising Alec to her, raving about how great he was, how strong, how much they all needed him.

She knew all that. *Don't tell me that. I don't want to hear how we need him. I want to know how he needs me.*

Alec was great at playing the rescuer, he was great at taking care of things. But Jenny didn't want someone else to rescue her, she wanted to rescue herself.

Two days later Brian caught up with her in the hall. He tried to take her arm, but she pulled back. She didn't want him touching her. He was left with his hand dangling uselessly in the air.

He spoke anyway. "I admire your integrity."

"Integrity? What do you mean, integrity?"

"I guess that's not the right word. Loyalty, I suppose that's it. Steadfastness."

Integrity. Loyalty. Steadfastness. What was he talking about? Of course she had all of those qualities, but she had had them every day for the past fourteen years. And he had always taken them for granted. Why was she suddenly so admirable today?

"I have no idea what you're talking about," she said briskly. *And I don't care.* She hoped that was clear.

He blinked. "Oh . . . you know, what everyone's been saying . . . about you and Alec."

Dear God in Heaven. He thought this was about *him,* that she didn't love Alec because she was being loyal and steadfast to *him.*

She wanted to slap him.

There wasn't going to be an Emmy for Jenny Cotton this year. As wonderful as all the story lines were, she was having to rush every one of them. Her first boss, Flo Newman, one of the *grande dames* of daytime, called her with a gentle caution. Not that Jenny needed it. She knew what she was doing wrong.

And there was such a simple solution. Go to an hour. An hour would give her the time to tell each story properly.

She hated the thought. It would be the end of the family. How she had loved this place, loved coming in here, knowing that everyone trusted her, loved her, needed her. She would never know the new actresses as well as she knew Trina, Karen, BarbEllen, and Pam. From now on everytime she walked into the greenroom it would be like the cocktail hour before the Emmys. Too many people would be thinking of her as the head writer, as the one with power, the one they had to make nice to.

But she had to do it. *Why isn't writing the best show on daytime enough for you?* Alec had asked that. And the answer had a bitter twist. If she didn't let go of everything else she loved about the show, it no longer would be the best show on daytime.

She picked up the phone to call George. *Tell the network we'll do it.* She hung up. There was a letter she wanted to write first.

January 21

Dear Alec,

You'll soon be hearing rumors that we are taking the show to an hour. They are true.

Jenny

He would know what this meant. He would know how reluctantly she was doing this. He would understand.

He didn't answer her letter.

I am not going to be here for you. I cannot. It would hurt too much.

This was what he had meant.

* * *

The network had to have their usual endless meetings before officially approving a schedule change, but within days the money started to flow. The unfinished space on the third floor was being turned into additional dressing rooms. No longer would all the actors be housed college-dormlike on a single, friendly floor. A new director, Diane Southfield, was hired to do one show a week. Visually she copied Terence and Gil's style; her true interest was in character. The actors started asking her the questions that they once would have asked Jenny. That hurt.

Does this make you happy, Alec? Now we are like everyone else.

No, of course, it wouldn't make him happy.

It was too late for him and her. Even if she woke up one morning, passionately in love with him, it would be too late. She could feel that through Hastings's character. Hastings was dying emotionally. His noble self-denial was costing him too much. He was deeply in love with an unattainable woman, and he accepted that completely. He never questioned her unattainability, he never strove to alter the relationship.

"Why can't he get angry?" Jenny overheard Brian asking the new director. He was worried about his character's future.

"Because he has no hope or expectation," Diane answered. "Without that he cannot be angry."

Alec had been angry for a moment, for one flashing, red-hot moment, he had been angry at Jenny. He wasn't angry anymore. And it was a form of death.

* * *

My Lady's Chamber
Script, Episode #717

MOLLY: Mr. Marble offered you a job, didn't he?
HASTINGS: Yes, but I'll not leave His Grace's employ. Ever.
MOLLY: (GENTLY) Another household might be more congenial.
HASTINGS: (STIFFENS. HE KNOWS SHE IS TALKING ABOUT AMELIA. HE DOESN'T WANT HER SYMPATHY) It is out of the question.

Molly's love for Hastings had now fully blossomed. She grieved for his unhappiness. She wanted to help him, but he wouldn't let her. Her love was generous, warm, expansive in contrast to Amelia's love for him which was born out of fear and despair.

Brian kept trying to add a warmth for Molly to his performance. He didn't want his character to become unsympathetic. But every time he tried to have Hastings soften toward Molly, the directors, acting on Jenny's instructions, clamped down on him.

"You're making yourself into the ideal white knight," Jenny overheard Diane Southfield say. "We want people to see the cost of that."

Diane was a poised, glossy Long Islander. Because she only came in one day a week, Jenny felt like they hardly knew each other. But no one had ever understood her material as completely as Diane did. The best show on daytime was better when Diane directed.

And Jenny was surviving. It was no fun to go home to an empty house. It was no fun having people treat her differently. She was lonely.

But she had been lonely before. She did exactly what she had done when she had been lonely as a child—she made up stories. It looked like the show would go to an hour at the beginning of the May sweeps. She needed to outline all the new stories and write audition scripts for the new characters.

Other shows were calling, wanting to know if Alec was being released from his contract. *Passions* wanted him back. They wanted him to work with Chloe again. His character's body had never been found. He could still be alive. *Day by Day* wanted him too. They were still reeling from the loss of Zelda. His character on that show had clearly died. They had had a body, a coffin, a funeral, everything, but they didn't care. They would figure something out.

Less than a year ago he had been unemployable. Now everyone had forgotten all about *Aspen*.

I did do that for you. I did help you clear your name.

But that wasn't enough. The new director was right. The white knight paid for his gleaming goodness; he moved too far from the muck and ashes, the passion and shadows that made up real life. Jenny could see that happening to Alec. He would become the elder statesman of daytime, respected by all, the one who got things done, the one everyone else leaned on. But there would be something empty and distant about him.

She longed to help him. Her heart mourned for him, for the lost possibilities.

How close this was to love. But if it was love, where was the delight and the sparkle? This was all dried roses and regret.

They were too young for that. She thought about the night on the third floor of her house. The roses had been blooming that night, their roots thrust deeply in dark, rich soil. Jenny remembered herself picking up the knife to slit the sleeves of her shirt. Where had she gotten that passion?

From her imagination. It had fired her that night; it was keeping her warm now.

Where do you get your ideas? People asked her that all the time. *It's involuntary,* she always answered. *They just come.*

But they came from somewhere, they came from her imagination. *You have your mother's imagination,* that's what her father had always said.

Lily. Her mother. She was just a name to Jenny. A name and a few pictures. Jenny had imagined her to be the loveliest, most feminine of creatures, as graceful as her name. But Lily hadn't chosen her name. And she hadn't liked the people who had.

Her mother had been the first character Jenny's imagination had created. The character had been a source of comfort to Jenny, but she had also been a standard by which Jenny had measured herself. *My mother would have been good at this; I am not.*

What did she really know about her mother? One important thing—that she had fallen in love with Jenny's father.

He had been a professional pool player and he had taken Lily on the road. Jenny knew the road. It was great fun, but there were roaches and cheap food and people stumbling outside to vomit near the Dumpster. How could someone elegant and fastidious enjoy that?

Lily Cotton had loved it.

Jenny fumbled in her dresser drawer, taking out the slim photo album that her father had given her when she had left Oklahoma. It held copies of the few dozen pictures he had had of Lily. Jenny knew the pictures by heart, but she needed to look at them again, look at them through new eyes. What would have Alec noticed about these pictures?

Lily was laughing. That was the first thing that anyone would notice, that Lily was always laughing. What else was there? Jenny forced herself to blot out Lily's features and look at the rest of the picture—how she was dressed, how her hair was done.

Her hair was long and straight, parted down the middle. In none of the pictures did she have flowers in it. She was never wearing earrings, she never had on a necklace. She didn't have a collar flipped up in an interesting way. She was simply laughing.

You were probably exactly like me.

Jenny was dumbfounded. But it was true. Of

course it was. Lily Cotton very likely was the same blurt-it-out, talk-too-much tomboy that Jenny was. Yes, Jenny's life would have been far, far easier if Lily had lived, but there was no guarantee that Jenny would have been any better dressed. Why had she always assumed that Lily would have taught her how to hang drapes and sew? Lily might not have known that herself.

And so what? What was the big deal about hanging drapes and sewing? Jenny liked herself as she was.

Because she had an imagination. You could get a fashion consultant to tell you what to wear. You could hire an interior designer to pick out curtains. But if you didn't have an imagination, there was nothing you could do, there was no way to get one.

And Jenny had one. It was from her mother.

You were there for me, weren't you? All those times when Jenny had felt so alone and she had retreated into the world of her imagination, her mother had been there with her. She might have died, but she had left her daughter with the one thing necessary to survival, her imagination.

She had been wrong all these years. Her ideas didn't "just come." Her mother sent them to her.

And now she needed another one. She needed to reach Alec. She suddenly felt strong and confident. Able to help him. *I did have a mother all that time. When you believe in your imagination, someone doesn't need to be sitting in the room for you to know that she is there.*

Alec had been right to walk out of the show. He needed to stop feeling like he had to take care of everything. But he seemed to think that doing that was enough, that that was the end of the story.

It wasn't. And as long as she was thinking about narratives—something she knew a lot about—there was another problem with the way he was telling the story. There were two strands which he had twisted up into one. One strand was about responsibility; the other was about love. At the same time he had quit carrying the world on his shoulders, he had also quit hoping that she would love him. He thought that they were one and the same. They weren't. Giving up responsibility freed him from being the model for Hastings; giving up hope locked him into it.

This was his problem. He needed a better storyteller.

Suddenly she remembered something from *Peter Pan*. Why had the Lost Boys wanted Wendy for a mother? There was all that stuff about making pockets and sewing on shadows, stuff that Jenny was no good at, and no doubt her mother wasn't any good at it either. But what else had the Lost Boys wanted? Something that Jenny was absolutely terrific at.

Do you know stories?

Oh, yes, Peter, Wendy had answered. *I know lots of stories.*

It was late afternoon. It would be time-wasting folly to take a car into Manhattan at this hour. So Jenny took the subway, sitting near the map so she could tell which station to get off at. At the top of the exit was a flower vendor. Tall galvanized buckets of imported and greenhouse flowers: tulips, ginger blossoms, freesia, and carnations were kept warm by portable heaters.

Jenny hurried past them, heading toward Alec's house. Then she stopped, turned, and fumbling with her purse, bought an armful of lilies.

Eighteen

For her the lilies said it all. She loved him. She knew what he needed. She was the only woman on earth who did. It all seemed perfectly clear to her.

It might not be to him. He might not even let her in.

Even if he did, it wasn't going to be easy. He was still too close to Hastings. He would try to turn her into Amelia, the quietly doomed, desperately needy Amelia. That kind of relationship was what he understood—the slowly dying younger sister, the high-strung fragile wife. But he didn't want that anymore. Jenny was sure of it. If he had, he would have fallen in love with Karen, not with her.

She was on his doorstep now, the paper sheath of lilies under her arm. She lifted the door knocker.

This wasn't going to work. She muffled the knocker, replacing it silently.

She was asking a man to forget more than twenty-five years of conditioning, twenty-five years of being the knight who picks up his arms in service of the weak and defenseless. *You must forget all that because you have gone and fallen in love with a woman who is neither.*

There was a coffee shop on the corner. A minute later Jenny was inside at the counter, begging for a piece of paper.

A scene was unfolding before her. It was as if she was watching it, knowing no more of how it would end than did any viewer.

A party of young gallants was calling on Isabella, but of course it was Sophie they were paying attention to, bright-faced, tomboyish Sophie. The party disperses. Isabella exits. The camera's on Sophie.

I'm Sophie. Energetic, tomboyish, full of insight and fun. Sophie was a portrait of herself. It suddenly seemed so obvious. *That's me at my best. That's me when I like myself.*

She started to write again. Sophie hears a footstep.

It wouldn't be Hastings. Hastings wouldn't love Sophie, any more than he would have loved Jenny. He would have been repelled by her spirited excesses. Jenny began the next line.

ROBIN:

Yes, of course, it would be Robin. Robin had fought for his country, he had borne arms, he had done battle, but it hadn't robbed him of his soul in the way that Hastings's long struggle was robbing him of his. Alec had sometimes joked about wanting to play Robin.

ROBIN: (OFF CAMERA) My gloves, I believe I forgot my gloves. (ENTERS. LOOKS AROUND ROOM, SEES

> THAT HE IS ALONE WITH SO-PHIE. COMES TOWARD HER, HANDS OUT) Well, dear wife.

Yes, that was it. Robin and Sophie were secretly married. The two liveliest, warmest characters on the show were already married to one another.

The viewers would love it. They had been fond of Robin since the earliest shows, and now they were enchanted with Sophie.

Okay, Alec, this is it. Here's how it works. If you want to be Robin, instead of the dour, dutiful Hastings, if you want to hold on to your warmth, your spirit, your enthusiasm, you have got to let me love you. I am your only hope.

She dropped some money on the table, jammed her lilies under her arm, and marched back to Alec's, boldly hammering on the door. A moment later she heard footsteps.

"It's me," she called out. "You don't have to look through the peephole." She felt a familiar bubbly confidence rushing through her. This was it, this was right.

The door opened, she thrust the lilies at him. "Here, these are for you."

He caught them instinctively, the natural response of an athletic man. But he kept his arms out, he didn't look at them, he didn't want them. "Jenny, I asked you not to come here."

His voice was weary and overly controlled.

"But I'm here," she pointed out. She was the kid who had sat by herself on the schoolbus for all those years. She wasn't afraid of a little rejection. "And you're too gallant to leave me out on the doorstep."

"It would be better for both of us if you—"

"I'm cold."

It was a lie, but it suited the purpose. He had to let her in. He stepped back, and after closing the door, he turned the sheaf of lilies right side up. They were glowingly beautiful, veins of pink streaking the waxy white petals. Of course, an hour in Jenny's company had left them the worse for the wear. One of the blossoms was bent at the neck, another was bruised, and there was a coffee-cup circle on the florist paper.

Who cared? Alec had had visual perfection before—Chloe Spencer wouldn't smash flowers—and he hadn't thought it worth the effort. Jenny grabbed the lilies and pitched them onto the hall table under the portrait of his little sister. "Read this." She thrust her pad in front of his face.

He took it, blinking, bewildered. "It's a restaurant order form."

That was the only paper the waitress had had. "Turn it over. It's a script. Read it."

He flipped the pad over, but he was still confused. Instead of turning the whole pad over and treating the last blank back sheet as if it were the top, Jenny had turned each page over one at a time.

Next time she sat down in a coffee shop to write a script on the back of an order pad in order to propose to a man, she would do it differently.

She crowded in close to him and found the start of the scene.

(MARBLE'S DRAWING ROOM. ISABELLA, SOPHIE, JASPAR, ROBIN, OTHERS)

"Why am I reading this?" Alec asked.

"Because I love you."

It was as if his body heard it first, she could feel the constricting surprise in his tendons, in his veins, in air that shot out of his lungs. But when he spoke, it wasn't his surprise speaking, it wasn't joy. It was Hastings.

"I don't want you to come to me out of guilt, Jenny."

He had a point. For a long time she had felt guilty for not loving him. But that wasn't why she was here now. "Didn't you try to figure out what you were doing wrong? I know you had this theory"—and it had actually been more than a theory, he had been right—"about me being too obsessed with the show. And, of course, you're right. But that makes it all my fault. Don't you think maybe you were doing something wrong?"

"Of course. Certain defects of character must have—"

Defects of character? She was just in time. He was almost entirely Hastings. A few more weeks, and even her stories might not have been able to bring him back. She interrupted him. "You didn't need me."

He drew back, puzzled. "Don't need you? Of course I need you. I love you."

"Then tell me how. Tell me how you need me."

"I just do. Isn't that enough? You don't want a list, do you?"

"Yes, I do. Tell me exactly and precisely. I, Alec, need you, Jenny, because . . ."

"This is absurd," he protested. "How could I not need you?"

"In fact, you do, but it's taken me all this time to figure it out, and I'm good at this sort of thing. I don't think you have a clue."

He started to speak, then stopped. He didn't have the right answer and he knew it.

Hastings would hate not having the right answer, but Hastings had probably been an only child. Alec had been in the middle. He knew that no one ever had all the answers all the time. He knew that life was about being wrong, laughing about it, learning from it.

Jenny knew that two things could happen right now. Alec could protest and grow impatient with her, frustrated because he wasn't in control. He could refuse to take another step until he was in charge, until she admitted that he knew best.

Or he could let go. He could trust her enough to follow the scent of the lilies. He could come with her on a little green lane that would twist past chicken coops and carousels. He was at a crossroads.

She couldn't see him make the choice, but she could feel it. Everything about him, his shoulders, his arms, the muscles in his neck and back and legs, seemed to warm and open.

"I'm not doing very well here," he acknowledged. "I need someone to feed me my lines." He pointed to the order pad. "Are they in here? Is this going to explain it to me?"

"It explained it to *me,*" Jenny admitted. "But not everyone may be able to follow my logic."

"Then clearly I do have an answer. I need you to explain to me how I need you."

That was the right place to start. Jenny wanted to hug him. She wanted to throw her arms around him and let him swing her off her feet. She wanted to laugh and shout. She wanted to tear the paper off the lilies and throw them in the air and let the blossoms rain down on them.

Instead she pushed him into the living room and, after knocking a gym bag off the wing chair, shoved him down. She perched on the coffee table in front of him.

"There are two ways in which you could need a person, Alec Cameron. Your first impulse is to need her to be weak and helpless so that you can go on playing the wonderful big brother to the sick little sister. That's what you're used to, that's what feels normal to you, that's how you can justify being the One With Talent. It's like you think you earned your talent by being great to Meg, and you have to go on earning it by being equally great with the rest of us."

Alec blinked and started to frown. He needed to think about that.

He could think about it later. She wanted to get on to part two. "But if you really wanted needy and helpless this time, then you picked the wrong cupcake because I can't stand feeling that way. You fell in love with me because you wanted to stop being responsible for the whole world all the time. You don't want to be Hastings."

"Hastings?" Alec was bewildered. "What does he have to do with anything? You're going too fast for me, Jenny. I'm lost."

She supposed that that was understandable. She was kind of blitzing her way through this. But she knew stories, she understood narrative momentum and the sequence of scenes. She had a pretty good idea what kind of scene was going to follow this one, and admittedly she was rushing to get to it.

"Have you been watching the show?" She didn't wait for an answer. Of course he had been watching the show. "What do you think of Hastings?"

"He's getting harder and harder to warm up to, but you can't blame him. It's admirable the way he's doing his duty."

That was completely, totally, one hundred percent, the wrong answer. "What do you think of his rejection of Molly?"

"It's not very sympathetic, but what else can he do? He loves Amelia. It's very consistent and believable."

Of course it was consistent and believable. Jenny had written it, hadn't she? But consistent, believable behavior could still be borderline pathological. "Who is your favorite male character? If you could play any other part, whose would it be?"

"Edgar's. James Marble."

She swatted him on the knee. "You're lying. You're just saying Marble because you think it's not dignified to hanker after a character younger than you. Robin's your favorite character."

"That's probably true."

There was no "probably" about it. "Then think about him. What would happen if year after year he never got a story, if he just stayed the dashing, not-so-young bachelor?"

"Ray would quit."

He had a point. "No, think about the character. What would happen to the character?"

"He probably wouldn't be so much fun anymore. He'd—" Alec stopped. "Oh, I'm getting it." He rapped his forehead with his knuckles. "I'm finally getting it. He'd either get absolutely dissolute or he'd end up all noble and stiff. He'd turn into Hastings . . . who is not a character you are as in love with as you used to be."

Hastings would have never seen that. Hastings would have never seen that spirit and dash, a sense of fun, can be just as admirable as sterling character. Sure, silver is going to tarnish a little bit if it's left out all the time, if it's used. But what's the point of gleaming polish if the brightness is locked up in a cabinet? Alec understood all this.

Jenny wrinkled her nose. "So what if Robin married Sophie?"

"Sophie? Zelda Oliver's character?" Alec's eyebrows went up. "Is that right? Have you told

Ray? He'll be thrilled. If he liked working with me, he'll love working with her."

"I haven't told him. I haven't told anybody. I just thought of it. But don't you agree that it's a great idea? That Sophie and Robin's best chance of being really wonderful people is if they are married to each other?"

"And I suppose we're to conclude from that that my best chance of being an acceptable human being is to be married to you?"

"That was the direction my thoughts were going," Jenny acknowledged.

Alec had hold of her hands. The next scene was about to start. "I can see that you're Sophie. That's been clear to me since Zelda's first scene. But I don't get how I became Robin all of a sudden. I thought I was Hastings."

"You are. I mean, you were . . . and I suppose you still could be if you don't watch yourself. But, Alec, who would *want* to be Hastings?"

He was pulling on her hands, and she was on his lap. "Better him than Lydgate."

"That's true. Fortunately the two of them aren't our only options." She was leaning back against his arm. His face was all that she could see. It filled her visual universe, the wide-set eyes, the narrowing, lean lines. "I love you, Alec. I really do."

"I guess I am starting to believe that." His arm grew tighter around her shoulders, but instead of pulling her closer, he leaned back so he could look at her straight. "We were talking about Robin and Sophie getting married. That's what I want for us too. I don't want this to be a 'relationship,' Jenny. I'm not Brian, I don't need to be free. I don't want to be free. I want us to be married."

"And I suppose you want to try the baby thing again?"

"I do. But I want to marry you regardless."

"No, no, I want to try it." She had used the flip language because she didn't know how good she was going to be at this wife/mother bit, but she was determined to give it her best shot. And when you grew up in a pool hall, your best shot ended up pretty damn good.

After all, you didn't have to be good at the "girl stuff" to be a wife and a mother. You needed to be a woman.

Nineteen

"I do wish everyone at the studio already knew," Jenny sighed.

They had come back to Brooklyn the night before. Alec hadn't actually tacked a FOR SALE sign on the front door of his place as they had left, but he certainly had done so in his own mind. Her house had a bigger yard, there were more families on her block, it was a better place for children.

"Let's start out as we mean to continue," he had said to her. "Say what you like about Brian, his taste is a whole lot better than mine."

"It would be symbolically correct for us to get a place of our own," she had pointed out, "one with no history."

"It wouldn't have curtains or furniture either, and if I know us, it never would."

She couldn't deny that. Getting married was not going to suddenly make her interested in interior design.

So the next morning they awoke in the blue-striped bedroom on the third floor of Jenny's house.

Alec propped himself up on his elbow and

looked down at her. Her hair was wildly rumpled, sticking up every which way. "Why do you wish everyone already knew? It won't be so bad. People will be surprised. They won't get a blessed thing done for two days, but in the end I think they'll be pleased for us."

"I know they'll be pleased, but . . . actually"—she was sounding sheepish—"I'm not sure they'll be so surprised."

He did love the way she looked when she knew she had made a mistake. "Oh?"

"Well . . ." She sat up and ran a hand through her hair. "I wouldn't have done it except that the stairs were being carpeted—"

"That excuses everything."

"Thank you. Anyway, everyone was wondering where you were—"

"What am I, a carpet layer?"

"—and so I sort of . . . well, I guess there wasn't any 'sort of' about it. I flat out told everyone everything. It was a mistake. I really regretted it. But I did it."

How like her. "What happened? Did people get a little overly involved?"

"You might say that. It's all they talked about. Maybe I should just keep this new stuff a secret for a while and then distribute a memo on my next day off. That's how people did it during the Regency days, put a notice in the *Gazette,* and then sat back and watched the fireworks. Do you think I can keep my mouth shut that long?"

"No," he said bluntly. He flung the covers open and swung his legs out of bed. "But this is going to be too interesting to pass up. I'm coming to watch."

"You're a brave man," she said. But she knocked her forehead against his arm. If he showed his face at the studio, she wouldn't have to say a word. Everyone would know.

Indeed the security guard's face lit up when he saw that it was Alec holding the studio door open for Jenny. He was reaching for the phone to spread the word even before the door had swung shut.

Alec thumped his hand on the guard desk, a wordless but affectionate greeting. Then he followed Jenny down the hall. Down the *carpeted* hall. Fancy.

He and Jenny had talked about Lydgate long and hard last night. And they both agreed that whatever the cause, this was a clear-cut case of a character who wasn't going anywhere. He didn't even have the energy and drive to be a good villain. The story would be more interesting without him than with him. So Alec would stick around for however long it took Jenny to dish out some interesting and well-deserved fate for His Grace, and then Alec would move on. It was a shame. It seemed like after all they had been through to get together, that they ought to be able to go on working together. But Alec knew that he couldn't play Lydgate much longer. It would be creative death.

And how much did it really matter where he worked? He had Jenny.

The message light on her phone was flashing madly. "Thirteen messages," she groaned after listening to the voice-mail prompt. "I left an hour and a half early yesterday and I have thirteen messages."

Clearly something had happened. "Then I'm out of here." He wasn't Brian. He wasn't going to give himself quasi-producer status because of his relationship with her. "Let me know if I can help."

He went downstairs. Dressing Room Six looked the same as ever. The coffee table was still crowded as close to the chairs, the cinderblock walls still needed painting, the dressing counter was still a churning welter of scripts, fan mail, toothpaste, and bottles of mouthwash.

But in the middle of all that clutter was a phone. An almond-colored, push-button phone. It couldn't be a prop. They didn't have telephones during the Regency. And this one had a cord running out the back and into a phone jack. Alec picked up the receiver. There was a dial tone.

The door burst open. "The guard said you were here, that you came in with Jenny." It was Ray. "Does this mean what I think it means?"

"Where did this come from?" Alec held up the phone. "Did everyone get them?"

"Jenny had them put in. We all have them." Ray didn't care about the phones. "Have you and she worked things out?"

Respectfully Alec replaced the receiver. What a difference phones would make. No more standing in line out in the hall. No more having the entire cast know how many calls you were making. He turned back to Ray. "Yes, we have. We're getting married."

Ray let out a delighted yelp and clapped Alec on the shoulder. "Actually married? I thought Ellie and I were the only ones who did that anymore."

Before Alec could answer, the door popped open again. This time it was Karen and Trina, both speaking at the same time, their words tumbling out, all mixed together.

"You're back. This is great. We missed you."

"You came in with Jenny. What happened? She said you didn't need her. Tell us everything."

"Yes, yes, you have to. Tell us everything."

Alec put his arm around Trina and kissed Karen's hand. "Not a chance, dear ladies. It's none of your business."

Trina swatted him across the chest. "Don't be like that. Come on, we *live* for stuff like this. You *have* to tell us."

"No, I don't," Alec answered.

A moment later Francine swept in. She took one look at Alec and went straight into character. So it was the proper but warm-hearted Lady Varley badgering him to tell everything. Finally she too gave up. "It's no use," she told the others. "If he isn't going to tell the Countess Varley, he isn't going to tell anyone."

At 7:15 they swept Alec up to the rehearsal hall, and there Alec discovered that he was already old news. Late last night David Kendall had received a sudden and glorious film offer, a featured role.

David was the young actor who played James Marble's valet. He had been the new character who had prompted all the recapping that Rita had crashed and burned on. And he was, everyone knew, slated to take on a dual part, the valet's look-alike noble half brother.

But if he was going to take the film, David needed to be in Toronto tomorrow. The movie was already in production. He was a replacement for an actor whose drug problems had gotten the better of him. Someone was needed immediately. But David's new character was going to be introduced within a week; the cast already had the scripts. Jenny couldn't drop a major sweeps-month story at a moment's notice.

What lousy timing.

It was 7:35, and it didn't look like the table reading was going to start any time soon. David—who was in the prologue and five scenes—was still in the production offices, and Gil was talking nervously to two of the production assistants. Everyone else was standing around in groups of twos and threes. Except Zelda Oliver. She was at the table, her script open. She wasn't fidgeting, she wasn't pointedly glancing at the clock. But her impatience was clear. She wanted to get this show on the road.

It wasn't his problem. He wasn't responsible for making the new star happy. He wasn't in charge of making the trains run on time. He wasn't going to do Gil's job for him. He walked out.

He went down to Jenny's office. She was on the phone. "How is it possible? . . . February sweeps start tomorrow, we have four February shows in the can already and David's in every single one of them . . ." She went on in this vein for another few minutes and then promising that she would do her best, she hung up and dropped her head down on the desk.

"Having a nice day, are we?" he inquired of the top of her head.

She groaned. "This story was gigantic. It was going to unite everyone, the Viscount was . . . oh, Lord, I just don't see what I can do."

"Then don't do anything. You're not always going to be able to find a solution that's perfect for the show and for every individual in the cast."

"I know that," she sighed. "But he really wants to do this. And isn't that how you came to appreciate daytime, by doing stage and film too?"

Alec couldn't deny that. Actors who had only done daytime—like Brian—tended to romanticize other kinds of work. "It is a tough break for him, but you can't solve everyone's problems all the time."

She made a face at him. "You're a fine one to talk about that."

"What do you mean?" he protested. "I left the rehearsal hall with the table reading so far from starting that it isn't even a gleam in its papa's eye."

Automatically she glanced at her watch. It was nearly quarter to eight. "Why did you have to start this mental health kick *now*?" she complained. "Couldn't you have at least waited until noon? You wouldn't believe the overtime bills we ran up while you were gone."

"It's not your job to tell David the bad news. It's George's."

She shook her head. "I don't mind telling David." She had plenty of courage. "It's his idiot agent. She'll scream for half the morning."

"Then have George make that call."

"Maybe I will."

He left her and went down to makeup and wardrobe to say hello to the people in those departments. If the table reading still hadn't started, he didn't want to know about it.

It was strange being here without anything to do. He observed more than he might have otherwise. The place was changing. People were spending more time in their dressing rooms. There was less hanging out in the greenroom, less milling around in the halls.

It was partly the phones. Installing the phones seemed to give everyone permission to have a life outside the show. And it was also the knowledge that the show was going to an hour. Everything would change. There would be more Zeldas, more fully professional actors and actresses who would view this as a job.

It was ironic. Alec hadn't approved of the way the show was run. He thought it was too claustrophic; roles and lives were too intertwined. But all that was changing now. It was getting on a more professional track . . . just as he was leaving.

He went back up to Dressing Room Six to call his agent. He had not exactly been her favorite client the last couple of weeks. She'd be glad that he finally had some definite plans. He was picking up the phone when he heard his name blaring out over the intercom. "Would Alec Cameron please report to makeup? Alec, makeup."

That seemed strange. Why would anyone want him in makeup? A surprise "Welcome Back" party would be in the greenroom. He hung the phone up and went down the hall to makeup.

The room was packed. Half the cast was there. Jenny was perched on an overturned waste can, frantically scribbling. George and Gil were reading over her shoulder. The senior makeup artist has talking to Brandi, Alec's favorite makeup girl. A line drawing of his face was taped to the mirror, and the two of them were experimenting with shadings and shadows that had nothing to do with Lydgate's makeup.

One of the wardrobe girls was bearing down on him with a tape measure. "Did you gain any weight while you were off?" She whipped the tape measure around his waist. "Good. Good for you." She spun him around and stretched it across his shoulders. "You've been working out, haven't you?" Her tones were accusatory.

"Not deliberately . . . wait a minute, what's going on?"

"More brown tones." Brandi pushed him in the chair. "Wouldn't he be thinner?"

Wouldn't *who* be thinner? What was going on?

"Here." Jenny stuck a legal pad in his face. "Learn this."

He took it. At least it wasn't a restaurant order form.

(ACT ONE B. MARBLE DRAWING ROOM. JAMES MARBLE, MR. NORDEN)

"Who's Mr. Norden?"
"You."

JAMES: Your references are excellent, but you have no town experience.
NORDEN: Resourcefulness can often compensate for routine.

Resourcefulness can compensate for routine? That was a fine piece of Regency bullshit. Alec liked it.

JAMES: (LAUGHS) We may do well together, young man. I didn't grow up to have a butler, and I don't know as how you grew up to be one.

"Are you serious?" Alec lowered the pad and stared at Jenny. "I'm playing this Norden fellow? Today?"

"It's a perfect solution, isn't it?" Jenny was so pleased with herself that she was almost dancing. "Instead of having a new viscount who looks like James's valet, we have a new butler who looks like an old duke. The same look-alike, half-brother story. Same sorts of problems, same sorts of impact on other characters. We can let David go, we get you to stay. He'll be a great character, Alec. I promise, one that you can go the distance with. The only problem is that you've got to start today, but you don't mind, do you?"

Alec felt like he had been hit by a truck. "Tell me about him. Who is he? What's he like?"

"I don't have a clue. A wise rogue, I don't know. Just get through today and we'll know more by tomorrow."

He was going to get to stay on the show. He was getting it all, the same show, but a new part. If he could have envisioned the ideal, absolutely everything he wanted, this would have been it. It was so perfect he hadn't even thought of it.

But Jenny had. She had thought of it. She had made it work.

"I need an accent. Where's he from?"

"I don't know. Where do you want him to be from?"

"Kent." Brandi spoke as she twirled a makeup sponge in a little pot of foundation. "Have him be from Kent. I've always liked the sound of that. It's my brother's name."

That was a good enough reason for Jenny. She wrote "Kent" on the back of the legal pad and circled it. Alec knew that by the end of the week, this guy—Alec had already forgotten his name—would be so Kentish in speech, manners, and psychology, that it would be impossible to imagine him being from anywhere else.

"Okay, Alec," Brandi said, "I need you to hold still."

"What do people from Kent sound like?" he asked. He only had the vaguest notion of where that county was.

No one knew. "Fake it today, and we'll find you some tapes by tomorrow," Jenny said.

This was what Alec loved the most about daytime, the harum-scarum improvisation, the headlong rush to do the best possible work in the least amount of time.

"This really does have possibilities." She was rubbing her hands in glee. "What if Amelia has a miscarriage and can't get pregnant again? She could seduce the look-alike half brother."

That didn't exactly sound in character for her. "So Lydgate isn't going to die?" Alec would not mind playing him occasionally, not as long as he had this other fellow.

"Who knows? Or maybe Lydgate could die, and the baby is so sickly that Amelia hires Norton to pretend to be Lydgate until the kid gets healthy."

Alec looked down at the legal pad. "I thought his name was Nor*den*. At least that's what you've written here." Alec held the pad out for her to see.

"Oh, so it is. Which would you rather have? You're going to have it for a long time."

"I don't care."

Brandi tapped him on the forehead with a makeup sponge. "I really need you to stop talking for a moment."

Jenny had moved her wastebasket to sit closer to him so that she could hand him pages as she finished writing them. Alec turned his head so that he could watch her work. She had pulled the collar of her turtleneck up over her mouth and chin.

Ever since Meg's death he had struggled and struggled to fix everything. Now in the last month he had learned to give up. He had learned how to be regretful, how to say, "I'm sorry. I wish this were different, but it isn't, and there's nothing to be done." And then what had happened? Someone else was making everything absolutely perfect.

There was a lot to be said for a woman with an imagination.

MEMO

My Lady's Chamber

TO: Susie Pritchard, Editor, *Soap Times*
FROM: Cathleen Yates, *MLC* Publicist

I tried and I tried, Susie, but Jenny and Alec refused to the end to let *ST* cover their wedding. Jenny says that we need all our publicity to focus on the new characters that will be coming when we expand to an hour. Alec said something more personal and more rude.

Anyway, the wedding was at Alec's parents' place on Prince Edward Island. Gobs of people from the cast and crew went up. We took over an entire motel. Actually it was a little compound of adorable guest cottages, all of them white with—this being Anne of Green Gables country—green roofs. People kept signing up to come until the very last minute so we had nowhere near enough space and we were all piled up on the sofas and everyone under twenty-five was in a sleeping bag. In the women's cabins you had to be a countess or higher to get a bed to yourself.

Brian O'Neill and Rita Haber-O'Neill were invited, but didn't come. Frankly—and don't you dare print this—I don't think they could afford the airline tickets.

The wedding was at the church Alec went to as a kid. Jenny's father gave her away. (Talk about your heartthrobs!! I'm ready to run off with him.) She did not make good on her threat to go to a discount department store and buy an off-the-rack confection dripping with polyester lace and plastic pearls. The girls in our wardrobe department wanted to make something for her trousseau, but Jenny, being Jenny, didn't have a trousseau. She asked them instead to make the actual wedding dress. It was Regency-inspired, of course—high-waisted and white, with a deep frill around the hem. She looked marvelous, very happy. I will send photos of her in the dress—just to make sure that she doesn't lend it out to extras next time the show gets in a budget crunch.

We all tried to get Alec to wear a kilt—his dad (another heartthrob!! All of us in the Girls' Cabin #2 decided we must be getting old since people's dads were looking so good) has one. But he refused.

There wasn't any glitz-and-glamour trappings, just a lot of people happy because the right man and the right woman were marrying each other. Although there was one bit of extravagance—the altar flowers and Jenny's bouquet (which afterwards she put on Alec's little sister's grave) were air-shipped up from New York the morning of the wedding. Apparently it was the only part of the wedding planning that she really cared about—she wanted to carry lilies.

NOVELS TO REMEMBER

- ☐ **SUCH DEVOTED SISTERS by Eileen Goudge.** Two sisters could scarcely more different—one of independence and one of sensitivity. Each desperately vying for the same man, who loves them both. Set agai the glamour of the chocolate industry, this is the searing story of a bl bond, of family secrets and betrayals. (173376—$5.
- ☐ **GARDEN OF LIES by Eileen Goudge.** Rachel and Rose grew up wo apart . . . until a terrible secret brought them face to face with the t about each other and themselves. (162919—$5.
- ☐ **SAVING GRACE by Barbara Rogan.** This intricate novel captures behind-closed-doors dynamics of a family in crisis, as it measures limits of love, loyalty, trust, and forgiveness. (170733—$4.
- ☐ **THE AUTOBIOGRAPHY OF MY BODY by David Guy.** An intimate, com ling, sexually graphic novel "of a man torn between appetite intellect."—*The New York Times Book Review* (172523—$5.

Prices slightly higher in Canada.

Buy them at your local bookstore or use this convenient coupon for ordering.

PENGUIN USA
P.O. Box 999 – Dept. #17109
Bergenfield, New Jersey 07621

Please send me the books I have checked above.
I am enclosing $_________ (please add $2.00 to cover postage and handli Send check or money order (no cash or C.O.D.'s) or charge by Mastercar VISA (with a $15.00 minimum). Prices and numbers are subject to change wit notice.

Card #__________ Exp. Date ______
Signature__________
Name__________
Address__________
City ______ State ______ Zip Code ______

For faster service when ordering by credit card call **1-800-253-6476**

Allow a minimum of 4-6 weeks for delivery. This offer is subject to change without no

Make some noise with the BOOKS THAT'LL BRING MUSIC TO YOUR EARS Offer and Sweepstakes!

Save the coupons in the backs of these Signet and Onyx books and redeem them for special discounts on Mercury Records CDs and cassettes.

June

RIPPER
Michael Slade

SPELLBOUND
Hilary Norman

July

CRIMINAL SEDUCTION
Darian North

BOUQUET
Shirl Henke

August

MATERIAL WITNESS
Robert K. Tanenbaum

FAN MAIL
Ronald Munson

September

THE SURGEON
Francis Roe

AGAIN
Kathleen Gilles Seidel

You can choose from these artists:

John Mellencamp
Vanessa Williams
Texas
Tony, Toni, Toné

or these:

Billy Ray Cyrus
Lowen & Navaro
Swing Out Sister
Tears For Fears
Lauren Christy
Brian McKnight
Oleta Adams

or any other Mercury recording artist

a PolyGram company